A NOVEL

LIVE FOR TODAY, LAUGH FOR TOMORROW.
LOVE FOREVER.

Noisy Creek

A NOVEL

LIVE FOR TODAY, LAUGH FOR TOMORROW.
LOVE FOREVER.

PAMELA FOSTER

FOYLE
PRESS

an imprint of

OGHMA CREATIVE MEDIA

OGHMA

CREATIVE MEDIA

Foyle Press
An imprint of Oghma Creative Media, Inc.
2401 Beth Lane, Bentonville, Arkansas 72712

Library of Congress Cataloging-in-Publication Data

Names: Foster, Pamela, author.
Title: Noisy Creek/Pamela Foster | Noisy Creek #1
Description: Second Edition. | Bentonville: Foyle, 2018.
Identifiers: LCCN: 2018946771 | ISBN: 978-1-63373-340-4 (hardcover) |
ISBN: 978-1-63373-341-1 (trade paperback) | ISBN: 978-1-63373-007-6 (eBook)
Subjects: BISAC: FICTION/Women | FICTION/Southern
FICTION/Romance/Later in Life
LC record available at: https://lccn.loc.gov/2018946771

Foyle Press trade paperback edition April, 2018

Jacket & Interior Design by Casey W. Cowan
Editing by Greg Camp

Acknowledgments

Thank you to the folks of Americus, Georgia who welcomed me into their big, rowdy, quirky, glorious, warm hearts and forgave me for talking funny. Or, kept their disapproval to themselves, gave me sugar, and blessed my heart.

Greg Camp's enthusiasm for the story made the editing fun, though he did delete Green Acres and Jax beer.

Casey Cowan welcomed me into the Oghma Creative Media family, opened promotional doors, and designed a beautiful cover.

My husband, Jack Jones, both encouraged me to believe in my writing talent and drove me to lock myself in my room and write.

And to Chesty and Rocca, whose snores accompanied the writing of most of this book.

This book is dedicated to my beautiful mother,
Joyce Brockmueller Foster Mulford Craig.

That all my heart I gave unto his hold.
He was, I say, but twenty winters old,
And I was forty, if I shall say the truth;
But always had an untamed horse's tooth.
Gap-toothed I was, and that became me well—
That was the print of Saint Venus's seal.
So help me God, I was a lusty one
And fair and rich and young and well begun.
And truly, as my husbands told me,
I had the best of things as might be.
For certain, I am all Venusian
In feeling, and my heart is Martian.
Venus gave me my lust, my eagerness,
And Mars gave me my sturdy hardiness.

The Wife of Bath's Prologue
The Canterbury Tales
Geoffrey Chaucer

Prologue

Folks around here tolerate newcomers, all right, long as they know their place. My mama, Shelby Powell Barr, never did know her place in Noisy Creek. She and the town both struggled with the challenge from the day my daddy, Clark Barr, brought her home from the University of Georgia. My daddy's people have been in these parts since before the War of Northern Aggression. Why Mama, a debutante from Dallas, was attending college in Athens, Georgia is one of those family stories that vary, depending on who's doing the telling.

Mama always claimed she fell in love with a young scoundrel in Dallas and as punishment, her daddy sent her to the University of Georgia. My daddy's mama, Gramma Missy, swore till the day she died Mama saw Daddy at a football game at that pitiful Texas school she was attending and chased him all the way to Georgia to trap him into marrying her. The upshot of all these variations of the truth flying like cottonwood in June is that both Mama's and Daddy's families think their babies married far beneath them. This makes for interesting holiday reunions, weddings, funerals, and birthday gatherings.

I admit Daddy compounded the feelings of his in-laws by insisting on naming my oldest sister Candace. Candy Barr. Mama did her best to rectify the choice by demanding Candy take her maiden name. My big sister is Candace

Powell Barr when she visits Mama's people in Texas. Here in Noisy Creek she's Little Candy Barr.

Not content with this mischief, a scant year later when Mama threatened to cut him off for all eternity if he didn't allow her to name her second daughter Selma after her daddy's mama, Daddy immediately nicknamed the new baby Snickers. A name which stuck like overcooked grits to a new pan. When I came along fourteen months later, Mama insisted I be named Alyson after Great-grandma Powell. Daddy smiled and agreed with that choice, slipped in Ruth as my middle name. Mama gamely called me Ally for a day or two and then just plumb gave up. I was and will always be Baby Ruth Barr. That ended the mischief as I turned out to be Mama and Daddy's last child.

This moniker was much cuter when I was younger. Now, at a gray-haired fifty-five, it is somewhat less adorable. Which matters not one wit to the folks here in Noisy Creek. Here I will always be Baby Ruth Barr. The name may well end up on my tombstone. I consider it a small price to pay for living where everyone either loves me, or, with true southern manners, pretends to love me to my face. Of course, my name hasn't legally been Barr for years. I've had three more last names since Daddy tricked Mama into my middle name that morning fifty-five years ago in the Caddell Hospital maternity ward.

The fact is three husbands have died out from under me. One figuratively and two literally. I can't be blamed for the fact that the throes of ecstasy sound remarkably similar to dying screams. It's even called "the little death," for pity sake. As my friend Ardell points out to those old ladies in town prone to a good gossip, both of those husbands went out with a smile on their faces.

My first husband, Kevin, was my childhood sweetheart. We shared an April 30th birth date as well as our first kiss. We were married on his eighteenth birthday and my sweet sixteen. A high school quarterback hero, once graduated, Kevin quickly grew disenchanted with his prospects for earning a living here in Noisy Creek. He took his good eye and quick reflexes to nearby Quimby and the nearest Army recruiting office. He never said a word to me or to his mama, Miss Bessie, until his name was on the dotted line. The thought of her baby boy leaving her sphere of influence sent Miss Bessie to bed for a week with a sick headache. I handled the news by agreeing to marry him before he left. It seemed the best way to tie him to me before he saw what other options he had out there in the big wide world.

We went across the county line to Monroe to a justice of the peace that Kevin knew about from a buddy he worked with at the brickworks. I was so dumb I didn't even wear white to the one wedding I was actually entitled to do so. A ten-minute procedure in an old shotgun house that smelled of collards and boiled peanuts mixed with the whiskey breath of the presiding government representative, and we were pronounced husband and wife. It turned out to be just as well I hadn't spent any money on a new dress. Less than five minutes after we opened the door to our room at The Cottonmouth Inn just off State Highway 4, my best navy blue church dress had a tear in the shoulder seam and was a wadded up mess under my butt where my new husband hiked it up to claim me as his own.

This was way back in 1966 and Quick Draw Kevin—as I secretly thought of him during our short and tragic eight months of marriage—had predictably signed up for the 101st Airborne out of Fort Campbell, Kentucky. Like so many boys of that time with more courage than good sense, he was killed over there in that steamy jungle country that never got mentioned back when we sat side by side passing notes in Mr. Jones's World History class at Robert E. Lee High School.

When he was on leave between training and shipping out, we pulled down an old Encyclopedia Britannica of his mama's with *V - Z* on its dusty spine and looked up Vietnam. A short, one paragraph description telling us that country was located in Southeast Asia and that its main export was rubber didn't do much to help us understand why Kevin was leaving me, his shiny new young bride who, less than an hour before, had managed to slow him down enough to understand why sex really was a pretty big deal.

The Army notified me he'd been killed on the same day I received my first letter since his arrival in Vietnam. I carried them both upstairs to my little attic bedroom and sat ramrod straight on my white chenille bedspread. What I remember most is the way the late afternoon sun spread the golden light of false promise equally across the death notice and the letter.

"Hey Baby," he wrote with squiggly blue lines on tissue-paper-thin airmail stationery. "My sergeant says I got here just in time to kick some gook butt!"

He'd named me on his $10,000 life insurance policy, and his indomitable mama didn't speak to me for the rest of her miserable life because I refused to share that money with her. Instead I paid my tuition at the beauty college over in Rockport and put a down payment on a tiny cottage on Jeff Davis Boulevard which I fixed up as cute as a doll house with a hair salon in front and my bedroom in the back.

I loved that little bitty place, and it didn't take long for me to have more business styling hair than I could handle with only the one chair. In lots of ways those years between my first and second husband were my best. That doll-sized shop was always buzzing with gossip and hairspray and the purring laughter of women being fussed over. I bought a comfortable love seat and overstuffed chair from the local second-hand store, and Snickers and I spent a week covering it in pink corduroy. I kept a pot of coffee fresh-brewed and carried in fat, sticky cinnamon buns from the Magnolia Tree Bakery down the street each morning. We were part hair salon, part coffee shop, and a whole lot of fun.

My second husband, Billy, was elected county sheriff a few months before I started seeing him. I hadn't voted for him because my best friend Ardell's older brother Lemuel was running against him, but I went to school with Billy's younger brothers, Bobby and David, and I knew Billy to speak to when I saw him around town. He seemed like just another good ole boy until Ardell and I saw him climbing out of the water at the dunking tank they always set up next to the Confederate soldier on town square during the Watermelon Festival. That man had the best chest of any of my husbands. I blew twenty dollars before finally connecting on a throw and dumping the grinning redhead into the water. It was worth every penny to watch him crawl out of that tank dripping wet and shaking his head like some beautiful, sleek animal.

He showed up at the salon and asked me out the next morning. Lord, it was just like in a movie. The women all sitting around watching and grinning and him in his uniform coming in the door, all awkwardness and pretended confidence, with a potted petunia in one hand and clutching his Smokey Bear hat to his beautiful chest with the other. We were married seven months later at the Jesus the Redeemer Baptist Church down on Montgomery Drive. This time I wore a pale green linen dress that matched my eyes. Standing up there at the altar in front of God and friends and family, nervously promising to love and honor, I thought he would be my second and last husband.

Married to Billy, I came into full bloom. We were happy and young, surrounded by people who loved and respected us, both of us working jobs we looked forward to getting to each day. When, lying in bed one Sunday morning after what Billy called our own private worship service, I found an innocuous looking black mole behind his left ear, neither of us worried. We paid it no mind until he got his hair cut a month or so later. It had grown and changed shape dramatically, and I insisted he make an appointment with Dr. Shaw.

Dr. Shaw was in Panama City visiting his oldest daughter whose family has one of those condominiums on the beach. Billy could have seen the young partner, but Dr. Shaw delivered both Billy and me. He was our family doctor. We trusted him. So we waited until his return three weeks later before Billy went on in to have him look at the mole. Even when Dr. Shaw sent us to a specialist in Atlanta we weren't really worried. Lots of folks went to Atlanta to confer with one medical specialist or another. Things usually turned out just fine.

The specialist operated four days after we sat in that over-cooled exam room and heard the words, "melanoma" and "cancer," spoken right out loud in the full light of day without even a "God forbid" to lighten their weight. Sometimes it still feels like the rest of my life has been a dream, and we never really left that doctor's cubicle, me on a chair with wheels that kept slipping around the white linoleum and Billy, still in his wrinkled gown, perched on the crinkly papered exam table. Even when the doctor found me in the waiting room after the surgery and told me he had removed the melanoma and taken seven lymph nodes and that we'd know better in a few days how to plan the rest of our attack, even then I wasn't really worried.

Billy was young and healthy. I was always a little anxious about my sheriff husband getting shot by some bad guy passing through from some big Yankee town up north. But a tiny black dot of skin just behind his perpetually sun-peeling left ear, surely that couldn't really do much damage. The doctors tried to kill the cancer without killing Billy. I begged and pleaded with Jesus. My prayers and the medical poison both failed. Less than four months later–months filled with desperate, failing hope–on the first warm morning in spring, one of those dawns when you wake and remember the taste of cold lemonade and the smell of jasmine, I finally did what Billy had been begging me to do for a month.

I brought him what he wanted and opened the bedroom windows. I forced myself to look outside, took deep breaths of the cool morning air, while he swallowed and swallowed and swallowed. Fresh cut grass was just beginning to warm in the morning sun. When I turned from the window, the bottle of pills beside the bed was empty and Billy was smiling. I let my robe slip to the floor then and came to him. As gently as I could I covered his poor wasted body with my own. Once we had the fit, I rocked slowly against him. I felt him swell inside me and looked down through tears to see his sweet smile for the last time. I was left alone again with a life insurance policy as cold comfort for the loss of my husband.

Eventually, I remembered that life was worth getting up in the mornings to live. One morning in January, I smiled over my cup of coffee as I watched Buttons, the neighborhood orange tabby, pounce joyfully on scattered sunlight coming through the lattice of my front porch. My first genuine moment of joy since I watched the light leave Billy's eyes forever. In March, I bought the old Marshall place, a neglected antebellum rambler on the shady side of town square across from the courthouse. My cousin Lorilee was fresh from earning her architectural degree, and she and I turned the ramshackle old house into a combination gym, spa, and hair salon. Membership at the gym bought you one free massage or facial each month. My idea was to create a beautiful place for women to come and be pampered or just sip coffee or tea or white wine away from the demands of their jobs and men and children. The town bankers all stopped by to study the construction and explain to me in great boring detail that I was not suitable as a merchant and that I was frittering away the money I'd gained from the premature death of my beloved husband.

Luckily, I didn't need the bankers to complete the project. We opened on Mother's Day, 1979. I gave every woman in Noisy Creek a gift certificate for one free day of pampering. Within a month I was the owner/operator of a successful small business. In July, one of the Forester girls, visiting her mama and daddy from Atlanta where she worked as a reporter for the Georgia Sentinel, came in with her mama and two of her sisters for the package I called The O'Hara. After a day of deep tissue massages and avocado facials, pinked nails, and freshly cut and styled hair, the subsequent story in the Sentinel further cemented the monetary success of my dream.

The busier I stayed during the day, the less chance I had of crying myself to sleep that night. My goal was to fall asleep on my feet just before I lowered myself into my big, lonely bed each night. It rarely worked, but the strategy did gain me a wildly successful business which, in five years, I expanded with two more spas, one in Columbus and the other in the home of the Georgia Bulldogs, Athens. At thirty-four I still had the occasional lonely night, but I was enjoying the life I had created. I wasn't looking for husband number three.

John Goodin came looking for me. He grew up right here in Noisy Creek, but he boarded a bus at seventeen and put us hillbillies behind him. He retired from the Marine Corp as a Sergeant Major six months before his wife died of breast cancer. After kicking around the country for a year of drunken misery, he claimed to have organized his shit and came looking for his roots. At fifty-six he was flat-bellied with steel gray hair cut short. Quiet and solitary, his pale blue eyes revealed hints of good natured cynicism. He introduced himself to me while I was enjoying a slice of pecan pie at Reb's Café.

"Oh, lord," were my first words to the man. "Your middle name isn't Blaine, is it?"

At his puzzled nod, I went into a fit of giggles.

"My daddy has always admired your daddy's skill for naming younguns. I'm Baby Ruth Barr," I told him through my laughter. "I'm glad to meet you Johnny B. Goodin."

Mama was harder for him to win over, but it was no surprise that, despite the age difference between me and him, Daddy approved of the match. We kept company for going on four years before I agreed to marry him. I sold my businesses in Athens and Columbus, but kept the salon in Noisy Creek. I still loved going to work each day, but I wanted more time with Johnny, so I turned over a lot of the operations to Snickers who had gone to work with me after her divorce a few years before.

We traveled all over, Johnny and me. We spent a month in Thailand one year. Lord, but those folks over there have got the temples to their gods. We saw enough gold- covered idols to blanket the whole town of Noisy Creek. We hiked mountains in Nepal and swam under waterfalls in Hawaii. One year we drove the whole length of Mexico, and when we got to the Caribbean Sea, Johnny taught me to scuba dive.

On our ninth anniversary, we went to New York City. Johnny got us a room at the Plaza Hotel, and we took one of those horse-drawn carriage rides in that park they've got right in the middle of that big ole city. You hear all kinds of frightening warnings about that town. My mama feared I'd be knifed and raped, and she'd not even have a body to bury. But Johnny and I had a grand time. We saw the Statue of Liberty and the Brooklyn Bridge. That place has got more tall buildings than Georgia has peaches and pecans.

Johnny was sixty-nine that summer. We still enjoyed each other's bodies from time to time, maybe not as robustly as we once did, but the tenderness more than compensated for a certain lack of vigor. We fought some, usually over some silly thing that neither of us really cared that much about. We just both hated to be wrong. We'd been back from that trip to New York for a little over a month when we got into a row because Johnny paid too much atten-tion to a sweet young University of Alabama coed who was visiting my uppity cousin Ginny. Ginny lives on the edge of town in that new subdivision, Mag-nolia Acres. She has the only swimming pool in Noisy Creek. To show off the pool, Ginny and her husband Gene always throw a big party after the parade and before the fireworks on the Fourth of July. Ginny says that way everyone leaves before dark so as not to miss the town fireworks that you surely can't see from way out there in Snob Village.

Johnny and I discovered the first Independence Day we were in our house that we could see the fireworks from our bed, all but the highest displays framed by the French doors that led out to the patio. We had our own private way of celebrating the birth of our nation. Back from the party at Ginny and Gene's and revved up by the bikinied coed, Johnny wanted to follow tradition. I, on the other hand, was angry over what I perceived as the disrespect he had shown me at the party by flirting with Miss Alabama Boobs. I yelled. He got angry. I screamed some more. Eventually we wore each other down.

He cocked his head in that way he had that I could never resist and said he had his hands full with the spitfire he married and why would he be interested in some twenty-year-old bimbo. I smiled. He grinned. We managed to make it to the bed before the fireworks were completely over. I was thinking I had actually benefited quite nicely from his attraction to Bouncing Boobies when his cries of pleasure reached a pitch I hadn't heard before. Unfortunately, they coincided with my own yelps of pleasure. I lay there under him for a minute or two before I realized he wasn't breathing. Then I waited another minute, praying for the familiar rise and fall of his chest. By the time I rolled him off and called 911, I didn't need the paramedics to tell me my third husband was dead.

Grieving is not something that gets easier with experience. I sorrowed then, not only for my wonderful Johnny, but also all over again for my sweet Billy and my long lost Kevin. I would have given up The Baby Ruth Barr, but Snickers refused to let me sell it. She ran the business, and Candy left her Baptist preacher husband and her grown-up engineer son on their own in Stone Mountain and came back home and moved herself right on in with me. Snickers, always a big Simon and Garfunkel fan, said the two of them were my bridge over troubled waters. Candy only rolled her blue eyes in her head and reminded her that Jesus was the buttress that supported the whole dang bridge.

Eventually, scant minutes before being smothered to death in the love of my family and friends, I began to recover. I came back to work sixteen months after Johnny died. Work at The Baby Ruth Barr helped me finish my grieving. Today is my fifty-fifth birthday. We've closed the shop, and Snickers and Candy have a party planned for me out at Traveller's Park. I have promised to be suitably surprised when I arrive a little over an hour from now. According to Snickers, there is a man coming to the party that has been asking to meet me. Candy says that given my history with husbands, the guy must be either the dumbest or the bravest man in the county.

MAGNOLIA TREE BAKERY
STICKY CINNAMON BUNS

<u>Dough:</u>
- 1/4 c warm water
- 1 T Peach Blossom Honey
- 1 pkg active yeast

If you can't make it out to Sinclair's Orchard on Route 3 to purchase this Noisy Creek treat, any mild sweetener such as clover honey can be substituted. Pour the water into a large, deep bowl. Add the honey, and stir gently to dissolve. Sprinkle the yeast on top, and stir. Let it proof. If your yeast is good, the whole mess will bubble up like the sulfur springs out back of Old Man Russell's place.

<u>Add</u>
- 1/2 c Peach Blossom Honey
- 3 fresh duck eggs
- 4 to 4 1/2 c all purpose flour
- 5 T butter melted and cooled
- 3/4 c buttermilk at room temperature
- 1 1/4 t salt
- 1 T vanilla

Duck eggs are reputed to give more lift to baked goods, but Mama always uses hen's eggs and swears there's not a difference in the world long as they're fresh.

Add the flour a cup at a time, beating with a large wooden spoon after each addition until the mixture is too stiff to stir. Turn the dough out on a floured surface, and knead in additional flour until the dough is smooth and slightly sticky.

Clean the bowl, and grease it with butter. Return the ball of dough to the bowl, cover, and let sit in a warm place for an hour or until doubled in size.

Punch dough down, and let it rise an additional 30 minutes.

Filling:
- 3/4 c brown sugar
- 1 t cardamom
- 1 T cinnamon
- 1/2 t nutmeg

Combine in a small bowl, mix well. Melt 6 T of butter, and keep separate.

Topping:
- 1 c brown sugar
- 5 T butter
- 4 T Peach Blossom Honey

Put topping ingredients in a sauce pan. Cook over low heat until the butter is melted and the sugar and honey are dissolved. Mixture will be smooth.

Assembly:

Generously butter a 9" x 13" baking pan. The last step is going to be to tip this very pan upside down so all this work pops out as a treat to fatten up your friends so you'll look skinnier standing next to them. When I say generously grease, I mean generously. And if you have a non-stick pan, use it. Pour the topping mixture evenly in the pan. Sprinkle with 2 cups of chopped pecans.

Gently roll the dough into a 12" x 18" rectangle. With a pastry brush, evenly distribute the 6 T melted butter onto the rolled dough. Sprinkle the filling over the surface. Beginning with the long side, roll the dough into a tube. Seam side down, slice the cylinder of dough into 15 even rolls. Arrange on the topping mixture. Cover loosely with plastic wrap. Refrigerate overnight.

The next morning, remove the rolls from the refrigerator, and let them sit at room temperature while the oven preheats to 375 degrees. Remove the plastic wrap, and bake for 35 minutes. Take the buns from the oven, and immediately turn the pan upside down onto a flat serving dish.

These buns are irresistible. We have been accused of serving them at The Baby Ruth Barr spa as a form of job security. Snickers claims to have calculated that it takes four hours of strenuous exercise to burn off the calories contained in just one of these Sticky Buns.

One

Noisy Creek is right proud of its parks. We have four. For a little bitty town, that's a heap. Confederate Square is downtown, bordered by the courthouse, police station, and jail on the front side and two blocks of restored antebellums on the other three sides. When I opened The Baby Ruth Barr there in 1979, most all these old houses were boarded up and waiting on the wrecking ball. But in 1986, the town accidentally elected Crazy Colonel Connery as mayor.

He wasn't really a Colonel. He was one of those Civil War re-enactors. With a twist. Dressed in a dirty rebel uniform, he was a fixture in the park. Used to stand to the right of the statue of The Confederate Soldier and speak against war. All war. Grandpa Barr used to say Ole Connery had a rant for every war going back to Neanderthal versus Cro-Magnon. The town up and ran him for mayor as a protest against the incumbent who had been embezzling. That old mayor bought himself a pontoon boat to buzz around out there on Lake Blackjohn. Paid for the contraption with our hard-earned tax dollars. We cast our vote for the Colonel to put a scare into the old thief. Only we made a slight miscalculation. When the votes were counted, we had ourselves Crazy Colonel Connery as our brand new, duly elected mayor.

Turned out the Colonel was crazy like a fox. He discovered, and by discovered I mean invented, an obscure skirmish in the War Between the States which occurred, as luck would have it, smack dab in the middle of our little town square. Which made a convenient rallying point for those Civil War buffs who came first as a trickle and then, after The Colonel finagled his way onto the Tonight Show, as a moneyed flood.

"You know," my mama once scolded the Colonel, "you can go to hell for lying, the same as you can for stealing."

The Colonel appeared to study on that for a moment before he grinned at Mama and told her, "Miss Barr, if these folks is foolish enough to be nostalgic for something as bloody horrible as war, I'm betting even the Lord is tickled to see us take their money."

Besides Confederate Square, we've got Lee Park which is out past the old Piggly Wiggly Market near the county line. Snickers lives out that way, and in the spring when the magnolias are waxy dollops of cream in their shiny green canopy, she and I sometimes walk the trail along the creek. The walk is our way of pretending to burn off the calories we know dang well we're going to consume when, after our stroll, we sit in the shade across from the standing bronze of Robert E. Lee and enjoy a pulled pork sandwich from Goggins Barbeque.

Noisy Creek's third park, Jeff Davis Square, is out near the new Big Johnson Super Store. Its stern statue of the man himself looks out at what is now Martin Luther King Boulevard. Corrosion has given Old Jeff a more and more puzzled expression over the years, but then again, maybe that's just my imagination. Sometimes it seems to me our whole country has been teetering on the corner of Jeff Davis Avenue and Martin Luther King Boulevard for near forty years now. I drive out there sometimes to pick the wild scupanines that grow in the sun along the path behind the picnic tables. Daddy makes scupanine wine each year with the plumb dusky fruit. Just the one batch. It's ready to drink by his birthday just before Thanksgiving when the whole family raises glasses of sweet liquid amethyst and toasts another year in the life of Clark Barr.

Last but far from least is Traveller's Park where my fifty-fifth birthday party is being held. That's the one with the equestrian statue of Robert E. Lee. It's a way out yonder by Mama and Daddy's place. When we were kids, that whole section of Noisy Creek was known as Leeville, but over the years the town has moved on and left Leeville to itself. There's still not much out there but old farm houses set on biggish plots of land. Long time ago, it was piney woods, but except for a hundred-acre lopsided rectangle on the other side of the creek from Mama and Daddy's, it's mostly been cleared and planted in cotton or peanuts or soy beans now. Though the last few years of drought have turned a good bit of Leeville into a kudzu jungle.

It's difficult to act surprised when, in order to find a parking spot, you have to drive past a hundred cars belonging to your closest friends and relatives who've all come to help you celebrate your birthday. Luckily, Mama raised me right. I cover my face with my hands in mock confusion, squeal with pleasure, and everyone goes along with the charade by pretending to believe my act. I do not, however, have to feign delight in the party itself. If there's one thing we know how to do in the Barr family, it's throw a party. Counting second cousins, which we most certainly do, we have one hundred and seventy-eight individuals in our family. Even doubling up on the birthdays and anniversaries and graduations from pre-school, karate class, and junior varsity championships, we have one sort of family celebration or another near about every weekend. So we have a lot of practice having a bang-up good time.

Except for one or two parties each year held in one home or another where the guest list is restricted by the size of the house or backyard, we nearly always have well over a hundred and fifty souls at these gatherings, most of them right here in Traveller's Park. A bunch of us get together once a year and freeze enough peaches to keep us supplied in peach daiquiris and peach pies. Sometimes Uncle Earl camps for a week in the park and puts a pig in the ground for the best barbecued pork in South Georgia. Over the years we have informally organized ourselves to where we always have a well-balanced blend of greens and meat and sweets so that we all waddle back to our cars in the dark and go home to sleep on our backs, our tummies stretched as tight as ticks.

Tonight is no exception. Ardell has strung fairy lights from the lower branches of the pecan and magnolia trees. Six long folding tables are covered with Gramma Barr's picnic linens, all laden with love offerings of delicious food. By dark-thirty my stomach aches from too much food and laughter. I have a slight buzz from the daiquiris. Ardell has brought me three little glasses of the sweet poison. Or maybe four. I'm sitting between Mama and Candy with a baby girl about two years old on my lap who I believe was put there by my niece, Mary Lynn. Though whether or not the child is hers I do not know. Or care. The baby is warm against me with her head on my left breast, her thumb in her mouth. A gentle honeysuckle-tinged breeze stirs my hair. The male fireflies glow mightily in competition with the fairy lights. I am surrounded by love, supported by friends and family, content to be turning fifty-five and settling into the life of a small town widow.

So when my nephew, Jimmy, brings me what turns out to be the real surprise of my birthday party, I'm not really paying attention. Jimmy is my cousin Ed's boy. It can't have been more than a year or two ago that we celebrated his return from the Marine Corps. Except I seem to remember a party to celebrate him getting his contractor's license, and didn't he just finish that big development up in Columbus? Was that last year? I'm too tired to cipher it out right now.

"Aunt Ruth, this is a buddy of mine from the Marine Corps, Colin Jenkins."

I'm waking up a little now. From the look on Candy's face, I can tell this is the man who's been wanting to meet me. The man about whom, sometime before my third daiquiri, Snickers whispered loudly and, I must say, somewhat drunkenly in my ear, "I just met someone who looks a lot like your fourth husband." Since I've only been married three times this confused the bejeezus out of Great-aunt Minnie who was sitting next to me at the time.

Looking at the man standing beside my nephew, I am confused. Colin Jenkins is right near six feet tall. His straight honey-blond hair is cut neatly, a little longer on top than on the sides. It's impossible to know his eye color since it's full on dark by this time, but they sparkle enough to let me know his smile is genuine. He's wearing jeans and a dark shirt with the sleeves rolled up, exposing long and well-muscled forearms. Mr. Jenkins seems just about perfect to me. For one of my nieces! One of my much younger nieces! This child cannot possibly be more than thirty-five years old.

Mary Lynn materializes from the darkness behind me, scoops the warm child out of my lap, and giving me a quick kiss on the cheek, disappears back into the night. The air is warm and humid, fetid with rotting leaves and the sweet smell of cigar smoke coming from the uncles gathered just over yonder. The warm child gone from her place against my breasts, my nipples harden as the night air seeps through my thin cotton dress. A shiver runs through me. I cross my arms and try for a matronly smile. The last thing I want is for Colin Jenkins to think that I am one of those silly older women who foolishly get all hot and bothered by gorgeous younger men. Because I most certainly am not.

Candy jumps up from her canvas chair so quickly the dang thing collapses in a heap as it falls backward onto the grass. "I better go and have me a word with Aunt Grace about her Brunswick stew. Y'all know how agitated she can get."

A good bit of Aunt Grace's Brunswick stew remains in her big ole enamel orange pot. Cousin Sally's contribution has been gone for hours. This is an old competition, and as far as I can recall, one in which Candy has never before gotten involved.

"Time I cleaned up that there mess a' tater salad," Snickers mumbles before she vanishes into the night as well, purportedly on her way to clear away the dish that Cousin Bill and Uncle Earl fell into earlier while scuffling over some obscure NASCAR statistic. Which leaves me to make conversation alone with this perfectly lovely young man of whom I am old enough to be his, well, maybe not his mother. An aunt perhaps. A young-looking older aunt.

Decades past girlish coquettishness, I simply ask him why he wants to meet me. His face registers a moment of surprise, then he shows me his smile, extends his hand, and asks if I'd like to go for a walk, "out from under these trees, over there on the grass where we can see the stars."

This seems a lovely idea to me. An action which I know will cause little gasps of surprise from my watching family. A lady does not walk out into the night alone with a man she has only just met, leaving her party guests to their individual active imaginations. Of course, the decision to act on this small indiscretion might be influenced by that fourth peach daiquiri. Or I may just be reacting to his grin. I have always been a sucker for a man with a good smile.

Either way, we wander into the night, leaving seventy or so of my relatives to watch us disappear. Half of them have cell phones which they'll be dialing before we walk out of sight, calling to report my indiscretion to those relatives who left early.

The cool night air carries Snickers's distinctive giggle and the soft hum of Candy's chuckle. Well, of course, this is all a big joke. One in which this handsome young man is playing his part quite charmingly. If we weren't all good Baptists, I'd think my crazy sisters hired this young hunk, and he'll be starting his strip tease any moment now. Instead he walks politely beside me until we're far enough away from the party that we can no longer even hear the speakers thumping out Willie and Waylon.

"Jim says you know all the constellations," he tells me as we stand without quite touching and look up into the night sky.

The grass here is taller, still damp from an early afternoon rain. The fireflies are thick, miniature beacons breaking around our legs like phosphorous waves on some tropical beach. It was my Johnny who knew the constellations. He taught me a few over the years on one memorable occasion or another. One such moonless night in the Mexican Caribbean, we floated side by side, the ocean inky black beneath us, the sky ablaze with the bright promise of unending tomorrows.

Here in the soft night, I am alone with a handsome young man close enough that I could reach across a small space of darkness and touch him, run the tip of my finger down the length of his forearm. For the first time since Johnny died, I let myself realize how much I miss having a man in my life. How much richer life is with the scent and sound and touch of a man.

I breathe the wet night air deep, hope to clear my head of the effects of the daiquiris. The deep bass voices of my Uncles Neil and Earl blend to send an old Eddy Arnold song floating out over Traveller's Park, calling me back to reality.

"Is that why you wanted to meet me? So I could show you the Big Dipper?"

My voice is softer than I intend it to be. My question comes out less a joke than an intimate challenge.

Colin Jenkins takes my hand. His is rough, hot enough to burn my skin. He steps behind me, lifts my hand with his as its guide, and points up into the sparkling infinity.

"That one. Right there," he whispers. "That's the only one I know."

His body is solid behind mine. The air charged with electricity. The dark defeated by our closeness. I nearly lean into him as I sight along his index finger, let him guide me all the way to Venus.

COUSIN SALLY'S
BRUNSWICK STEW

Ingredients:

- 2 pounds of meat, cubed
- 4 cloves of garlic, chopped
- 1 c onion diced
- 1 pound spicy sausage, sliced
- 1 quart jar of canned tomatoes
- 1 pint canned corn
- 1 c okra sliced into rounds
- 1 c carrots diced

Cousin Sally likes a combination of chicken, venison, and beef, but she says she's had right good results with young goat as well. Aunt Grace has accused her of using opossum or even armadillo when she can get it, but Cousin insists that was only the one time as a kind of experiment.

Simmer the meat, garlic, onion, and sausage in enough water to cover for three hours. Add the remaining ingredients, and cook another hour. Let the whole mess set until it's cool so the flavors can marry together. Skim the fat if you're so inclined. Then heat it once again, and serve it hot.

Two

This time of year in Noisy Creek, the mornings can be depended upon to dawn crisp and clear. This morning was probably no exception. I wouldn't know. I slept until well into the first morning service at Jesus the Redeemer Baptist Church. By the time I pried one eye open, my left one as I recall, Mama and Daddy had their hearts and voices raised to Jesus. No doubt praying fervently for my back-sliding soul.

I force myself out of bed, intent on making it to the eleven o'clock Drunkards' Service. It's not really called by that name in the church bulletin, but everyone knows it's the service Pastor Coleman added when so many of his congregation persistently missed 9:00 services due to the tops of their heads threatening to blow off if they moved too quickly. Barrs, of course, go to the early service that my mama calls "the real church service."

Well, Barrs don't generally gallivant out into the night to stargaze with inappropriately aged men, either. If I'm going to have to endure a Come to Jesus meeting with my family over Sunday dinner, I may as well add to the sins from which I'll be repenting. Three cups of coffee, followed by the old family hangover cure, and I'm feeling almost human when Ardell calls.

Ardell has been my best friend since first grade when she smashed Davey

Mullings over the head with a bright yellow Tonka bulldozer for calling me Booger Barr. I repaid the favor two days later by punching Gary Grear in the stomach when he chased her around the Longstreet Elementary School playground in a failed attempt to look up her skirt. The two of us have been tag-teaming the men of this county ever since.

We have very few secrets from each other, and that includes those of, shall we say, a sexual nature.

"How'd it go out there under the stars with that handsome young Colin Jenkins? Is he a good kisser?"

"Being a good Christian woman, I wouldn't have the faintest idea how the very young Mr. Jenkins kisses."

"Ah-huh. You on your way to the Drunkards' Service?"

I hang up on my best friend. I'll see her in two hours at Mama and Daddy's for Sunday dinner, and besides, the raw egg in that old family hangover cure is threatening to come back up on me. I can hear her laughter as I replace the phone on the receiver.

I check myself a final time in the full length mirror before I leave the house. At five foot eight, I'm the tallest Barr sister. I suck in my belly, smooth my bias-cut, summer-weight, gray, wool-blend skirt over my hips. My height and B-cup breasts weren't a big hit with the boys when I was in high school, but both attributes are allowing me to age well. I touch my wavy shoulder length hair, toss it back over one shoulder to see if I've still got the flick move down pat. I have no idea what my natural hair color is anymore. It was mahogany red when I was younger, but the more gray I've discovered over the years, the heavier the butterscotch and honey highlights have become.

I've been told, and not exclusively by men trying to get into my britches, that I look like a young Blythe Danner. This morning, hung over, with every piece of fried chicken, catfish, and cake from the night before settled lumpily along my hips and belly, I'm afraid that Blythe Danner reference is only going to work if I concede that I'm a curvier version. Some of those curves aren't exactly in the right places, either. This morning that similarity is going to require a distance of a half-block, and to be on the safe side, it wouldn't hurt if the viewer squinted his eyes up into slits.

I do manage to drag my back-sliding body to church minutes before the start of the Drunkards' Service. Though I end up way down in front because the other, less conspicuous pews are already full by the time I sneak in the double doors just as the choir is opening with "Washed in the Blood of the Lamb." I can hear the whispering as I take my seat and smile innocently up at Pastor Coleman. It's not so much that folks here are judgmental as it is that they're delighted to have attention shifted away from the last damn fool thing they went and did. Also, we Noisy Creek folks are easily entertained.

The nearest movie theater is sixty miles away in Americus. Of course, we all have metal satellite dishes stuck on our roofs or hanging off the sides of even the tiniest shotgun shack. I keep expecting the rate of some obscure birth defect or leukemia or cancer of the ears to go way up. There can't be a single spot in the entire county where a person can stand and not be bombarded by microwave, satellite, and cell phones. So far I haven't noticed any significant changes around here. Though we do seem to have a few more Republicans than we used to have.

Remember when they first came out with those dishes? When they were bigger than a hay wagon? Daddy bought one from a fellow that came around in an old green Studebaker truck. Fellow had the franchise for these parts. Smooth talker. When Mama saw the monstrosity sitting smack dab in the middle of her view of the cornfield from her kitchen window, the one over the sink where she swore she spent nigh on to twenty long, hot years of her life, she was madder than a wet hen.

I don't think Daddy had any idea how big the thing was when he bought it, but once he'd gone and paid cash money for it, there was no way in thunder he was going to return it. Ten years ago when The Dish Network came around selling the smaller version, Mama paid to have one put up on the roof with her own social security money. I never did find out what happened to the old metal giant. Daddy swears Mama ran over it with the John Deere until it was nothing but a crumpled heap of twisted metal. Which could be true. It's a fact that it don't do to piss off my mama.

But even with a hundred channels to choose from, we've been raised to make our own fun. Sitting in a dark room and watching some fool in New York or Los Angeles or Miami pretend to get themselves into interesting situations is not our idea of a good time. Especially when our very own friends and neighbors, not to mention relatives, are some of the most downright entertaining folks you'd ever wanna meet.

So I'm not surprised or angered by the churchy whispers that I know for a downright fact are going to be following me everywhere I go for a day or two. It don't mean I'm not loved. It just means folks are interested in me. And happy it's me and not them that's caused tongues to waggle. As long as I don't actually date Colin Jenkins or some such foolishness as that, time will transform my star-gazing incident into just another funny story about the incorrigible Baby Ruth Barr.

By the end of The Drunkards' Service, I am feeling uplifted and right with the Lord. Just in time to hurry over to the home of my childhood where I'm sure Mama will be serving fried chicken, okra, and turnip greens, along with a small helping of worry, topped with just a sprinkling of disappointment over my recent uncharacteristic behavior. I'm doing a little girding up of my loins, spiritually speaking, as I walk outside the church into an already hot, late May day and come face to face with Colin Jenkins.

"What? I… did you go to church?" I choke out when I eventually untangle my tongue.

"I did," he assures me. "Sat right beside your parents and the rest of the family at the earlier real church service."

I always try to be gracious. I do. Give people the benefit of the doubt. See the good side of folks. But I assure you the man's smile when he delivers this news can only accurately be described as wicked.

Since I'm rendered speechless, he follows up with, "Your mom sent me to pick you up and bring you to dinner."

I could not be more surprised if I'd opened a door in a familiar room and stepped out onto another planet. Maybe Venus. He offers me his arm as if he's been raised his entire short life south of the Mason-Dixon. I honestly can't think of a single thing to say or do, except to slip my arm through his and let him lead me to his car. Which turns out to be a truck. With a side step that folds out from under it automatically when he opens my door.

Now I have no trouble whatsoever getting myself into and out of the standard redneck jacked up 4x4, but I happen to be wearing a dress and heels so I admit I hesitate for a moment before stepping up.

"Want some help?"

He actually waggles his eyebrows at me when he asks this. I'm not making a word of this up. Those soft blond arches over those blue eyes most certainly do waggle.

I am not so much worried about getting up in the truck as I am wondering how much of me is going to be exposed when I do so and yes, I admit it, how much of my upper thigh in all its cellulite glory is going to be on display. While I'm pondering on this, he places his hot hands on my waist, picks me up, and sits me in the truck. I try my hardest to be angry about this action, but it is difficult when all I can think about is the heat of those hands and how effortlessly he lifted me. By the time he strolls around the front of the truck and slips behind the wheel, I've recovered my breath.

"So tell me about yourself. Where are you from?" My voice catches in my throat, comes out in a ragged stammer. Like a blushing sixteen year old instead of the older aunt persona I'm shooting for.

"I'm from a small town in northern California. Arcata." He cranks up the truck. Blessed cold air blasts from the dash vents, blows up my dress, rippling the light-weight wool. We both reach to readjust the passenger vent at the same time, his warm hand covering mine for one electric moment. He clears his throat, pulls out of the church parking lot behind Miss Nadine in her 1968 Buick Regal.

"Anyway," he says. "Arcata is an interesting blend of down-home rednecks such as myself, 60s drop-out hippies, eco-terrorists, and, like pretty near everywhere else these days, retired Los Angeles Yuppies."

"So how did you end up here in Noisy Creek?" I'm relieved to hear that my voice has returned to normal, though for some reason, my accent is asserting itself, the way it often does when I'm talking to a good-looking man.

"I was in the Marine Corps with your cousin Jimmy. Over there in the desert. We kept in touch over the years. I went to Cal-Poly after the Corps. Have a degree in architecture. Was looking for someplace where I could afford to buy a small chunk of land, build a few beautiful eco-friendly houses. Make a little money in the process. Jimmy suggested I come out here and take a look."

We're skirting Lee Park. He seems to know his way to Mama and Daddy's. The sun has burned the morning's deep blue from the sky, the way it does when rain clouds are hunkered down over the mountains, building strength, making us wait for their sweet relief as the day grows hotter and hotter.

"So have you found what you're looking for here?"

He takes his eyes from the winding road, looks full at me, flashes that irresistible smile. "I believe I just may have, yes."

I ignore his obvious double meaning. "You've bought land? Are you building houses?"

"I am. I'd like to show you my project sometime."

I nod and smile, but my mind is elsewhere. We pull up under the cottonwood in Mama and Daddy's side yard, and I still do not have a definitive answer to my most burning question.

He comes around to open the door for me, reaches up as though it's the most natural thing in the world, and lifts me out of the truck, setting me down in front of him. Very close in front of him, kissing close. I decide the time for pussyfooting around the elephant in the room had passed.

"How old are you, Colin?"

"Does it matter?" His voice is as soft as a magnolia petal dropping on rain-drenched red earth.

"Uh-huh. It most surely does matter," I insist, though, right this second, I cannot think of a single reason why.

"I'm thirty-five," he says matter-of-factly. A thirty-five-years-young man standing close enough that I can smell his lime aftershave, revel in the way it mingles with his orange mouthwash to make an intoxicating sangria.

I take one giant step backward.

"My birthday last night? It was my fifty-fifth," I inform him. It's time to put a stop to any peculiar ideas he might have in his honey-blond head.

"Yes," he says as though a twenty year age difference isn't in the least shockingly inappropriate. "Look Ruth, I felt like I knew you before I ever hit town. Remember all those letters you wrote to Jimmy when he was in the Corps?"

I nod my head. Most all us Barrs are good letter writers. Snickers does a good bit of emailing, and we all talk on the phone as if we own stock in Southern Bell, but when one of our own is in the service, we do us some real letter writing.

"Jimmy shared those letters with me," Colin tells me. "Reading them let me feel like I was right in the middle of this homey, slightly crazy world of Noisy Creek. Compared to the sand box we were in right then? This little section of South Georgia seemed like paradise."

I think about pointing out to this gorgeous man that any one of my nieces would be delighted to show him around the county. Instead I take his hand and lead him inside to Sunday dinner.

THE OLD BARR
HANGOVER CURE

Ingredients:
- 8 oz tomato juice
- Dash of Tabasco sauce
- 1 fresh raw egg

I suspect this cure was originally concocted as a punishment, and a rather harsh one at that, for some husband who had over-imbibed the night before.

Pour the juice and Tabasco together, break a raw egg into the glass, hold your nose, and drink it down. I generally follow this up with one of those mega dose B-vitamin pills and a pot of coffee. It should be noted that when I was compiling this book, Uncle Earl pointed out to me that I had left out the main ingredient. He says the true Barr hangover cure is all the above ingredients chased with a can of warm beer.

It needs to be noted also that salmonella poisoning from store-bought raw eggs is on the rise and has the potential to kill you dead. If you didn't pluck the egg out from under your own hen while it was still warm, don't try this cure.

Three

Folks can surprise you. Not often. But enough so life stays interesting. Mama is the very last person in Noisy Creek I expected to be delighted with the idea of my dating a man young enough to be my. . . nephew. But here she is. Greeting him like some long-lost soldier returned from a popular war. Sitting him next to Daddy at the dinner table. Instructing me to sit across from "my young man" in what is now and has always been Snickers's place at the table. Seating herself, the queen mother, on Colin's right where she can serve him extra big portions of "our simple southern food." Like he's the Sultan of Brunei and accustomed to dining on the hearts of rare golden-toed monkeys or some such foolishness.

Midway through the meal, Colin, in glorious northern ignorance, asks, "I was wondering about Traveller's Park. It's a cool idea, a place for travelers to stay, but I didn't see any campsites yesterday at the party."

Mama serves him a third helping of chicken, politely explains without so much as a raised eyebrow, "It's called Traveller's Park for General Lee's horse, Traveller."

"Ah. The statue. General Lee on the horse. I get it now."

Then, because except for Mama, we Barrs have no mercy at all, the rest of us recite in unison with great feeling and appropriate hand and body movements the description of Traveller General Lee wrote to his sister-in-law, Markie Williams.

"If I was an artist like you, I would draw a true picture of Traveller, representing his fine proportions, muscular figure, deep chest, short back, strong haunches, flat legs, small head, broad forehead, delicate ears, quick eyes, small feet, and black mane and tail. Such a picture would inspire a poet, whose genius could then depict his worth, and describe his endurance of toil, hunger, thirst, heat and cold; and the dangers and suffering through which he has passed. He could dilate upon his sagacity and affection, and his invariable response to every wish of his rider. He might even imagine his thoughts through the long night-marches and days of the battle through which he has passed. But I am no artist Markie, and can therefore only say he is a Confederate Gray."

Grandpa Barr made every child in the family memorize this speech for his eightieth birthday. We Barrs love the prose, and given a set up like the one Colin has just provided, there is no way we can pass up an opportunity to trot it out. Besides, these days, revering General Lee or Jeff Davis or flying the Stars and Bars is fraught with complications about which most of us don't even care to think. I heard a televangelist say one time that the southern white man is like a child who, to keep warm and heat his food, brought fire into his home. But the flames got away from him, and while he labored heroically to save his family, his home has been consumed. By his own hand.

Well, all this guilt and resentment and nostalgia for a way of life none of us can remember and most of our ancestors never even experienced in the first place, not to mention the collective psychic memory of Reconstruction, and the ongoing meddling of Yankees who insist on believing they know better than us how to live our own lives, all this has made us leery, careful of how we express our love for our land and culture. Traveller is a safe vessel. Even the most hard-core Yankee doesn't object to the veneration of a horse. Ol' Confederate Gray Traveller only did what he was told to do. Let love and his earlier training, and, undoubtedly, his need for food and shelter carry him into bloody battle for a cause he could never understand or even question. We identify with ol' Traveller. Yes, we do.

So amidst all the laughter and the self-parody there at Mama's Sunday dinner table, while we Barrs prance in place and shake our heads to throw our imaginary manes off our arched necks, hangs something small, sharp-edged, and unspeakable. When we finish our little act, Colin looks around at our flushed faces and says, "That horse must have been something to see."

Which is about the best response to the whole deal you're ever going to get from a person raised up north.

Mama has outdone herself with dessert. She serves up pecan, peach, and rhubarb-strawberry pie. Even uses Gramma Powell's pie plates, the ones reserved for special occasions. Colin is the perfect guest. He questions Daddy about the battle that was fought in Noisy Creek. The one Crazy Colonel Connery employed to revitalize the downtown area. We all know it's a made-up story. Even so, we like to hear it. It may not be technically true, but the essence of the legend is dead on. Besides, storytelling is a tradition in Noisy Creek, and Daddy is one of the best there is at it.

"You are never gonna hear the term, Civil War, uttered by anyone born and bred in Noisy Creek," he instructs Colin. "The War Between the States. The War of Northern Aggression. The Late Unpleasantness. Whatever its name, it was a bloody awful mess, and it left the South defeated militarily, but never conquered. Toward the end of it, the North was beginning to draw the same conclusion that Truman came to when he gave the order to drop the atomic bomb, that Johnson understood when he chose not to run for re-election in 1968, that the Soviet Union finally understood when they withdrew from Afghanistan, and that the U.S. is coming to see in Iraq—them locals ain't gonna stop fightin' until ever last one a them is dead."

Mama and Snickers order me with thick glares and raised eyebrows to stay put while they clear the table, brush away the pie crumbs, and create a general nuisance refilling coffee cups.

None of this fuss slows Daddy's telling of the story.

"So by the time that devil, Sherman, marched his army of invaders through our great state, there weren't many left to resist him. Young boys, old men, and woman. Most of Sherman's troops burned their way through up northeast of Noisy Creek. But a depleted squad of marauding Yankees did pass by here.

They followed the Chattahoochee River and got themselves lost in the piney woods up near Sweetwater. By the time they staggered into Noisy Creek, they were hungry, tired, and feeling even more ornery than usual.

"It was Miss Bessie Smith that saw them first. The men folk, what was left of 'em, were out near Greens Prairie on a hunting expedition. Miss Bessie gathered up the women, and they marched right up to those Yankees, though the story is that one or two held back and positioned themselves around town with long barrel rifles. The rest of the women had politely brought an offering of tea and cornbread. Which, seeing as how the whole town had been on short rations for going on two years, was mighty hospitable of them."

All this reciting of tall tales is giving me ample time to study on Colin's rapt face as he follows Daddy's story. Lord, it is a dirty shame I am not a few years younger.

"Well, now, all that good southern food did not agree with those northern boys." Daddy's mouth is serious, but his eyes sparkle with mischief. "Within an hour, every one of them Yankees was sick as a wormy dog. Just in time for the old men and boys to arrive back from Greens Prairie, carrying a doe and four wild turkeys they'd surprised from under the ancient oaks out yonder there on the far side of Riley Creek. You know where I'm talking about?" Daddy asks me. "Where we had that picnic for Jimmy's eighteenth birthday party?"

I do my part. I nod my head. Nothing like throwing in an actual physical location to dress up a fine story.

"There are a couple different ideas on where those Yankee boys are buried. Some folks say that patch of green grass that's always thicker and higher there next to the Rotary Club welcome sign as you hit town. You noticed that spot?" Daddy asks Colin who grins and nods. "Other folks are sure them boys ended up in Traveller's Park. Right about there where you and my youngest daughter were gazing up into one of our fine southern nights."

By the time Daddy has spun this yarn out to its last drawled syllable, even I am feeling a little sorry for Colin, whose eyes, by the by, have revealed themselves in the light of this fine day to be a pale blue. The sort of washed-out blue that calls to mind a cloudless day in August. One of those sweltering days when the sweat runs down your back and into your waistband and all you can think about is taking a picnic to the creek, stripping out of your clothes, and plunging into a deep pool of leaf-speckled water.

Thoughts of rolling sweat and the removal of clothing bouncing around in my head, I get up from the table so quickly and, in my defense, from a place I don't usually sit that I knock my chair against Mama's hutch, making every last lovingly displayed plate jiggle and bounce with enough noise to wake the dead.

Ardell, sitting at the far end of the table, as far away from me as Mama could place her, laughs evilly and calls down the table to Colin, "It's okay, honey. She does that kind a thang all the time."

A joke the two of us have shared since we were gangly, awkward pre-pubescent twelve-year-olds. The shared memory causes me to laugh. Until I see the look on Mama's face. Then I quickly finish clearing the table.

The women in my family have other plans. Every last one of them spring up from their chairs like grease speckles that jump at you when you lay down a cold catfish fillet in a hot fry pan. Snickers pushes Colin and me out the front door where the early summer heat just about takes my breath away. My very own mama shuts us out into that sweltering mess with instructions that I am to "take my nice young man down to the creek and show him where Daddy caught that fat brown trout last fall."

COLIN'S FAVORITE
RHUBARB-STRAWBERRY PIE

To make the real thing, you're gonna need lard. Not the rancid cubes you buy in markets either, not unless you want your pie crust to taste like bacon. You need leaf lard which is the hard white globs of fat around the kidneys of young pigs. I know this is off-putting if you weren't raised on a farm. So, incidentally, is half of what we carry home from the air-conditioned supermarket to eat all wrapped up nice and pretty under plastic wrap. We've all grown used to not thinking about where food actually comes from.

The first time I helped my Uncle Earl butcher hogs, I was twelve. Since I'd been eating his famous pigs-in-the-ground at family gatherings since my baby teeth popped through my gums, Uncle said it was time I learned where all that goodness came from. Hog butchering is generally done after the first cold snap. You want the meat to keep, plus the smell alone would no doubt choke you to death in the heat and humidity of a hot summer day. The first year Daddy carried me with him to do the butchering, we didn't get our first freeze until late November. For me, the weekend after Thanksgiving is always going to be the day the hogs died.

Before we even went out back to where Uncle had the pigs penned up–oblivious, one hopes, to their fate–he and Daddy let me sit with them at the kitchen table and sip milk coffee. Back then, folks drank coffee all day long. I rarely stepped into a kitchen in my childhood there wasn't a pot bubbling thick on the stove. Us children were allowed a share on special occasions. In general, men in the Barr family drank their coffee black with plenty of sugar, and women drank theirs with a splash of cream and sometimes just a kiss of sugar. Children's coffee was a little more complicated. For us, an adult would warm fresh milk on the stove until it was steamy, then pour that frothy, yellowy white into a cup with a tablespoon of sugar and a jigger of coffee.

I wasn't allowed this treat very often, but the day the pigs died, Uncle served a cup up to me and told me to remember that he makes a deal with his pigs.

They eat good, enjoy each day of their lives, and he makes sure that at their death, "ain't nothing left of 'em don't get et but the squeal."

Feeling any better about the leaf lard now?

Pie Crust
- 4 c pastry flour
- 1 1/2 T sugar
- 2 t salt
- 1 3/4 c leaf lard

Use Crisco if you must. Not everyone is lucky enough to live in Noisy Creek and have an Uncle Earl.

- 1/2 c ice water
- 1 T white vinegar
- 1 fresh egg

Put the flour, sugar and salt in a bowl. Add the lard in small batches until the mixture looks like coarse-ground cornmeal. In a small bowl, stir together the water, vinegar, and the raw egg. Make a hollow in the flour mixture, and pour the contents of the small bowl into the depression. Using a wooden spoon and then your floured hands, gently fold the flour around the liquid until you have a smooth ball of dough. Cover the ball in plastic wrap, and refrigerate for at least an hour.

Filling
- 4 c rhubarb stalks, cut into 1/2 inch slices
- 1 1/2 c strawberries, stemmed and sliced
- 1 1/2 c sugar   • 4 T quick cooking tapioca   • 1/4 t salt

Do not use the leaves of the rhubarb. Mama never even gives them as scraps to the animals. They are poisonous. Remove all strings from the stalks before slicing. Combine all ingredients, and let sit while you roll out the pie crust.

Line the pan with the bottom crust. Pour the filling into your pastry-lined pie pan. Roll out and then gently fold the top crust in half, and move it to your pie. Open it so that it covers the filling and hangs down around edges of the pie pan. Trim, crimp, and cut vent slits.

Bake in a 375 degree oven for an hour. If your crust is golden before the pie is cooked, protect it with a tent of tin foil. Mama saves a twist of foil to lie along the crimped edges of the pie which sometimes brown faster than the middle.

Four

Clouds as black as the thoughts I am entertaining about the women folk in my family build out on the amber horizon. I am wearing my church clothes, for pity sake. I might be a dyed-in-the-wool country girl, but there is no way in heaven I'm going to fight my way through the gnats that, by the by, are as thick as soup and walk to the creek in heels and my best gray skirt. I'd turn myself right around and beat on the door until Mama lets us back in, except I'm pretty sure she'll pretend not to hear me knocking.

"Want to sit in the truck and listen to music?" Colin chokes out, swallowing two or three hundred gnats in the process.

I am from around here. I know better than to open my mouth in a gnat storm. I nod my head, and we run for his truck. Once inside the cab with the air conditioner blasting cold, bug-stunning air, Colin turns the radio on low, and the cab fills with the sounds of Toby Keith and Merle Haggard growling low about some woman that ain't hooked on them no more.

The land out here is flat with just a few folds and wrinkles, like those left on a bedspread after a nap in the heat of the day. We watch the storm come on in a direct path toward us, as though homed in on his truck. The clouds bleed streaks of tarnished silver that don't quite reach the ground. Sunset colors overshadowed by the rushing clouds. Pearly black ink spilling across a canvas of lilac and gold.

A crack of thunder makes me jump, and we are enclosed in rain. It pounds on the metal roof of the truck, drowns out the radio, covers the windshield with liquid pewter, shakes the truck in its delight in breaking free of the clouds that imprisoned it. Colin reaches across the cab, cups my face in his hands, hesitates for the breath it takes me to lean into him and then I taste his warm mouth.

The ground is steamy when we pull apart, the rain shower spent. He puts down his window. Warm air, charged with the smell of ozone mingling with wet Georgia clay, fills the truck cab, reminds me of where I am. The radio plays Trisha Yearwood's "Georgia Rain." It's not that big a coincidence. The station is just over yonder. They play the song pretty near every time it rains. Even so, it's nice, hearing it here with Colin after our first kiss.

I wait until the song's over before I ask, "What are we doing here, Colin?"

He looks out the side window, turns his head away from me. "A minute ago you seemed to know what you were doing."

The gnats are making a recovery. He lets the window back up. I see the silhouette of three faces framed in Mama's living room window all looking this way.

"Will you go out to dinner with me Friday night? Jimmy says there's a nice place out by the river."

I picture myself walking into The Plantation House on his arm. Hearing whispered words like "cradle robber" and "old fool." Think about how, for the first time in a long time, I am excited about life. Wonder if I might have mistaken resignation for contentment, growing old for aging gracefully. I know Mama and them are still watching there at the window. I lean across the seat of the truck, wrap both arms around his neck, and give Colin the full benefit of being kissed by a mature woman who knows what she wants.

Mama's washing the last of the coffee cups when I step into the kitchen. Seventy-eight years old, and she still won't allow her daughters to help her out hardly at all around the house. I tried moving these Sunday dinners over to my house a few years ago. "So long as the good Lord allows it, I'll be fussin over my kin and enjoyin ever minute of it," is the way she put it and not in that gentle a voice, either, so I just backed on off that idea.

Tonight, though, I can see she's tired. She folds a tea towel and hangs it on the front of the oven to dry. Its soft white cotton is decorated with two blue birds on a branch of cherry blossoms. She embroidered those pale-blue birds and pink flowers when I was just a little bit of a thing. Her hands are gnarled now, tweaked by arthritis and years of taking care of her family, keeping a house, and working her garden. But back then, sitting in her ample lap, watching those smooth hands pull the needle in and out of the material stretched tight in the hoop, cuddled against the warmth of her body—the touch of those hands seemed the best thing in the whole wide world.

Mama has not left the state of Georgia since marrying Daddy. Only been out of the tri-county area but three times since she arrived as a young bride. She did cross over into Dawson County to go to their Catfish Carnival a few years back when she and Daddy were in the middle of some mid-life crisis deal that scared the bejesus out of all of us girls. The year our cousin Tucker took his Angus to the state fair she traveled on up to Atlanta to see the child show that steer. The last time she left home was when me and Snickers and Candy carried her to Lookout Mountain for her birthday. That trip was something she talked about wanting to do for years until we just up and made the arrangements. She worried so about Daddy the whole time that I'm not sure she even enjoyed herself any. Though she surely did show off those pictures to The Ladies' Guild at the Jesus the Redeemer Baptist Church once we got her back home.

Colin left hours ago with a carry-home-for-breakfast plate of four hardtack biscuits and a slab of ham left over from Daddy's supper the night before. Snickers and Ardell finally grew tired of teasing me about that lovely kiss and went on home. Daddy's snores coming from his recliner in front of the TV periodically drown out the voice of David Attenborough. Mama sits across the kitchen table from me, smoothes the red and white checked oil cloth. Nearly every serious conversation Mama and I have ever had has taken place right here.

"I'm pleased you're keeping company with this man."

Her skin is crinkled tissue paper. Watching her in the yellow kitchen light, I picture her smoothing the wrapping paper of a hundred gifts over the years, saving each piece carefully to cover the next offering.

"He's too young for me, Mama. People will talk."

It isn't that I need her approval exactly, but my whole life I seem to have kept her soft voice in the back of my head, whispering her love and acceptance. I do not want to disappoint her now.

"Alyson Ruth Barr, if you think folks are whispering and watching because they don't approve of this match, you have sorely misjudged those what love you."

SOUTHERN
HARDTACK BISCUITS

These are not the fluffy Bisquick variety of biscuit. Those are made with buttermilk, and we usually eat the whole batch of them with butter and honey before they have a chance to cool. Hardtack biscuits are denser, they travel well, and are better the day after they've been made. Daddy once carried a batch on a ten-day hunting trip up near Buck Point. He came back with enough venison to fill the spare freezer and the claim that those biscuits were just as good the last day of the trip as they had been the first.

Growing up, Candy, Snickers, and I carried a good many of these flat, rock-like biscuits along with whatever meat we could rummage from the ice box down to the creek or in our school lunch boxes. The best thing that can be said for these circles of baked flour is that they're good for keeping the meat grease off your fingers, and I agree with Daddy, they're just as good after two weeks of being folded up in a dish towel and stuffed in a saddle bag as they are fresh from the oven.

Ingredients:
- 2 c flour
- 6 T cold lard

Do not waste your leaf lard on these. Any bacon flavor added by regular ole lard will be a blessing.

- 1 t salt
- 1 T baking powder
- 3/4 c water

Put the flour, salt, and powder in a bowl. Cut in the lard. Add the water, and mix gently just long enough to combine the ingredients. The trick to making any biscuit is to handle the dough as little as possible. Turn the dough onto a lightly floured hard surface, and pat it gently to a thickness of about an inch. Mama uses a jelly glass to cut the dough into rounds, but you start your own tradition. Use whatever you have that'll make the biscuits the size you want them for making biscuit sandwiches. Some folks even cut the dough into squares. Place the cut dough into a pan with the sides not touching. If they touch, you'll have soft sides which is glorious for buttermilk biscuits, but not what you want for hardtack. Bake at 425 degrees for fifteen minutes or so, depending on the size biscuit you've chosen for your hardtack.

Five

LuAnne Jones was the first negro woman to ever get her hair done at my salon. Course she wasn't a negro woman then. This was back in 1972. At that time, LuAnne was an Afro-American. This was a good number of years after Miss Rosa Parks sat her tired self down in the front of that bus in Selma. A fair piece of time had passed since Mr. Johnson pushed through that Civil Rights Act that repealed all those Jim Crow laws that had allowed the maintenance of some fairly peculiar traditions in our neck of the woods.

Noisy Creek stayed out of the civil rights fray for the most part. Though, for a fact, it was in 1969 that Mama moved our family from His Holy Name Baptist Church out in Leeville into Jesus the Redeemer Baptist Church here in town. I was busy running my first tiny business, and I missed most of the excitement. But as I heard tell, Mama stood right there in front of God and everybody, smack in front of the doors of the Baptist church where she'd been married and where all her children had been presented to the congregation and flat refused to shake ole Pastor Griffin's hand after one too many sermons where he shouted about God having placed the mark of Ham's shame on the brow of the Knee-gra.

The story was all over Noisy Creek by nightfall, and this was in the days before cell phones.

Folks told about how Miss Shelby Powell Barr told Preacher Griffin, "We are all God's children, sir. I no longer want to be instructed about the love of our Lord and Savior Jesus Christ by a man who believes that heaven is segregated based solely on the color of the skin into which we are born."

This whole deal wasn't as shocking as you might think. Remember Mama wasn't from around here. The majority of the town gossips believed this was Daddy's comeuppance for marrying an outsider. Also, there wasn't hardly a soul in Noisy Creek that Mama hadn't done something kindly for at one time or another. Besides, the Jesus the Redeemer Baptists had been trying to get us Barrs to switch churches for years. They managed to take credit for Mama's good judgment without actually endorsing her precise reason for moving.

So, when LuAnne Jones walked into The Baby Ruth Barr and asked for a haircut, she was one brave young woman. Not because she had any thoughts that I might refuse to cut her hair based on the color of her skin, but because I had no idea in the world how to cut or style negro hair, having never received a single class or instruction about it at beauty college. Which, come to find out, was just what LuAnne was counting on.

She was the first black stylist I hired. While I was still over at the original shop with just the one chair, LuAnne came in to work on weekends and after hours. All her customers were black women. But when we moved to the new place, she had her own chair during regular hours, same as me. At first, black women seemed to be just as uneasy as their white neighbors about this new arrangement. LuAnne and I talked about it and decided the thing to do was to just ignore the whole deal and go about our business.

Which we did. Folks will usually come around to change, long as you don't preach or push them along too quickly. Since just about half the population of Noisy Creek is black folks, over the years I have hired more stylists knowledgeable about their hair type. By 1987 the salon was split just about fifty-fifty, black and white. For years the black stylists had their chairs on the right side of salon , the side away from the windows that look out onto Confederate Square, and the white stylists worked along the left side of the room.

Gradually though, as one stylist left and was replaced with another, that has changed. In this twenty-first century, as LuAnne says, "the whole place looks like a salt and pepper jumble now, baby." Beauty Colleges teach all their graduates to cut all types of hair these days, and when you work side-by-side, knowledge gets passed around so that today we even have some black women who prefer white stylist and visa versa. Times change.

When I come into work on Monday, LuAnne, who's been my salon manager for five years, gives me a grin that lets me know that even the Noisy Creek grapevine now crosses race lines. Over coffee she tells me how, two years ago, she dated a younger man for a while. LuAnne is sixty, though that's hard to believe. When I look at her, I still see the skinny young woman that waltzed into my shop almost forty years ago asking if I knew how to cut nappy hair.

"How young was he?" I ask.

She looks at me over the top of her glasses. "Child, he was so young his idea of a date was to carry me to Six Flags Over Georgia."

I laugh, picture the always proper LuAnne, her straightened hair flying out behind her on some wild roller coaster.

She grins. "Honey, we was upside down and sideways until I was screamin' for mercy."

Snickers, who has come in behind us and helped herself to a cup of coffee, deadpans, "We still talkin' about roller coasters here, or have we moved on into the good stuff?"

"I did not have sex with that young man," LuAnne imitates our beloved Bill Clinton, "Lordy! After that day at Six Flags, I was convinced that boy's enthusiasm was likely to kill me if we ever did the dirty deed."

That's pretty much how my day goes. Every stylist, masseuse, manicurist, and cosmetician is booked solid all day by women who flock in to trade tales about younger men they or their sisters or cousins or great aunts have dated. Every last one of them has a story. Judging by the bits and pieces of conversation I overhear when I venture out of my office, pretty much every story is risqué.

By noon I have finished with my bookwork, and I come on out into the parlor. This is where clients sit after their appointments, drink coffee or sip wine, and relax a bit in the company of other women. I call it the Decompression Chamber. LuAnne claims it's the Transition Room. Either way, it's where, after being pampered and beautified, our clients prepare themselves to enter the demands of the real world again.

The light here comes from windows that run along the top of the room on three sides. The older I get, the more I appreciate indirect lighting. The wood floor glows around the edges of peach and cream carpets. Everything here is soft colors. The couches and plush chairs are apricot and peach and the palest yellow. Nobody but Snickers knows how much I paid to have the walls painted. I hired me a women from Atlanta who worked five days to create an illusion of the softest crushed velvet the color of sweet cream.

Today, this room, my favorite at the spa, is filled to bursting. A cacophony of women's voices punctuated with raucous laughter greet me when I walk in. For a few minutes they take turns giving me a hard time.

"Honey, does his mama know you kept him out so late the other night watchin' them stars?"

"You gonna marry him, Ruthie, or just go ahead and adopt him?"

Then, obligatory hazing over, they gather round and tell me how happy they are that I am seeing someone, how worried they've all been that I was just never going to get over losing three husbands. Which, given that I thought I was doing just fine being a widow lady, surprises me a bit.

"Ah honey, for some women being alone is fine and good. But child, you have always enjoyed the company of men."

This I get from Nancy Burton, who has brought in a plate of her famous pralines. Her proclamation is immediately greeted with a veritable chorus of "uh-huh" and "you got that right." Followed by more hazing.

"My cousin up in Cordell, when she was seeing a younger man, she got herself one a them Brazilian waxes. You gonna do that, Ruth? Make your puddy look like a fortune cookie for your young beau?"

I console myself by nibbling on a praline and trying to imagine how bad things would be if these were not all good Christian ladies. But they've gotten their point across. My mama was right. Folks aren't judging, they're just happy I've come out of my self-imposed isolation from the opposite sex. That and every last one of them are voyeurs.

—

Colin's working up near Columbus, finishing up a deal to build twenty-six luxury homes out on the outskirts of town. He calls them McMansions. Two-story, plantation style homes with lots of columns and narrow windows, granite counter tops, plastic Jacuzzi tubs and nearly three thousand square feet of living space, a third of which is a three-car garage. Not what he prefers to build, but it's what people want to buy.

He calls every night. On the phone, without his physical presence to distract me, I find I enjoy talking to him. He makes me laugh, which has always been my first prerequisite in a man. Okay, second after the nice smile.

"What I really want to build are site-specific homes. Beautiful, comfortable houses with non-toxic insulation. Built in small developments that share solar and wind power."

"That all sounds good," I tell him, "but can houses like that be built so ordinary people can afford them?"

"Absolutely, and I'm going to build them. Just as soon as I find me a partner who shares my vision." His laugh is more self-effacing chuckle than belly shaker. "And money. Somebody with a shared vision and lots of money. That's what I need. Else by the time I've saved enough to finance my first green development, I'll be in danger of breaking a hip falling from a step ladder."

"There ain't a lot of that kind of money around here," I warn. "Hard-working folks with Christ-loving hearts, we've got a plenty. But money enough to finance a small experimental housing development? For that you're gonna have to fish in bigger waters."

"I've got a few lines out in a deeper pond or two." He clears his throat, drops his voice into a sexy growl. "I can't wait to see you Friday."

"Ah huh." I'm curled on the sofa, watching the rain halo the streetlight on the corner. The paper-towel wrapped glass of iced tea in my hand tilts at the change in the tone of his voice. I set the sweating glass on a coaster. I have always been a world-class flirt. So why do I suddenly feel ridiculous, unable to form a coherent sentence without seeing a caricature of myself?

"It's funny," he says, "you look pretty much exactly how I pictured you when Jimmy and I were sitting on our bunks over there in the desert, and he was sharing those letters of yours."

"Maybe he showed you a picture."

"Uh-uh. I never saw you until Jimmy and I were sitting in my truck at the Piggly Wiggly the other day, and he pointed out this fine woman in nicely filled jeans. You were strutting along like you owned the world. When he told me who you were, I just felt like, 'Yeah. I have got to meet this woman.'"

On Wednesday, he calls after going out for a few beers with the guys. Just before we hang up, he begins to talk about how much he likes my green eyes with their tiny flecks of gold, my full mouth, that hollow at the base of my throat that leads down into my. . . . I tell him good night before he can sink any lower. It takes me a good long while to fall asleep.

MISS NANCY'S
PRALINES

Miss Nancy has lived here abouts since she was a young bride, but her people are from Mobile, Alabama, just across the bay from New Orleans. It's been rumored that when you look up "southern gentleman" in the Daughters of the Confederacy dictionary, there's a picture of her white-haired husband Robert. It's possible. Especially seeing as how it was Miss Nancy who helped write the book.

When the French were settling that beautiful and recently devastated crescent, the bayou country of Louisiana and southern Alabama, they brought their love of almond pralines with them. With no almonds available, the women used the abundant local pecans to create a new version of this delicacy. There's a knack for making them. Miss Nancy warns it'll take a couple of tries before you get the blend of sugar and cooking time exactly right to create this creamy treat.

Ingredients:
- 1 1/4 c sugar
- 1 c brown sugar
- 1/3 c butter
- 3/4 c cream
- 1 3/4 c pecans
- 1 t Southern Comfort whiskey

Put everything but the nuts and whiskey in a pan, and bring to boil over a low flame. Stir until the mixture reaches the soft ball stage. This is when a trickle of syrup dropped into a saucer of room-temperature water will form up into a nice soft ball when you roll it in your fingers. Add the last two ingredients, stir until the mixture turns cloudy and thickens. Then quickly drop by teaspoon onto wax paper. If it hardens too quickly, add a teaspoon of warm water, and stir. Miss Nancy says you can store these candies in an airtight container for weeks, though they never last more than an afternoon when she brings them into The Baby Ruth Barr.

Six

By the Fourth of July, Colin and I are ambling our way slowly toward being an official Noisy Creek couple. In this relationship, I am still what my niece Samantha calls a technical virgin, but the center isn't going to hold much longer. Folks seem to have passed through some sort of social values warp where they believe a woman dating a man twenty years younger than herself is finer than frog's hair.

It's Miss Moira Caldell who sums it up for the whole town. Miss Moira seemed older than red dirt back when I was a kid. She still lives alone in the old Caldell place that sets back in that grove of pecan trees as you come into town. Children still sidle past her house on Halloween with nervous looks over their shoulders. She sits in the back pew, aisle seat, of Jesus the Redeemer Baptist Church each and every Sunday where she packs Red Man snuff, sings in a pure soprano voice that can make you believe in wrinkled angels, and leaves before the preacher can make his way down the aisle so as to never shake hands with the man who, "opened the door to all this here foolishness." By which she means employing anything other than an organ as an accompaniment for making a joyful noise unto the Lord.

I run into Miss Moira as I am leaving Longstreet's Hardware. She grabs my arm as I come out of the store with a grip that could crack pecans. I'm telling you it left a mark on my arm like she'd used a vise.

That sweet, clear, and completely incongruent voice of hers floats out into the thick heat as she croons out, "Honey, maybe you finally found one that won't die off on ya."

For a while it seems that I am the only person in Noisy Creek who has reservations about the age difference between Colin and me. Then I talk to Daddy.

"It ain't natural," is the way he puts it to me.

Even though I've been having some of the same thoughts, it gets my back up, him saying that.

"What about Johnny and me? The age difference between me and Johnny was almost exactly the same as it is between me and Colin? How come this is different?"

Daddy and I do disagree from time to time. I won't try to tell you different. Mama says both of us can be as stubborn as Georgia mules and just about as ornery. But my daddy has always been my biggest supporter. So it surprises me, plus it hurts my feelings, him telling me I am too old for Colin Jenkins.

The two of us wander out to the back pasture where Daddy raises a couple of Angus each year. He leans against the wooden gate while I feed scraps from Mama's apple pie fixins to this year's sacrificial duo. The hair between the horns of an Angus is curly and coarse. I've never known one yet that didn't like a good scratching in that spot.

"I agree with you," Daddy says, his voice low and cracking along the edges. "It is unfair. Might even be, as your nephew Jake says, 'sucky.' But there are different rules in life for women than there are for men. Older man, younger woman is the way of the world. Younger man, older woman is a bad joke."

"That's a mighty odd statement," I counter. "It being you raised me to believe that I could do anything I wanted with my life. 'What's holdin' you up, Ruthie?' is, I believe, what you used to ask me. 'Fear or old age? If you want something, go out and get it.'"

The smallest calf pushes his hard head against my hand. The air smells of heat-drenched pines and sweaty livestock.

"The world ain't fair," he pronounces. "It'd be a fine place indeed if all God's children, regardless of gender or race or any other dang thing, were judged by the same rules. I wish we lived in that world. We do not." He reaches over, brushes the hair out of my face, sums up succinctly, "Wish in one hand, daughter, shit in the other. See which hand fills up quicker."

Up until now, my anger has been on a low simmer.

"The one thing I'm going to forbid." He stares off across the pasture, says the words like he's speaking them out of love and concern. "Do not be fooled into giving that young man any money."

This decree turns up the heat under my anger, possibly because I've had the same thought a time or two myself. The humid air is suddenly too thick to pull down into my lungs.

"So, what? You're saying the only reason Colin would be interested in me is my money?"

I ask this question a little louder than I intend. The calves both look up from where I've dropped apple peels, pull black ears forward on their broad heads, and study me to see what disturbance I might be up to next.

"You know better than that," Daddy says in a voice so soft I have to lean in to hear him. Which is such a difference from the volume I've just used to fling the question at him that it shames me some.

I can see Mama coming towards us from the house. Still in her apron, her black and white Wyandottes and orangey-yellow Orpingtons think she's bringing them kitchen scraps, and they make a feathery clucking flurry at her feet. She shoos them away with her apron and comes on a steady path for Daddy and me. Daddy's face reveals clearly that he has been advised not to have this conversation. That he's chosen to do so against Mama's wishes convinces me of his worry.

I step across the gap we've just built with our words, a barely visible fissure really, and rest my head on his shoulder. He wraps his arms around me. We watch Mama come on, swirls of red dust replacing the disappointed hens.

—

Ardell, my best friend in the world, has what good Baptist ladies call a seducing spirit. I assure you this is not meant as a compliment. If this ability to grab the attention of any man between the age of twelve and death has eased off any as she's gotten older, it's not so as you'd notice. Her appeal is not based entirely on her looks, though she does have, as my second husband Billy was fond of confiding, a mouth that looks like it could suck the chrome off a trailer hitch. Plus she also has really big boobs.

But it's her attitude that attracts men like bees to honey. When Ardell speaks to a man, she focuses every last bit of her attention on him, and her drawl gets thicker than sorghum in winter. If the man is attractive, you're going to be spoonin' sweetener out of the jar 'cause that drawl is going to be way too thick to pour. Now, all this is not to say that she is promiscuous, but she has been with a few men, and this, coupled with her aforementioned attitude, means that between the two of us, she is the *de facto* expert in the field of sexual attraction.

Colin and I have not yet made love, and Ardell is her usual sensitive self when we discuss the situation over Garden of Delight salads at Reb's out on Route 6. This, by the way, is the vow that has kept both of us within one size, okay two sizes, of our homemade senior high prom dresses–we never eat anything but green salad unless eating in the presence of a family member.

"I can't quite get my head around the whole age difference thing," I tell her as I munch rabbit food and gaze longingly at the platter of catfish and hush puppies that Ella May Spaulding is wolfing down at the table next to us. Ella May tips the scales at well over 250 pounds. Which encourages me somewhat to keep chewing my shredded lettuce. Though it doesn't improve the taste any.

"Honey, just because you've married every man you ever slept with, that don't mean you can't change that pattern of behavior at this point in your life. Just enjoy the gorgeous man. Quit over-thinking it."

In an attempt to pull my eyes away from Ella May's catfish, I happen to spot the pie case. Reb's famous sweet tater pies cover the top two shelves.

"Did I tell you what Tricia Rayland brought me when she came in for her weekly facial and massage?"

Ardell, who is putting yet another packet of sweetener in her sweating tea glass, just waves me on.

"A chocolate mess that is reported to be so good they call it 'Better than Sex with a Younger Man' Pie."

"Oh, Honey, there ain't no such a thang!"

"You're probably right. Tricia told me she brought it in special for me so I could try a bite and let her know if the name is justified."

"See," Ardell tells me triumphantly. "Everybody in town already thinks you're sleeping with him. You may as well get some enjoyment out of your tarnished reputation."

It isn't that I don't want to have sex with the man. Lord knows he's pistol hot. I like him. I like him a lot. I might even be falling in love with him. Something I thought I'd never do again. But much as it pains me to admit it, Daddy's right. The age difference going in this direction does feel a little unnatural. I lie in bed at night and try to picture Colin and me together.

I take advantage of owning a spa. I exercise, my skin is exfoliated and moisturized with each new miracle anti-aging claim that comes down the pike. I'm almost the same size as I was in my thirties. Well, all right, that right there, that's part of the problem. I'm nearly the same weight, but the pounds have shifted around on me since menopause.

"The thing is," I whisper across the table to Ardell. "I'm nervous about him seeing me naked."

"Oh for pity sake," Ardell's voice booms into the café. "Just turn out the lights, and get it over with!"

TRICIA RAYLAND'S
SEX WITH A YOUNGER MAN PIE

<u>Crust</u>
- 1 c flour   • 1 c butter
- 1/4 c sugar   • 3/4 c finely chopped Georgia Pecans

Using a mixer, beat these ingredients until creamy. Pour into a 9" x 13" baking pan. Bake at 350 degrees for 10 minutes. Remove, and cool completely.

<u>Second Layer</u>
- 1 c heavy cream whipped to stiff peaks
- 1 c powdered sugar
- 8 oz cream cheese

Mix thoroughly, and spread evenly on cold crust.

<u>Third Layer</u>
- 1 3 1/2 oz package of chocolate instant pudding
- 1 3 1/2 oz package of butterscotch instant pudding
- 3 c whole milk

Mix it. Pour it on the second layer.

<u>Fourth Layer</u>
- 1 c heavy cream whipped to stiff peaks

Spread it over the top, and sprinkle with chopped Georgia pecans. Refrigerate until served. I want to go on record as saying that this pie is good, but it most certainly does not live up to its name. Also, I feel obligated to point out that while Tricia is a little bit of a thing, when she carried it in to share at the salon, the clients who simply adored this treat were those in our Big-boned and Beautiful support group, who, as luck would have it, were meeting in the lounge that very morning.

Seven

I decide to skip the Fourth of July celebration this year, the third anniversary of Johnny's death. For two years running I set up lawn chairs on the sidewalk in front of the salon. I took my place among family and friends, waved to the Peach and Pecan Princesses as they balanced precariously on the back of the shiny red 1968 Cadillac Seville convertible that Bud Pierson from over at Pierson's Cadillac and Buick dealership keeps just for this occasion. Raised my eyebrows just a hair to let the rest of the womenfolk know I understood that ole Bud's shit-eatin' grin wasn't all about civic mindedness.

I ate barbecue and slaw and slurped beer from plastic cups while the Kiwanis Club, the Daughters of the Confederacy, and the Martin Luther King Middle School Marching Band passed by for inspection. I even made my appearance out in Magnolia Acres at my snooty cousin Ginny's where I kept my smile plastered steady on my aching face. But this year, I'm skipping the whole production.

I have demonstrated beyond reproach that I am handling Johnny's death in a reasonable fashion. Proven that my grieving is genuine, but not excessive. Shown that I have accepted his dying as the will of our Gracious Lord and Savior Jesus Christ and am getting on with the business of living. This year, I plan to stay home and spend the day saying good-bye to my husband. After three years, it's time to let him go.

My plan works well, to a point. I tell Mama I've come down with a summer cold and am going to spend the day curled up with a book. She pretends to believe me. Colin will be in Columbus. He's just finishing up the McMansion deal and is going to spend the day with someone he calls his money man. I tell Ardell the truth and as a reward receive only an eye roll of exasperation and a parting shot about some folks' need for a pity party. But it isn't pity, exactly. Soon now, Colin and I will be lovers, and before I can take that step, I need to say one last ritual good-bye to Johnny.

At dawn I sit on my back porch on the slide swing, Johnny's place vacant beside me. I let myself remember how he would lay his hand on my leg just above my knee and how I'd lean my head against his shoulder so that the backyard bird feeder looked skewered, the early morning birds breakfasting on a slant. I linger over the old photo albums. Dredge up his slightly spicy scent, the deep timbre of his voice, the way he'd roll up the sleeves on his dress shirts, making the movements almost a strip tease as he exposed his forearms.

By nightfall I am cried out, empty. I lie on Johnny's side of the bed, pull my legs up near my chin, and watch the fireworks burst up into a waiting sky and then fall spent to earth, glittering tails marking their path. I sleep well that night and am not all that surprised when Colin calls the next morning as I sip my first shot of caffeine and asks if I'll go to Savannah with him for the weekend.

I say yes.

—

I had been to Savannah with both Johnny and Billy, so I expect to be ambushed a time or two by the distorted déjà vu you sometimes experience in a familiar place with a new lover. But I have never before been there in the summer, and the city seems to me new and unexplored.

We drive to the coast in Colin's redneck truck, the radio blasting Toby and Alan, Waylan and Willie. Our talk is a smidgin nervous as we pass through a succession of small towns where folks go about the ordinary business of living and loving. I watch sunlight filter through streaming rain to make pale streaks of light across Colin's face, and know that I'll never again be able to ride in a truck in the rain without feeling this same sense of discovery and fear, anticipation and nerves.

The rain doesn't let up until we hit Chatham County, then the sun dances with the clouds and turns the light pearly and iridescent. Savannah is fresh and washed clean when we pull into town. Colin has reservations at The Gastonian Inn. Its elegance surprises me a little. Makes me think I am maybe reading Colin wrong. Putting so much emphasis on his youth that I am missing part of who he is.

We have never actually talked about money. I have simply assumed, because of the little trailer he rents out by Lee's Park, and I suppose, based on his youth, that his finances are restricted. But The Gastonian is not a hotel where we are going to run into anyone trying to squeeze a nickel into dime. I surprise myself by being almost disappointed by this. Having gone to the trouble of talking myself into enjoying the role of affluent older woman, I am caught off-balance.

Savannah is a wonderful city for walking. We find a map in the lobby and amble through the city, peer in through ornate iron gates at blowsy plantations and rambling antebellum homes. Our favorite is the Mercer House, which was the inspiration for the book, *Midnight in the Garden of Good and Evil*. Colin talks of southern architecture, of porticos and Greek columns, while I luxuriate in the feel of his body brushing mine as we walk arm in arm.

We pass a coffee shop advertising low country biscuits and gravy, his voice sparkling with excitement as he updates me on his plans for a green housing development. "I've designed a series of ecologically friendly homes built on large plots. A hundred acres of virgin land out in Leeville is what we're looking at."

For this dream project, he's talking about a parcel of land that bumps up against the back of Mama and Daddy's place. I listen to the excitement in his voice, am impressed by his knowledge and expertise. I've been seeing him through a veil of my own expectations based mostly on his youth. Here, away from Noisy Creek, I finally and for the first time begin to know him, not as a younger man, but just as a man.

We eat supper at an outdoor café across from the Forsyth Fountain. Hungry from our afternoon walking tour, we share grilled oysters and blackened sea bass and a shrimp éttoufée that leaves our mouths burning and nearly rolls our eyes back up in our heads in delight. We pick food off each others' plates while Colin tells me about his home town in northern California, and I try not to be distracted by random and seemingly uncontrollable thoughts of what we will be sharing a little later, back in our opulent room at The Gastonian.

I let myself luxuriate in the caress of his voice. "Arcata's all about fog and tall trees that meet along a wild, craggy coastline. Once every two or three years a Great White Shark mistakes a surfer for a seal and makes an indelible impression on some daredevil."

I'm floating on sexual anticipation, my belly filling nicely on rich food. I almost miss his next statement.

"Mom, who still lives just outside of Arcata in a farming community known as Elk River, she's coming out for a visit the end of October."

The picante heat of the éttoufée nearly chokes me to death. Once my coughing fit has passed, I force myself to ask sweetly, "And how old might your mother be?"

He is swallowing an oyster from our third batch when I ask, and it takes him long enough to answer that I come close to passing out from holding my breath.

"She is sixty-eight, I think. Why?"

Thirteen years older than me. Thank you, Sweet and Merciful Jesus.

"No reason. Just wondered."

Colin suggests a carriage ride after dinner, but I am going to need all my strength as well as the full effect of the oysters if I plan on making it through the night. I can't get the vision of LuAnne's Six Flags roller coaster tale out of my head.

Back at the hotel, I lock myself in the bathroom, tuck my hair into a butterfly clip, and shower with the elegant body gel provided by the hotel. Apricot pits hand-ground by virgins and infused with organic Madagascar almond oil, the soap is slick and smooth and warm against my skin. Music that sounds like the wailing of a cat in heat seeps through the walls and is quickly replaced with Dean Martin crooning "That's Amore."

How old does Colin think I am, anyway?

My stomach aches a little, and I laugh at myself realizing, even here in the privacy of the shower, I'm sucking it in.

Oh God, what am I doing?

I dry carefully with a creamy white towel so soft it feels like kitten fur. A mirror runs the length of the room. I preen and turn, lift my breasts and straighten my shoulders until the automatic fan begins to clear the shower steam. Then I slip on the peach silk nightgown I spent two hours shopping for in Americus. My sister, Candy, assures me that very soon now I will develop cataracts which will soften my image enough that bathroom mirrors will again be my friends. For now, I turn my back on the dang thing, pull my stomach tight, and step out into the bedroom, thinking of the long and lovely night ahead of me. This expectation, once again, turns out to be a false assumption based solely on his youth.

I admit it is partly my fault. I haven't made love since the night Johnny died. During that murky three-year stretch, I have passed through the change of life. In my mind I may be a dewy young lover, but my body needs external lubricant if we are going to pull this deal off without a good bit of discomfort. Lubricant I haven't thought to bring. But, hey, there's more than one way to lick a cat.

So we might have been able to work around that dry little obstacle, except that Colin, bless his ignorant, horny little soul, has no idea what the hell he's rushing through.

I have lived my life under the assumption that if a man is sensitive, then his thoughtfulness and desire to please will transfer into the bedroom. Lord, did I have that wrong. This young man has hands like a milk maid and a tongue he uses only for grunting the same boring phrase into my ear for the two minutes it takes him to accomplish his goal. My cry of genuine pain as he enters he takes for passion, and that sends him over the top.

All this I might have handled if, while I'm lying there trying to figure out if any of my nether parts had been actually broken, he hadn't flopped back on the pillow, grinned like a striped ape, and said, "So you liked that, did you?"

I wrap the two thousand thread count sheet up to my chin, sit straight up as though propelled, and explain to him about the old International Harvester I used to drive for my Uncle Paul each spring. I instruct Colin on glow plugs.

Explain how the oil in one of them old diesels takes a long and sluggish time to work its way through the engine parts. Talk about how the process cannot be hurried. Tell him how a gentle intuitive touch is needed to get the old piece of equipment up and running. Make clear to this handsome, technically challenged man, that if started improperly, the engine will seize up and refuse to start for you at all. Tell him how, if he is patient, if he respects the machine and listens carefully, it will tell him when it's ready. And then and only then, it will go for many long and wonderful hours, steady and true, until he finally wipes the sweat from his face one more time, gives up, and calls it finished.

When I stop talking, Colin pulls me over on top of him, nuzzles my neck, and whispers, "So I guess you didn't like it then, huh?"

Which makes me laugh. We agree to try again tomorrow, after we've located a drug store. We've flooded the engine now. Best to leave it alone for a while.

COONASS
SHRIMP ÉTTOUFÉE

That fancy restaurant in Savannah refused to share with me its recipe for breathtaking éttoufée, but I promise this one is a genuine treat. Coonass, just in case you ain't from around those parts, is French for bayou redneck.

Cousin Marlene and her husband, Bud spend one week a year in a time-share beach house in Gulf Shores, Alabama. She says that week is the only time she makes this recipe, since it is just an affront to the good Lord to use anything in it but fresh shrimp.

Ingredients:
- 8 T butter
- 3 garlic cloves chopped
- 1/2 c green bell pepper
- 2 1/2 c water
- Pepper flakes or Tabasco sauce to taste
- 5 lbs large shrimp, tails, head, and whiskers left on
- 1/2 c red bell pepper
- 1 c diced onion
- 1/2 c okra sliced
- 4 T flour
- 1 bay leaf
- Cooked rice.

Cousin Marlene says her boy, Jeffrey, calls this dish Whisker Stew.

Melt the butter in a skillet. When it's bubbling nicely, add the flour a tablespoon at a time, stirring constantly. Keep stirring until your roux is browned nicely. Add all the vegetables, and cook until everything is tender. Add the water, seasoning, and shrimp. Taste as you go now to determine how much pepper flake or hot sauce you'll want. Simmer uncovered for about twenty minutes or until the shrimp are cooked and your sauce has thickened. Serve over hot rice.

This is not a meal for the dainty eater. You are going to pick the shrimp out of the sauce and peel it with your fingers. I suggest you put on some zydeco music while enjoying this treat. An authentic coonass will suck the heads right out of the shell and swear on the Virgin that "this he-ah is the best paht, y'all."

Eight

In the cool early morning air of the Botanical Garden, Colin runs his index finger along the rise of my collar bone, does a good job of kissing me. When we separate, I watch a purple-chested hummingbird feed in the deep throat of a red Trumpet vine. We drive out to Tybee Island and eat soft-shelled crab on sour dough for lunch. Colin is attentive. With the slightest encouragement he talks more about his dreams for the green project. After lunch we splash our bare feet in the salty waters of the Atlantic and watch brown pelicans dive-bomb a swirling ball of silver bait fish flashing just below the surface of the opaque blue-green water. He kisses me thoroughly, demonstrates all the right moves.

But the night before has spooked me. Brought his age back into my head. Made me wonder if my much older naked body simply wasn't an inspiration for him. All day—as he touches my cheek or spoons the last bite of pecan pie into my mouth or holds me against him in a way that makes me ache to believe in him—all day I hear Daddy's voice in my head.

"Don't you give that boy any money!"

I do my best to drown my misgivings in a day that is glorious even by Georgia standards. Try to lose myself in the luminous quality of sun on azure water, the pure glow of light revealed in each small wave at the moment of cresting, so quick and so joyful that, each time, I suck in my breath, almost can't believe I've seen it. I nourish my shaken confidence with each look and touch from Colin, every hope and fear he shares with me.

We take a carriage ride that night. I'm not ready to go back to the room. I'm worried the old engine isn't going to crank at all. More worried that Colin doesn't have the patience to operate vintage equipment, or worse, that he doesn't have the desire to learn. My uncertainty has made the whole day feel a bit like being underwater. Hard to see clearly when the light is being bent and warped by a medium in which I'm not used to being surrounded.

Huddled together in the carriage, a sliver of moon sliding in and out of thin trailing dark clouds, Colin bestows on me one of those deep kisses that make me forget everything but the feel of his tongue, the way my body responds to his touch. When we separate, the salty air cools my wet mouth, and I am momentarily bereft. Then, finally, leaning in close, his words hot in my ear, he offers an apology for the night before.

"I was nervous. Worried about how I'd. . . perform," he confesses. "I, um. . . I had trouble with some. . . sexual stuff with my last girlfriend. I guess my worrying about it made it worse, and we eventually broke up over it."

In the dark, with the clomp-clack of the horses' feet on cobblestones as a staccato back beat, I whisper the two words a nice southern woman is never supposed to say to a man—erectile dysfunction. He doesn't gasp. He may have blushed.

"Yeah." Breath hot on my ear again. "That was pretty much the problem. But then last night I was relieved, you know to not have that. . . difficulty. You are so hot, and I just got into it and didn't think so much or worry about. . . you know."

I can't remember ever being described as hot.

In the dark his soft confession tickles the tender spot behind my ear. "I think I was already half in love with you, reading your letters to Jimmy. In a funny way I feel like I knew you long before I ever met you in person. When I saw you coming out of the Piggly Wiggly, from that first moment, when I had a body and face to put with the words of your letters, I've been fantasizing about getting together with you. It took me two months to convince your overprotective cousin Jimmy to introduce us at your birthday party."

The carriage lets us out in front of The Gastonian. In our lovely room, with its king-size bed and soft sheets, I discover that he is trainable. For my part, the old engine cranks right up, purrs smoothly on into the night. The next morning the gilded mirror over the bathroom sink reflects a woman I haven't seen in over a month of Sundays. My eyes glow, my mouth is slightly swollen, bruised by our enthusiasm. Colin looks like every man in the world who has spent the night making his woman happy. As we pack to leave, our hands keep reaching to touch each other, to find again those secret places we discovered in the dark.

Feeling languid, nearly boneless, I lean against Colin while he checks us out at the front desk. A large, gray suited man startles me by putting his hand on Colin's shoulder, flashing a Rolex as shiny as greed. Colin does not seem pleased to see this wide and grinning gentleman. This, it turns out, is the money man. Preston Yates. The investor who helped Colin put together the McMansion deal and is thinking of coming in also on the green project in Noisy Creek. The one who, it soon becomes clear, has paid for our room here at this elegant hotel. The man on whose credit card Colin has undoubtedly put our candlelit meals and romantic carriage rides.

"So," Preston Yates bellows at me as though he's calling hogs. "What do you think of our boy's idea for this e-co-logical project?"

I am chilled, as though suddenly struck with some nasty debilitating flu.

Oblivious to my sudden need to get out of the air-conditioned lobby, Yates barrels ahead. "It's gonna make us a ton of money. Be good for everybody. Be smart if you got in on the ground floor."

I experience a vivid out-of-body sensation. I no longer stand in a fancy hotel lobby beside a man to whom I have made love less than an hour ago. Instead, I huddle in a rocker, a shawl wrapped tight around the shoulders of my faded housedress. In a quaking voice I tell a sympathetic reporter how that nice young man insisted he needed my life savings up front to buy the aluminum siding.

The image lasts only a moment, a flash, like the afterburn behind your eyes when you stare at a golden sunset a fraction of a second too long. The image remains only the time it takes me to remember that I am Alyson Ruth Barr from Noisy Creek, daughter of Clark and Shelby Powell Barr. I tighten my grip on Colin's arm, more a wrestling move now than a lover's touch.

In my thickest drawl, I tell Preston Yates, "I am just tickled to death to meet you, but now I need to speak with our boy alone."

I stomp with Colin in tow through the lobby and outside. The air is dense with the mingled smells of blooming honeysuckle and the salty tang of the sea.

My anger is a physical thing. It grips my pride and shakes hard. That hideous phrase, there's no fool like an old fool, is an endless gloating tape in my head. Colin hasn't known me long enough to keep his mouth shut until my adrenalin level has dropped to somewhere below the bloody murder stage.

"Look, Ruth, it's not what you're thinking."

I release my death grip on his arm. Take a step back and then change my mind and charge forward until we're face to face, as close as lovers.

Colin edges back until he's up against the brick wall behind him. My voice is low and ugly. Even as I hiss at him, I know I am caught up in an anger that is not based solely on his deception about who has paid for a hotel room or even why that person has done so. I throw at him all my insecurity about the difference in our ages.

This morning, when he stepped into the shower with me, had I seen a look of distaste pass over his eyes when he saw me there with no way to disguise my body? No way to cover those little deviations from youth that have settled over me with age. The slightly softened arm muscles. The left breast that falls just a tad lower than the right. The grouping of skin tags under my left breast. The ones that appeared one night after a hot flash like mushrooms after a hard rain.

"Your little tale of past impotence?" I shout. "Was that the truth or a handy lie to cover your repulsion at making love to an old broad like me in the hope of raking in some investment money? That extra glass of wine you had with dinner? Was it to settle your nerves, build up your courage before coming back to the room and being forced to have sex with me?"

I stand on that steamy sidewalk, my voice a hoarse cackle, and I mix a brew of my own insecurity with some righteous indignation, I stir in a pinch of self-pity with a bait of lost youth. I show no mercy. I do my best to cover him in the same shame that I now feel.

When my anger finally slacks enough that he can get a word in edgewise, Colin dares to trace my cheek with his finger. His touch burns my skin, and I slap his hand away before I can remember the feel of his hands on my body last night. The way he had transformed over the course of the night from an eager but clumsy boy into a man who made me feel beautiful and desirable again. I retreat back out of his reach.

"You're wrong." More than a touch of anger hardens his voice.

"Really? What am I wrong about exactly?" I say it mean, but part of me wants him to explain it. To make me believe again that he and I are just beginning a journey of discovery with one another. That he sees in me something other than an older woman with money who might be persuaded to help him out financially with a dream project.

"Everything. You're wrong about everything."

I almost believe him. If he had let himself get truly angry, fought back, it might have ended differently. Or maybe not. Maybe this was never anything but a sad little sexual fling. A last hoorah before I settle into my safe and settled life as a three-time widow.

LAST BITE
PECAN PIE

Every woman in Noisy Creek has a recipe for pecan pie. I gained five pounds testing them all before settling on this one from Uncle Hershel's wife.

Ingredients:
- 3 fresh eggs
- 1 c light corn syrup
- 1/4 t salt
- 1 t Southern Comfort whiskey
- 1 c dark brown sugar
- 2 T butter
- 1 1/2 c pecan halves

Make one crust from mama's pie dough recipe. Lay this in your pie pan, and crimp the edges, arrange the pecan halves on this uncooked crust. Whisk the eggs, stir in the rest of the ingredients until well blended. Pour on top of pecans in pie shell. Bake at 375 degrees until the filling is set around the edges, about one hour. It should be jello jiggly, not runny. You might need to use that twisted length of tin foil to keep the edges of the crust from burning before the filling has set.

Serve with whipped cream.

nine

Colin does his best to give me the keys to his truck. I throw them back and stalk away, head high, hoping my ass looks passable and that my triceps aren't jiggling in my new mint-green sleeveless sun dress. I have no idea where I am going, but the movement is doing me good. A red and blue Mason-Dixon Car Rental sign glints in the sun. I set my sights on it as though I knew all along that's where I was headed. A canary yellow Corvette convertible catches my eye, but at the last minute I talk myself out of it. How cliché would that be? A convertible sports car and what is apparently my own version of a midlife crisis. Instead I settle on a Nissan Altima. Steel gray. The color of a sensible old woman's hair.

The sun shines bright and mocking all the way home. The Nissan has one of those satellite radios. I hit the button for Classic Country and Western Women and sing along with Tammy and Patsy and Loretta. In Americus I stop for breakfast and flirt outrageously with the old man on the stool next to mine at the counter. He's eighty if he is a day. Apparently just my type. I order ham and eggs with red-eye gravy, grits, and buttermilk biscuits. It's the new me, relaxing into my age. By early afternoon I'm home in bed, the entire episode behind me. A nap seems the thing to do. Old ladies do that, right? A nice soothing nap in the heat of the day.

It's dusk before I drag myself out of bed. From the glider on the screened back porch, I watch the light change from palest gold to soft lavender and then, as the sun disappears for another day, the world is momentarily lusterless gray. I am beginning to frame the last few months as my folly with the boy. Having had sex with him seems now a betrayal, not just of my own self-worth, but of my love for Johnny as well. As though the act dishonored his memory. Well, as my daddy's sister, Aunt Trudy, says, "too much ponderin' ain't good for the soul."

I turn on a couple of lights and call Ardell. Ten minutes later she's established herself in Johnny's place on the glider next to me, both of us sipping mojitos, as I confess my tale of shame. One of the things I usually enjoy about Ardell is her short tolerance for fools. Tonight, this is not my favorite thing about her. She allows me to piss and moan until long after I have gone past sipping, am well into slugging back the mojitos. Then she leads me down the hall and tucks me into my big lonely king-sized bed. By this time her patience with me has left the building.

"I have three words for you, darlin'." She kisses my forehead and adjusts the covers around me. "Get over yourself."

She leaves me there in the dark with the room spinning slowly, a small rueful grin of acknowledgment on my face.

Pity party over, I go in to work the next day hung over and dreading the questions about my romantic weekend in Savannah with The Boy. That's the thing about Noisy Creek. Folks not only share your triumphs. They're quick to acknowledge your failures, shames, and downright foolishness as well. Quicker even. Being a Barr, marrying three good men, having my own business, and being independent enough to do pretty much whatever I dang well please–all these things put me high on our small town pecking order. So a lot of folks are of the opinion that I am maybe a little too full of my own self-importance and that, with this little fiasco with a younger man, the Good Lord has busted my britches.

There are times when I think they might well be correct in this assessment. Still, the fall from the pedestal of my own self-invented perfection isn't fatal. I may have behaved like a fool, but I am Noisy Creek's fool and folks rally around.

Colin calls two or three times a day for a week. At work, Snickers or Lu-Anne screen my calls. I can hear them worrying Colin on the phone, their voices low and growly like a pair of bulldogs protecting a favorite bone. I feel a little bit sorry for the boy. You'd think that tale Daddy told him about what happened to Sherman's boys when they wandered too close to Noisy Creek would have tipped him off. Being a Yankee and all, he really has no idea what he got himself involved in when he pissed on southern womanhood.

At home, I stand in the kitchen watching the evening light slant through my magnolia and chinaberry trees, lace the St. Augustine's with silver. I wrap a carefully folded paper towel around my sweating tea glass, make myself experience all over again that moment when Preston Yates casually tapped Colin's shoulder and shattered the spell I had been foolish enough to believe Colin and I were conjuring together. I sip my tea, enjoy the cool sweet flow of it. Only then do I push the button on the blinking answering machine. Colin's voice fills the kitchen. He apologizes. Sounds sincere, filled with energy and the hope of the young that all things can be put back together. Insists he has an explanation for everything. That I've misinterpreted the whole damn thing with the hotel room.

On Friday, just after dark, even before I peek out the window and see the monster 4x4 truck behind my car in the driveway, I know who is standing on my porch. He is fresh and clean from an after-work shower, his hair still a little damp, more amber than honey-colored. His blue long-sleeved shirt is rolled up to just below the elbows. Soft golden hair on strong forearms bring a rushing memory of our love-making. I let him inside, am careful to keep a good bit of physical distance between us. I don't know what to do with my hands, settle on folding them around my elbows, arms crossed over my breasts. He follows me to the living room where I turn on the overhead light and both lamps. On shaky legs I motion him to the sofa, while I sink into Johnny's well-worn leather chair.

He perches his long body on the edge of the couch cushion, keeps rubbing his right thumb along the ball of his left hand. Which, despite my best intentions, I find insidiously arousing.

"Look, I should have told you that Preston was paying for the hotel room."

"And the candlelit dinners and romantic carriage rides." I intend to sound spiteful and mean. It's possible I end up sounding more nostalgic than nasty.

Colin looks pitiful. He does. Like one of Uncle Maynard's hounds when the coon has done slipped away into the night. He keeps rubbing that thumb along his palm.

"I wanted to take you someplace special. Preston offered to pay for everything. Said maybe you'd be interested in getting in on a good investment with the housing deal. If not, well, we'd still have a great weekend on him. The man has more money than an Arab prince. I'm still working out my own financial stuff. It just seemed harmless. That's all. I should have told you all this. I know. I'm sorry, Ruth. I don't know what else to say."

Well, neither do I. Even if all this is true, even if his feelings for me are genuine, it doesn't change the age difference between us. It helps my pride, but it doesn't change things.

"Colin, I just can't see where this relationship can go. I don't do that California mess–friends with benefits. I've done my share of traveling around the world, and yes, I'm a successful business woman, but at heart I'm a fifty-five year old small-town southern woman. I'm not telling you that after three months I want a commitment, but I need for there to be a possibility for a long-term relationship. I can't see that happening with us. When I'm seventy you'll be—"

"Why do we have to project fifteen years into an uncertain future? Why can't you just accept that, right now, this very day, I love you?"

The first time the word love is spoken in a relationship, it shouldn't be during the break-up.

"Why is this age thing so damn important to you? It's like you wrap yourself up in it as a way to protect yourself against me."

I hate it when men see through me. I have never found it to be an endearing quality. Plus, when you come right down to it, I still have only the word of a proven liar that he hasn't been playing me all along. A gullible old broad with money. Maybe the truth is that when I'm with him, I just can't get beyond the image of myself as a ridiculous figure. An older woman clinging to the arm of a handsome young man, grasping at her own long-vanished youth.

"None of this changes anything, Colin. Even if you're telling the truth about not wanting money from me. I don't see a future for us, and I'm too old-fashioned for recreational sex."

His gray blue eyes widen in disappointment, yes, but also in anger. When he stands, the room seems to fill with his energy and strength. He covers the distance between us in two long strides. He pulls me up out of my chair, cradles my face in his hands. My mouth turns up to him of its own volition. His kiss is rough, thorough, tastes of spearmint and anger.

He pushes away while I am still tilted upward, open to him.

"So let me get this straight. At best you think what we've been doing is meaningless sex and at worst that I've been whoring myself out to you in the hopes that you might spare me some coin?"

I admit it does sound bad when he puts it that way. I can't think of anything to say, am still catching my breath from that kiss, still leaning slightly forward into the empty space between us.

"I'm real sorry you feel that way." His voice is soft. "'Cause I thought we had something special going on. Just so you know, I fell in love with your honesty and your way of looking at life before I ever met you, and when I saw you walk out of that Piggly Wiggly, you just flat took my breath away."

He's at the door when he stops, calls back over his shoulder, "I have never once thought of you as an older woman. You are the one with the problem about our ages. Not me."

He turns around then, looks at me standing there in the hallway of my home, my arms wrapped across my breasts. I feel at that moment completely barren. There is no sign of the relief I counted on for having successfully ended this folly.

I think in that moment that he will walk back to me, force me somehow to see myself the way he sees me. Instead, sadness floods his pale eyes, but it does not spill down his beautiful face before he shuts the door gently behind him and walks out of my life.

I eat a box of Milano cookies and take my pride to bed.

REDEYE
GRAVY

Red-eye gravy is always served with ham and grits and buttermilk biscuits. Anyone tells you any different ain't from anywhere around here.

 Fry a slice of country ham, fat untrimmed, in a cast-iron skillet. This recipe will not work in one of those new stick-free frying pans. For red-eye gravy you want those bits of browned fat that stick to the bottom of the pan for flavoring. When browned nicely, set the ham slice in platter, and add 1/2 cup strong black coffee to the ham fat in the skillet. Stir until heated, making sure to loosen the fat from the skillet. Pour over the ham, and serve with your grits and biscuits.

By the bye, never wash your cast iron skillet with soap and water, or everything you cook in it will soon carry a subtle taste of rust. Wipe it out after each use with a damp dish cloth, and store it in the oven where the heat will keep it nice and dry.

Ten

Snickers's birthday is August second. She always throws a themed party. One year it was Hawaiian with fake palm trees and plastic orchids. We all wore hula skirts and had plastic coconut knockers. Last year she went Oriental and the entire Barr family ended up banned from The Lotus Blossom up in Columbus when Uncle Joel set off a bottle rocket to punctuate the end of the traditional Happy Birthday song. It did seem appropriate for a Chinese-themed party, they having invented fireworks and all. Though setting the rocket off inside the restaurant was admittedly not the best idea. When a few of the multicolor sparks set fire to a string of paper lanterns hanging over the statue of Buddha, it sealed the deal on our expulsion.

This year she's celebrating with just Candy and me. The theme is Old Broads Gone Wild. We're leaving town, staying at Maggie's Marvelous Magnolia Manor in Buckhead. Snickers found this "unique and charming bed and breakfast" on the Internet. She has occasional insomnia, and lately she entertains herself during these quiet hours of the night by surfing the web. Maggie's is owned and managed by a convert. We used to call these folks carpetbaggers, but even us hillbillies can be politically correct when we choose to be. Born and raised in upstate New York, Miss Maggie crossed the Mason-Dixon less than five years ago after what she describes as one hellacious divorce and has since become more southern than the ghost of Margaret Mitchell.

Her B&B is a small plantation house lovingly decorated in southern kitsch. If Scarlet O'Hara and Elvis had a love child and then that child designed a bordello, Maggie's Marvelous Magnolia Manor is what you'd get. I am staying in The Jungle Room. My bathtub's clawed feet are gold gild, the porcelain painted to look like leopard skin. To match the bedding, I presume. Candy is in The Ladies Chamber. She has a laced canopy bed big enough for said lady to bed half the Confederacy and an actual fainting couch covered in pussy-pink suede. Snickers, because it is her birthday, got first choice. She is in The Crystal Palace Suite. Maggie draws open the brocade drapes over the leaded windows with a flourish to rival Vanna White. When the sunlight hits the over-sized chandelier and the crystals hanging from each and every lamp and drawer in the room, we are momentarily blinded by tiny rainbows of light. We all stand speechless, stunned. It's like being inside a kaleidoscope. I hope I packed Dramamine.

"Isn't it something?" Maggie enthuses.

We all agree that it most certainly is something.

Once Maggie is out of earshot, Candy asks in that deadpan serious voice of hers, "So, Snicks, why exactly did you choose this particular bed and breakfast?"

The question causes us to laugh ourselves into a fit, which ends with all three of us stretched sideways across the white brocade bed while a million tiny specks of brilliance dance around, over, and seemingly through us. Our bellies are sore with laughter by the time we get the answer.

"What attracted me," Snickers chokes out between lingering fits of giggles, "is that Maggie offers a deal called The Shopper's Package. Room, a car and driver, and a hand lettered guidebook to, reputedly, the most expensive shops and exclusive restaurants on the planet."

Candy and I sit up, suddenly aware that there may be a need to conserve our strength.

Snickers blows her nose on a tissue she plucks from a crystal embedded holder on the nightstand. "Of course, they don't sell anything in these stores that we could actually wear once we get back to Noisy Creek, but the point isn't to buy anything. My plan is to dream away the day window shopping, have a couple of glorious meals and then, under a fine southern moon, return happily to Maggie's modest B&B."

The limousine turns out to be a pink Cadillac. Maggie apparently honed her entrepreneurial skills up north by selling Mary Kay cosmetics. Eli, Maggie's twenty-year old son, is our driver. His hair is spiked and maroon. He sports enough facial piercing that I have to concentrate on not flinching in sympathy each time I look at him. He recommends a new restaurant a few blocks away for our lunch.

"There are edgier places, but, like, I think, for you ladies, more traditional is what you want, huh?"

We think that's what he says. Between the Yankee accent and the silver ball bearing through his tongue, it's a little like traveling in a foreign country. But it turns out that young Eli knows his stuff as a tour guide. We eat giant salads of exotic greens and shop until our feet swell to twice their normal size. Candy splurges on a silk tie at Hermes for her pastor husband, though she swears if his parishioners ever find out how much it cost, it will reduce the Sunday collection by half. Snickers, who collects silver plate, finds a cream pitcher dating from before the War of Northern Aggression in an antique shop. I sneak back and buy it for her for her birthday.

By late afternoon, we are collapsed at the round table of an ice cream parlor, our shoes kicked off helter-skelter on the sparkly black marble floor.

"So it's over between you and Colin?" Candy spoons peach sorbet into her mouth.

"I guess it is, yeah."

I can already tell I am not going to be able to get my pumps back on without significant pain.

"I may have misjudged him as far as the whole wanting money from me thing goes, but it worked out for the best. The break-up. I'm too old for him."

I choose to ignore the looks that statement sends flying across the shiny pink and gray granite table top.

The truth is, I miss Colin. I miss hearing about his projects, miss his energy and excitement. I miss the rush of pleasure I felt at his smile or the way he'd pull me against his length before he kissed me. I had begun to look forward to knowing him better, and I am saddened by the loss of that promise.

Candy rubs her feet. "I thought this weekend was called Old Broads Gone Wild? I ain't gone anywhere near wild yet."

We limp to our pink limo and our pierced driver who we instruct to take us back to our unique and charming B&B. We take a little nap and then go out into the hot city night and have ourselves a whooping good time. Meaning we eat real food for dinner instead of salad, drink a teensy bit more than we should, and when I refuse to share sexual details about the now infamous weekend in Savannah, my big sisters giggle themselves into a frenzy of naughty speculation. A handsome gentleman and his friends from South Beach, Florida send a round of drinks to our table, and Snickers gives him her best smile and her phone number before shooing him away. That's about as wild as the old broads get.

Two weeks after the Buckhead jaunt, I am on my way to Mama and Daddy's for Sunday dinner when at the junction of Lee St and Pecan Ave, where that hundred acres of pristine woods sits, I notice a sign announcing Jenkins Construction—An ecologically friendly development of quality homes. A bulldozer is already at work easing a winding road gently around the spreading magnolias, pecans, and mossy oaks. Happy for Colin, I pull over and watch the dozer begin to make his dream a reality. I'm struck with an ache to hear his voice, share his enthusiasm for this project, when my cell phone screen flashes his number temptingly across the lit screen.

I put the phone back in my purse and go on to Mama and Daddy's. It's late. Mama has made buttermilk fried chicken. They'll be wondering what's keeping me.

BUTTERMILK FRIED CHICKEN AND CREAM GRAVY

Mama always kills the chicken the day before. For frying she uses her young Rhode Island Reds, never her Wyandottes or Orpingtons. Chickens have all got their own personalities, individually and as a breed. Rhode Island Reds tend to be big, brawny, pushy chickens with feathers the maroon color of an Irish Setter. The afternoon sun can turn a scratching flock of Rhode Islands into a burnished copper and magenta wonder. Nearly every wild bird's nest I peered into as a kid had those soft red feathers woven into the pilfered twigs and pale green moss of the live oaks.

Ingredients:
- 1 fresh fryer cut into pieces
- 1/2 onion, about a half cup
- 1 t cayenne pepper
- 1/3 c mixed fresh herbs or 1 t dried herbs
- 2 c buttermilk
- 3 cloves diced garlic
- 1/4 t paprika

Mama favors basil and oregano.

Pour the buttermilk and herbs over the chicken in a bowl that you can cover. Put the bowl in the refrigerator overnight.

When ready to cook, heat an inch or so of lard in your skillet. Put about two cups of flour in a paper bag, and drop the pieces of chicken inside one at a time. Once the grease is popping, begin gently placing your flour and herb-coated chicken pieces into the pan. Remember the chicken is cold. It's going to splatter when it hits the hot grease. Grandma always told me you could tell a good cook by the overlay of tiny grease burns on her forearms. I suggest long sleeves and great care. Cook the chicken about fifteen minutes on each side, remembering to keep adjusting the heat so your grease stays hot, but doesn't start to blacken. For gravy, brown enough flour to sop up the remaining grease, add the leftover herbed buttermilk and salt and pepper to taste.

Eleven

On a day so sultry and heavy with wet heat that by ten o'clock the mocking-birds are panting in the magnolias along the edge of Traveller's Park, we Barrs gather ourselves together for our traditional Labor Day fish fry. The bronze statue of Lee's faithful horse gleams like molten silver in the thick air.

The whole family is there by the time I arrive. Mama and Daddy are laid out in folding lounge chairs set side-by-side under the ancient oak that shades the picnic table. Candy and Snickers fuss over the placement of various and sundry fried foods along the length of the cloth-covered folding tables. Dozens of cousins, nephews and nieces, and assorted other kin are already in cut-off jeans, doing their best to cool off in the creek's eighteen inches of tepid water.

The main attraction, however, is the deep fat fryer at the edge of the oak's shade where Uncle Neil holds court. Uncle Neil is Daddy's brother's wife's sister's husband. Not blood kin, but a fine half-assed relative. I don't believe I've ever seen him in anything but a ratty Braves ball cap and Dickie brand over-alls—the ones with the chimp's face on the bib. His unruly gray beard is per-petually stained with Red Man juice.

He is, despite what Uncle Earl may tell you, the best fisherman in the family. He is also a close runner up with Daddy when it comes to the rural art of twisting a story around the truth in a knot so tight and clean nobody is ever going to be able to separate the two. For our Labor Day blast, Uncle Neil has caught an Appaloosa catfish big enough fill all our bellies. He won't tell where he was fishing when he hooked into the monster, but he does relate a story to rival Melville.

"Ah had me that thar itty bitty ol' skiff what ah got offen Cooter Jones over yonder in Vidalia. Beauregard, ma new bulldawg pup, was with me, and that thar pup was fussin' over a squirrel he'd spotted in a big ole mossy oak on the lake bank. Drivin' me to distraction is what he was doin'. We was up on Blackjohn, way back yonder in one a them little fingers whar the water ain't much deeper'n a bathtub along the bank, but whar it drops off to China in the channel."

The smells of hot grease and fish fried crisp mingle on air already thick with honeysuckle. Uncle spits into his custom-molded Spam can, inhales a half can of Pabst Blue Ribbon, gets on with the story.

"Was about then, with the dawg still raisin' cane, ah hooked into this Appaloosa big as a young hawg. The cat headed deep into the channel. Ah just nearly come to follow him down inta that tobacco brown water afore ah could get myself untangled from the durn dawg. Well, son, it took goin on two hours to land that beast and then, when ah got it to the boat, there weren't room in the skiff for the fish and me and the pup all three.

"Ah pondered on this he-ah dee-lema for a spell. Popped me a top or two. The pup had been fussin' and barkin' and leapin' around the boat while ah was reelin' in that catfish, but once Beau got a good look at that ugly whiskered face, he commenced to whinin' and backin' himself up under the seat."

Cousin Billy blows on a chunk of hot catfish and cuts into the story. "By seat are y'all referin' to that two by six you wedged across the beam? The one with splinters long enough to put an end to a careless man's ability to pro-cree-ate?"

Uncle ignores this disrespect to his boat. "The way I figgered it, if ah managed to cram that catfish into the boat, young Beuregard was going over the side. That dawg had taken a permanent dislike to that ugly fish face. I drank me 'nother beer and thought on the situation some more. Long about the fifth PBR, the solution come to me.

"I took off my undershirt, tore it in strips, threaded it through the gills of that Appaloosa, wove the cotton strips around the tail. Slicker'n goose shit, I had me that catfish see-cured to the side a the skiff. Ah headed for the dock, real slow like and bein' right careful of submerged stumps."

My nephew Jake hits a softball into the kudzu, and I miss a portion of Uncle's tale beating the vines with a baseball bat, dwelling on cottonmouths, before I return to my canvass chair for the conclusion of the story. We never did find the ball.

"So, ah'm easin' along, real slow, Beauregard's whine just loud enough so's ah can hear it above the engine, when ah see a dark, lumpy log 'bout seven foot long following in the wake of the boat. That gator came on. Them yellow eyes, sprinkled with amber like they are, they kept ta watchin' me. Neveh blinked. Ah come ta believe that gator was plannin' to hep himself to ma catfish and finish the meal with the shiverin', whinin' Beauregard."

Uncle grins, throws back another Pabst. None of us move or utter one single word.

"Ah scavenged 'round in ma spare tackle box, found me the i-tems ah was huntin', all the while keepin' ma eye on that thar ole gator. That rep-tile, he kept to edgin' closer to the catfish. The fish, knowin' he was 'bout to be et, thrashed against the side a the skiff.

"Ah popped the tape ah'd retrieved into ma old cassette player, and while Hank Jr. sang about country boys from northern California and south Alabam', country boys who can survive, ah employed the .22 Smith and Wesson ah always carry in that second tackle box.

"That thar is how ah showed up at Johnson's pier, naked as the day ah come into the world. A whopping' catfish that weighed in at well over a hundred pounds tied to one side of ma skiff. A seven foot gator tied to the other side, gray and white Dickie denim plainly visible 'long its lumpy hide."

It's also how we all came to fill our bellies to bursting with fried cat fish, hush puppies, and fried gator tail.

Of course, in true Barr fashion, we also cover six tables with turnip and collard greens, fried green tomatoes, salads and beans, pecan and fruit pies, watermelon pickles, and fresh green beans and okra. Daddy and four of the uncles do the deep frying, and we eat until we are staggery with grease and good times. Aunt Eileen has been up to the Wal-Mart in Columbus. Just as night falls she extends the party by bringing out a tub of antacids for which we all promise to remember her in our prayers.

I've been watching all day. Cousin Jimmy is here. But not Colin. After the miracle of the antacids, I locate Jimmy with some of the other cousins skipping stones across the creek and trading stories.

"How's your mama and them?" I ask him.

"They're finer than frog's hair. They've got the trailer up to the lake today. Been staying up there most all summer."

"I heard that. Good for them."

We stare off into the dusk. Watch the fireflies for a while, work up my nerve to get to it. Finally, I ask about Colin. What I really want to know is if he misses me. But I can't figure a way to ask without sounding pathetic. Fortunately, Jimmy, being a Barr, understands that my pride is never going to allow me to ask, and he volunteers that Colin is right sorry things didn't work out between us. I can't figure out if that means he thinks about me or if it means he's moved on.

A week later I get my answer. I have already slid myself into a red leatherette booth at Rebs when I see them. Colin has his back to me, but there is no mistaking the set of his broad shoulders or that slight duck's tail of honey blond hair at the base of his head just in that little hollow where my fingers met when we kissed.

The first thing I notice about the girl is that layer of softness that only the young possess, baby fat transformed by estrogen to velvety curves. The second thing I pick up on is how completely focused she is on Colin's face. These two have slept together. Everything about this bitch child's demeanor shouts it out to kill my soul. Her thick-lashed eyes rapt on his, she doesn't notice the old woman across the room having some sort of fit where she can't seem to remember how to breathe.

I want to get the hell out of there. Every molecule in my tired body is screaming at me to move, now! Before he sees me and I am stuck trying to make polite conversation while recovering from what feels like a blow to the solar plexus.

A flash of memory provides me an image of myself as a scabbed-over four year old perched on the roof of an abandoned chicken coop. My skinny arms straight out from my sides, I have one of Memaw Barr's old table clothes tied around my neck. It must have been in autumn because I remember watching the leaves on the maples dance a mosaic of russet golds and tawny oranges. I wait for just the right gust of wind before launching myself out into mid-air. That feeling of nothingness beneath my feet, the air slamming out of me when I hit the ground—that's what I remember as I study this lovely young girl with Colin.

If I could have moved right then, I might have tore out of Rebs like a scalded cat. But by the time I rediscover how to draw breath down into my lungs and then remember to allow it to flow back out, by then I remember who and where I am. Not a soul in that restaurant is eating. Old Man Norris has a spoonful of Brunswick stew halfway to his mouth that has been hanging there so long it's lost its steam. Millie Craig has whipped cream on the tip of her nosey nose, a slice of peach pie, one bite neatly cut from its point, rests undisturbed in front of her.

Colin still hasn't seen me. I slide out of the booth and make my feet carry me to their table. It seems a long walk. Long enough for me to remember the look he gave me after I taught him the first secret to letting me catch up with him in bed. Long enough to see his grinning face again and hear him laugh at himself and say, "Well, I guess this time I don't have to ask if you liked it." Enough steps for me to wonder if he uses what I've taught him with this young girl. The one who thinks she's fooling folks with that over-highlighted blonde hair. I am close enough by now to see that she's wearing sandals with four inch heels, cut-off jeans, and a deep blue, midriff-exposing tank top. A tiny golden frog pierced to the curve of her bellybutton draws my eye to her flat tummy, makes me suck in my stomach, stand up straight.

"Hello, Colin," I manage as I come up behind him and touch his shoulder lightly with the tips of my fingers. He jumps as though sparks have flown, recovers enough to make the introductions.

The girl is Kristen Yates. Daughter of Preston Yates. The money man. So maybe the boy has come up smelling like a rose. Found himself a beautiful, if slightly trashy, young woman instead of an old broad to finance his project.

Kristen Yates is nobody's fool, though. She knows who I was.

"It's so nice to meet you?" she intones in that California accent with the end of each sentence rising up so that everything sounds like a question.

Irritating. That's what that accent is. And they think we talk funny. I'm standing at the end of the booth, blocking Colin's exit. He has to twist his head uncomfortably to look at my face. The tops of his ears are as red as beets. My hand still rests on his shoulder. I know I should remove it. I would, except this girl has begun to get on my last nerve.

"Colin has been telling me about how super nice you and your family have been to him since he moved down here to this little place? You know, how you showed him the ropes of living out in the sticks and all?"

"Well," I purr in my very best southern lady voice, "it was our pleasure. Really it was."

"So? Since you've lived in this place like your whole life? What do people do down here anyway? You know? For fun? I mean is there even like, a mall? Or a movie theater? Like, where do kids go for raves?"

I can feel Colin pushing against my hip, doing his best to bump me forward so he can escape the booth. I put my hand on his neck and pet the back of his head the way a woman will stroke a little dog who's demanding attention when she's engaged in something more important. Colin puts both hands on my waist and lifts me up off my feet and out of his way. He takes my hand and drags me toward the door.

I smile over my shoulder at Kristen Yates, call back, "I hope you enjoy your little stay in our neck of the woods. There's a heap a things to do round here. Why, we ain't near as backward as we used to be."

We stand in the gravel parking lot, little swirls of gray dust settling on our shoes from where Colin has kicked it up with his stomping.

He squares himself in front of me and demands, "What the hell was that?"

Now I don't know about Yankee women, but I guarantee you it is never a good idea to demand anything from a southern woman.

I step into him, intend to give him a piece or two of my mind. It's an old trick. Has always worked for me in the past. You step forward, forcing your opponent to step back, thus giving you the advantage. I forgot Colin has seen this maneuver before. He doesn't budge. Instead he rests his hands on the curve of my hip, runs them up to just below my breasts, leaves a trail of confusion in their wake.

"Ruth?"

I am afraid to look up at him, can feel all that adrenalin slamming hard into desire, leaving me flat and unsatisfied. Against all scientific understanding, with absolutely no orders whatsoever from my brain, my hands float up and push their palms against the long muscles of his back. Knowing I've decided to never do this again, I nevertheless, tilt my face up to meet his mouth. I push against this physical need to taste him just once more by resting my forehead against his chest.

"Kristen is Preston's daughter. I knew her out in California. I guess you'd say we—dated. Briefly. Very briefly. I have no interest in her whatscever. She's here because Preston is training her to work with him in the business, and he asked me to show her around."

My desire morphs just a bit when I hear her name come out of his mouth. Anger flares. I understand he's told me he's no longer sleeping with her, but the picturing the two of them, young bodies together, has me overloaded.

"I'm not sure Ms. Yates knows your little affair is over. I think she has other plans."

I force myself to push away from him. An organized retreat. Maybe I should have left it at that.

Instead I add, "It works out well for you, though, huh? This way you get the money and the trampy Daisy Duke imitator."

He flinches as though I've slapped him. Turns and leaves the gray gravel battlefield. Storms back toward the restaurant. I can see Millie Craig's mouth hanging open to every fly in the county. Ed Norris is standing to improve his view, his face all but pressed against the plate glass of Reb's front window.

I experience a momentary glimpse into another dimension, a parallel universe where I'd filled my mouth not with angry words but with the taste of Colin's mouth. The trouble is, much as I want to travel in that other world, I can't get beyond the kiss, can't make myself see beyond the physical bend in that other road.

UNCLE NEIL'S
FRIED GATOR

First off, Uncle Neil says to only eat the tail of the gator. The rest of the reptile he cuts up and uses for catfish bait. Once you've skinned the tail out and got yourself about ten pounds of gator meat, cut it up into steaks, and pour you some salt and pepper over it, then let it set awhile. Uncle says about a six pack's worth of setting usually does it. Mix you up a mess of cornmeal with a little flour added to smooth it out some. Throw in some more salt, pepper, garlic and onion powder, about 2 cups of powdered milk, and as much cayenne as you believe you can handle. Dredge the steaks in this here mixture. Heat up the oil in your deep fryer. Once its spittin, add the meat a few steaks at a time. Cook for no more than five minutes. Any longer and you'll ruin the taste of this here delicacy. I suggest long sleeves and great care.

Twelve

Mama calls and asks me to come over Saturday morning. I assume Snickers will be there, too, and we'll begin the plans for Daddy's eightieth birthday party in October. It turns out to be just Mama and me, and while she most certainly does want to talk, her agenda has nothing to do with Daddy's party. We sit on the front porch with a tin washtub of green beans between us, her gnarled fingers snapping and stringing twice as fast as my younger hands. The set of her jaw is enough to keep my mouth shut and my fingers busy.

It has rained earlier, and the air is hot, heavy with moisture. It condenses on our skin, runs down our faces and arms. When we girls were little, Mama told us that a southern lady never sweats. She dews up. If I dew up much more, I am going to have to wring out my cotton blouse. But I wisely keep that thought to myself. I hear Daddy stomp the mud from his boots and then the familiar twang of the screen on the back door slamming as he comes into the kitchen.

Mama doesn't say a word until Daddy is tucked into his rocker next to her, a cup of coffee in his hand, a sheepish look on his face. Then she fires her opening salvo at me.

"Child, I'd like to know when it was that you got so scared of living."

When I just stare at her blankly, she gives me a second hint.

"Colin come by earlier in the week."

Daddy fluffs out the story. "The boy brought her chocolates from some fancy smansy place in Columbus. Some naked lady name." He stares off across the front yard, sips at his coffee. "Godiva. That's it."

Mama's fingers never stop stringing. The green beans are heaped up in the bowl at her feet, the washtub still half full. I watch her cut her eyes to Daddy. He clears his throat, builds up his strength with one more swig of coffee.

"Baby Ruth." His voice is soft and slow, forced up out of a place he would have much preferred to keep private. "I may have misspoke when I warned you off that boy."

Mama's hands pause mid-bean. Daddy clears his throat again, reforms his words, "I told you wrong about that boy. I was wrong."

Mama drops another bean in the bowl and eases back in her rocker. Daddy tips his coffee for one final swallow, unfolds himself up out of his chair. Gives me a conspiratorial wink.

"I done said my piece," he declares.

The wooden planks of the porch vibrate as he strides back into the house. He reminds me of Colin marching across the parking lot of Reb's, kicking up little tufts of gray dust at each step. I can almost see the thoughts about the cantankerousness of southern women forming in Daddy's head, know those words are never going to see the light of day.

Mama points her chin at me. "You finish those beans now. My hands are paining me some."

I remember all the times Candy, Snickers, and I have heard that tone in Mama's voice. Can almost hear my sisters singing the childhood mantra—
"You're gonna get it!"

"It's no secret that you have always been your daddy's favorite. Don't look over here all shocked at me, Alyson Ruth Barr. It's a fact."

Not a good sign that Mama is using my full name. She's right though, Daddy and I have always been close. Candy, being the oldest, is the big sister. Even though we're all three as close in age as green beans in a pod, my oldest sister has been almost like another parent to me and Snickers. Snickers is Mama's girl. Been that way all her life. In a scuffle, Snickers ran to Mama for help. She still does. Me, I have always run to Daddy.

When I played salon with all of Candy's Barbies and gave them stylish new haircuts with the nail clippers, it was Daddy I ran to with Candy hot on my heels. Candy got to pick out two new Barbies on our next trip to Columbus. I got the Princess Hair Salon. It came with two dolls whose hair could be made to grow by turning a tiny crank on their anatomically incorrect butts.

When I snuck into the kitchen before the party and ate all the sugar roses off the top of Snickers's birthday cake, her first one ever from a real bakery, it was Daddy who saved me. Mama was fit to be tied. I heard her say as much to Daddy. Snickers was of the opinion that I should be stuffed in a weighted sack and tossed in the creek. Six eight-year-old girls coming from her third grade class, and I had ruined her beautiful cake. My position was that I had just gotten hungry, what with Mama so busy with the party for stupid Snickers that she hadn't even made me a peanut butter and blackberry jelly sandwich, not even when I told her and told her how hungry I was getting to be. I did miss the party that year, but Daddy snuck me down to the creek afterward where I stuck a wriggly old night crawler on my hook all by myself.

Mama's rocker creaks as she settles herself back into it. "Ruthie, your daddy has always been over-protective of you, and I have always let it pass. Because you never once allowed his worry to slow you down one whit. Do you remember your training wheels?"

When I was four, on a summer morning already thick with heat, I announced to Daddy that I wanted him to take the training wheels off my bicycle. Candy and Snickers and a heap of cousins rode their bikes to the creek every afternoon as soon as chores were done. The trainers on my red Schwinn Rocket got hung up on the roots and tangled in the grass, and the big kids wouldn't slow down for me. I was left in the heat and the gnats, struggling with the baby wheels, while listening to the rest of the clan squeal with joy as they swung out over the water and released the rope swing at just the right moment. Through my pitiful sobs, I heard them splashing into the cool water.

Daddy had refused to remove the trainers. He didn't want me following the big kids to the creek, thought I was too little to swing out over the swimming hole and drop just in time to splash into deep water. I opened his locked tool box with the hatchet Mama used for cutting kindling. It took me most of the morning, but I got the training wheels off my Schwinn. I bent up the wheels some and one of Daddy's screw drivers and two of his pliers were never the same, but I got the stupid baby things off. I would have made it to the creek with the big kids, too, except Snickers told on me to Mama.

When Daddy got home, I was hiding under the front porch playing with the doodle bugs that liked the cool red dirt down there. Daddy called me out and listened to my tale of woe about being left like a baby while the rest of them played and splashed and cooled off. He and I walked the quarter mile to the creek. At the age of four, that path of worn grass had seemed like an adventure no less exotic than a jungle trek ending in a hidden waterfall. I still occasionally wake from dreams of that silent trip to the creek with Daddy.

Once there, he held me tight against his chest as we swung out over the creek, let go of the rope at just the right moment to send us falling through the hazy, gnat-ridden air and into the joy of the cool creek water. Over and over we climbed the slippery gray rock, balanced on its ledge, gripped the mossy rope in our hands, and then swung out into nothingness. At first, Daddy released the rope, then he had me grip his waist tighter as a signal to him at the moment of release. It was dusk when I got it right. Six times in a row I squeezed at the exact moment when Daddy released the rope. The first time he let me swing out over the abyss on my own, I couldn't let go of the rope. I swung back into his arms. But the second time I got it right, fell alone through gnats and fear into the deep cool waters of Noisy Creek.

NOISY CREEK
STRING BEANS

There was never any trouble in our house getting us girls to eat our vegetables. This is one of my favorites. With a square or two of cornbread, these beans are a meal in themselves.

Ingredients:
- 1/2 pound of thick sliced bacon, cut in one inch pieces
- 1 diced Vidalia onion
- 4 cloves of chopped garlic
- 2 lbs of green beans
- 1 c chicken stock or water
- Salt and pepper to taste

You need a deep frying pan with a lid for this recipe. Your cast iron skillet will work great if you have a cover. Fry the bacon for about ten minutes over a medium heat. Add the onion and garlic, and stir, cooking until both are tender. Add the beans, and stir to coat with the bacon grease. Add the chicken stock, and bring to boil. Reduce heat, cover, and simmer gently for about ten minutes. Remove the beans to a serving bowl with a slotted spoon, and enjoy. I hope you made cornbread to sop up the pot liquor.

Thirteen

Besides the fact that I have somehow turned chickenshit as I've aged, I also discover at that Come to Jesus Meeting that Colin has taken to having dinner with Mama two or three days a week. His development bumps against our property with the creek as its border. Evidently he just sashays across a log, strolls through the orchard, prances across the yard, and joins Mama for soup and sandwiches any old time he feels the urge.

It does nothing to lessen my outrage over this violation when Snickers asks, "What do you care, anyway? You dumped him, right?"

We are supposed to be planning Daddy's birthday party. Snickers brought fresh greens from Mama's garden, and we're eating our salads on my screened back porch. She has an idea for the party, wants to do something she calls "The First Eighty Years." We have photos, and she has rounded up a heap of folks to talk into a video camera, telling stories from Daddy's life. She's organizing a PowerPoint presentation, for the love of heaven. So far she has forty minutes of friends and family remembering incidents while pictures of Daddy at the appropriate age flash on the screen.

It seems to me like something a person—an anal-retentive person it goes without saying—would do for a funeral, but Mama has signed off on the idea, and Candy says even if it is sort of a eulogy, why not do it now while Daddy is alive to enjoy the attention.

So I am sorting pictures, and Snickers is editing. Candy, up in Stone Mountain with her preacher husband, has the deciding vote. We call and put her on speaker phone each time the two of us disagree about whether to use Cousin Sally's story of how she and Daddy played doctor when he was six and she was four—I say no, Snickers thinks it's adorable—or whether to use that family picture from Mama and Daddy's fortieth anniversary, the one where the rest of us look normal enough, but Snickers appears to be coming off a four-day drunk.

The two of us have gotten on Candy's last nerve with our bickering. She's looking to change the subject.

"So—you and Colin still haven't made up?" her voice scratches through the speakers.

"It's not a question of making up." My voice comes out louder than necessary. I hate speaker phones. I try to pick up the receiver, but Snickers slaps my hand away. "I just think I'm too old for him, that's all."

"In what way?" Candy asks.

Snickers grins at me from across the room. These two have been tag-teaming me my whole life. I hate it as much now as I did when I was six and they tried to talk me out of entering my Easy Bake Oven chocolate cake in the county fair. For which I'm sure I would have won a blue ribbon if I hadn't yielded to temptation and eaten it on our way to the fair grounds.

"Cut the pastor's wife psychology crap," I tell her. "I don't want to talk about it."

"Too bad!" they both say at the same time, a duet of sisterly snootiness.

"Look." I capitulate. "I like him. Okay? I do. But I was never completely comfortable with the age difference and then, when the whole who-paid-for-the-room deal happened, it made me feel foolish. Happy now?"

"No." Candy's voice scratches through the speakers. "You may have chosen to feel foolish, but Colin did nothing to cause that feeling. You misread the situation and reacted out of insecurity about your own aging."

I reach across and hang up on my know-it-all sister. Then I threw her accomplice and her self-satisfied little smirk out of my house. The last thing I hear as I slam the door behind Snickers is her deep belly laugh. The one that usually makes me happy that she's my sister. Tonight, it makes me want to throw a vase at her.

I'm at my desk at the spa late the next morning, sorting through my mail and trying to decide if I want a salad or granola and yogurt for lunch. It's a difficult decision, since what I really want is to go out to Goggins and eat a barbeque sandwich, but I've already come in early and spent an hour on the treadmill to work off the weekend's catfish and gator fry. We have those new treadmills with the calorie counter and heart rate monitor and a dozen scenic views at your fingertips. I detest them.

When I stumble off the machine, dripping unladylike sweat, I don't enjoy being confronted with the hard truth that with my imaginary climb up Pikes Peak I've managed to work off the calories in exactly two chunks of fried catfish. This morning I stagger to the shower and crank the knob up to hot enough to scald the hair off a hog. Then I twist it the other way and make myself stand under the cold spray until my pores close up shop for the moment.

Part of what makes me angry around the subject of Colin is that I thought I was content before he showed up at my birthday party. Now I'm not so sure about settling into my age. I find myself questioning the joys of living alone. Plus, and this is the part that shames me some, I have always liked the way I look. I know most women don't. I've made a living turning brunettes into blondes and blondes into redheads. LuAnne and I have chuckled for years over blacks having their hair straightened right beside whites having theirs permed. I have built a tiny kingdom off young women working to get rid of that extra ten pounds that collects around their hips and waist and old women fighting to look like they did twenty years ago when they were struggling to drop ten pounds.

Now, I didn't go to college, but I do read, and I know that a big part of the reason for my liking myself, including my body, is that I grew up in a home where I was Daddy's little princess. I was married to three men, all of whom believed, most days anyway, that I walked on water. Certainly, I never heard a complaint about my looks. But with Johnny dying just as I started into menopause, I guess I missed all the little physical changes in my body.

I sure woke up to every last one of them when Colin kissed me that first time out there sitting in his big honkin' truck with the rain pounding all around us. Kissing ought to make a person feel beautiful. Instead, I was suddenly aware of all the subtle and not so subtle changes that have come to my body over the past three years.

I called Candy back after hanging up on her. I called late last night. Late enough that I knew Bill would be in bed and she'd be awake, working on one of her projects. We talked about how, when Mama had that lumpectomy five years ago, the oncologist had warned that none of her daughters was to even consider taking estrogen when they hit menopause.

We hadn't paid much attention before that time, but well over half our aunts on the Powell side have had breast cancer. Every one of them survived it, but, still, cancer hides in the genes is what they say. So all us Barr woman have since gone through menopause cold turkey. Not even any of that fancy herbal Chinese estrogen you can buy in those expensive health food stores in Atlanta. Estrogen is estrogen is what the oncologist warned us, and y'all can't take any of it.

I suspect my dear sister had been sipping the communion wine.

"I am thinking," she informed me, "of filing a class action suit against the pharmaceutical companies. The buggers finally figured out that estrogen ain't all that good for old women at the near exact same time they began marketing Viagra. So now we've got ourselves a nation of old men with hard peckers and a bunch of old women with dried up puddies."

She's not wrong. For years I struggled with the rise and fall of estrogen each month. Worked hard at not letting myself transform completely in those few days just before my period. Still managed to scare the holy hell out of my husbands until they learned to step away from the PMS. Scared even myself some months. So when my estrogen levels tapered off just before Johnny died, I rejoiced in the freedom.

People tell you about the hot flashes and the night sweats, but nobody talks about the rest of it. The whole package of changes that are as startling as they were when you walked this line going the other way at adolescence and the estrogen began its coup of your body. The loss of that layer of fat just under the skin that I never even knew I had until it was gone and no amount of exercise or dieting could bring it back. The sinking of my curves. My breasts dropping just a bit, waist thickening, hips spreading, butt flattening. And then, here's another thing that I don't remember anyone ever mentioning to me—no more hair under your arms or a few other places either. Of course that part wouldn't be too bad except that some of that coarse hair has found its way to my chin. My cheeks are now soft and furry. Without the aid of depilatories, I'm an adorable old monkey woman.

This whole menopause package I was living with nicely. Until that kiss. So it's no wonder I'm angry at Colin for bringing all this to my attention. Plus, I have no experience in being insecure with my body. None whatsoever. It's fine and dandy to remain sexual with a partner who knew you when you had pubic hair, but to begin an affair at my age, with a younger man to boot, well it takes more courage than I seem able to muster. So Mama and Ardell and my know-it-all sisters can say what they want, a relationship with Colin is just too much for me.

This morning, dressed in work clothes after my shower and back at my desk, I sort desultorily through the mail. Snickers is on her way to Atlanta to find a new computer for her office. That woman kills more computers than General Jackson killed Damn Yankees. She reports that the one in her office is acting peculiar again. She also tells me she and Candy just want me to be happy and that I'd seemed happy when Colin and I were carrying on. Which tells me my sisters have talked this morning. Mama always said she worried about having three children, that with three, one child would always be on the outside. But that's not how it works with us. Three always gives the other two something to talk about.

With Snickers on her way to the city, when Daddy phones from the hospital, it's me who takes the call. Except it doesn't sound like Daddy. For a moment's reprieve I think it's all a mistake. Some frightened stranger is calling with news of someone else's mama. I struggle to stay in that moment, but my daddy's scared voice drags me back.

"Baby Ruth, honey. Your mama fell. She's in surgery now."

I call Snickers on her cell on my way to the hospital over in Dothan, which is where Daddy said they've taken Mama. It's a seventy-minute drive on most days. I'm running through the hospital parking lot forty-seven minutes later with no recollection of the trip. It's Colin who meets me at the door. Daddy is inside waiting for his wife of sixty-four years to get out of surgery.

"I found her when I came over for dinner," Colin tells me. "Your dad was out back in his work room, finishing some living-room shelving your mom wanted redone. She'd climbed up on a step ladder. Said she was trying to reach a jar of canned tomatoes for the Mulligan stew she was making for dinner. She'd been on the floor for a while, assured me she felt fine except that she didn't seem able to get herself up off the linoleum. I called an ambulance and got your dad who rode with her."

I call Snickers and then Candy, tell them what I've learned. They're both already rushing toward the hospital. Candy is on the road coming out of Atlanta. She won't arrive until almost dark. Snickers is minutes away, racing blindly toward her mama. Colin and I are still standing in the hospital lobby when I snap my cell phone shut and slide it carefully into my purse.

I seem to be moving unnaturally slow, as though under water. The surrounding pressure here is evidently just a little thicker than the air through which I'm used to negotiating. I want to stay here in the lobby, in this sterile limbo, where surely nothing bad can happen. None of this can be real. Mama must be home doing her afternoon chores. Daddy, right this minute, is carrying her the newly refinished shelves for approval. Except how come I'm not at work with nothing more to worry about than the new Rorschach pattern of skin tags I discovered in the shower?

I don't know I'm shaking until Colin provides a ballast by wrapping me in his steady arms. We stay there, parting the folks coming through the entrance doors hurrying toward their own worries. When I feel strong enough, I step away. Colin hands me a clean white handkerchief, which makes me smile. What man under seventy carries a hanky these days?

"The doctor says she broke her hip," Colin's eyes are wet, and I would offer to return his hanky except I've already blown my nose on it. Repeatedly.

"She broke it when she fell?"

We move to a group of bright blue plastic chairs arranged around the focal point of a lopsided coffee machine. I want to go to Daddy, but not before I know what's happened. Not before I understand whether we might lose Mama or if she is going to be crippled, changed from my robust mama into an old woman needing constant care. I pray this will turn out to be just another episode we Barrs will use as a base for stories at family gatherings. Remember when Mama scared the bejesus out of us by falling off that step ladder in the kitchen? What were you reaching for again, Mama? Canned sweet corn? Stewed tomatoes?

"The doctor said it's more likely the hip broke and that's why she fell," Colin takes back his hanky which I am twisting and knotting into a soggy mess.

Snickers tears into the lobby, impatient with the slow-sliding automatic doors. Her face is white, as though all the life has just drained right out of her. She looks like Mama standing there in the slant of harsh sun from the entrance door. Her eyes, made up this morning before any of us knew what the day would bring, are wide purple smudges of fear. I have a clear thought, like a shaft of light piercing creek water, revealing the glint of a prize stone—this whole deal is going to be hardest on Mama's girl, Snickers.

MAMA'S
MULLIGAN STEW

This dish is never the same twice, but it always turns out delicious. Feel free to substitute other fresh vegetables for the suggestions given here. For us, of course, this meal is now always going to be "what Mama was makin' on the day she fell."

Ingredients:
- 1 pound of beef, cubed
- 1 onion
- 1 c mushrooms
- 10 cloves garlic
- 1 can of stewed tomatoes
- 12 oz dark beer
- 2 c carrots diced into 1" cubes
- 2 c potatoes cut in 1" cubes
- 1 c string beans, cut to about an inch long

Dredge the meat cubes in flour, and brown them in hot oil. Add onions, garlic, and mushrooms, and cook for three minutes. Add everything else, plus enough water to cover. Simmer until everything is tender.

Mama's canned vegetables are no longer kept in the shelf over the refrigerator that requires a step ladder to reach. I suspect Snickers glued that cupboard shut for all eternity.

Fourteen

Candy calls Mama the Bionic Woman. The surgeon replaced her hip, and he swears she'll be good as new. We have our doubts as we cluster around her hospital bed, trying not to see the tubes bringing liquids in and out of this shrunken woman who bears only a slight resemblance to our mama. I am sitting between Daddy and Colin, the three of us joined in a daisy chain of worry. Daddy's age-speckled hand is icy cold in mine. On my other side I can feel the callus along the ridge of Colin's thumb on my palm, his hand warm and strong.

Across from us are my sisters. Candy is slumped in an orange plastic chair Colin carried in from the end of the hall. Snickers is standing, stroking the back of Mama's arm just below the IV. Watching Snickers there gives me an eerie sense of dislocation. My eyes keep trying to tell my brain that it's Mama standing beside the bed, petting the limp hand of Grandma Powell, who, without a single sick day in her life to warn any of us, died of a heart attack eleven years ago on a visit to Noisy Creek. Here in this very hospital.

Mama was awake a few minutes ago, long enough for Daddy to kiss her forehead and for her to start issuing orders. "Go home. Get something to eat. Did anybody remember to turn off the Mulligan stew I was making before all this fuss?"

"I turned off the burner, Mrs. Barr," Colin assured her.

"Good boy," she'd cooed weakly before closing her eyes and drifting back into sleep.

Colin and I mean to take Daddy home just as soon as we gather ourselves together for the effort. Snickers will not be pried away from Mama. The doctor, having enough sense to know when he is beat, has given approval for a cot to be brought in so Snickers can sleep here. Candy has a room at The Rebel Yell Motel just down the road. If we weren't all numb, we'd give her a bad time about trying to get a good night's sleep in a motel with that name. As it is, we just say we'll see her in the morning.

Colin insists on driving. We take my car and leave his truck in the hospital lot. We all know we'll be making the trek back the next day. He can pick his truck up then.

It's funny that before today, I never thought about Mama and Daddy dying. I must have known they would. We all die, and they're definitely getting up there in years. But they seemed invincible to me, maybe even immortal. I suppose it's just hard to conceive of someone who's been there your whole life being gone. In particular when those people have raised you up real good, loved you every second of every day of your life and made sure you knew it, too. Losing three husbands, I should know all about death and loss, but this, the idea of Mama and Daddy being gone from this world, this is like looking into a dark bottomless abyss.

Orphaned is the word that keeps leaping into my mind as I sit in the dark beside Colin and listen to Daddy stretched out in the backseat, snoring like a tired old bear. I lay my hand palm up on the seat. Colin covers it with his, entwines his fingers with mine, drives one handed.

"I'm glad you were there to find her. Thank you for calling the ambulance."

"I've been coming over at noon a few times a week since I started the project. She makes a pitcher of sweet tea, pours what's left in a thermos for me to take back to work."

His voice is soft. I have to strain to hear him over the whoosh of the tires on the asphalt road to home. "Your mama is completely different from my mom, and at the same time, they're very much the same."

"What's different about them?"

"I told you my mom is a teacher. Well, she's actually a professor of comparative religions at the University of California. My parents split up when I was just a baby. I never knew my dad. Never knew to miss him. Mom raised me on her own."

He smiles, squeezes my hand as he negotiates the car around a wide curve. "She had two predominant goals as a parent. To raise a son who was respectful of women. And to make sure I learned to question authority." His teeth flash white, and his voice softens, lets me know how much he loves his mother, how close they are.

"In what ways are your mama and mine the same?" I ask just to hear his voice float across the car's darkness, soothe me for a moment longer.

"There's no way you can spend time around either of them and not feel the love and acceptance that flows out of them, sort of blankets everybody around. They both expect a whole lot from the people they love. But they expect it, not because they're demanding, but because they have a great belief in the ability of their loved ones to accomplish these things."

I unfasten my seatbelt, scooch across, and lay my head on his shoulder. His kiss on the top of my head is warm, comfortable. Without a word he pulls the car over onto the red dirt shoulder of the road, finds and untangled the middle seat belt, fastens me securely in place, pulls back onto the road home. My head on his shoulder, I fall asleep with the smell of sawdust and citrus aftershave in my nose.

Snickers and Candy stay right there in Dothan with Mama. They share a room at The Rebel Yell.

"Thank the Good Lord," Candy tells me. "The hotel has been erroneously named. I'm staying not to take care of Mama, who seems to be doing remarkably well, but to make sure Snickers eats and sleeps."

Just as I suspected, Snickers is in a panic over this proof of Mama's vulnerability. That Mama has broken her hip, that she isn't invincible, that she is in fact getting older—all this is a sort of bugle call, blaring the refutation of her daughters' ridiculous, but nevertheless hard-held belief that Mama is going to live forever. Even her breast cancer battle ten years ago didn't hit us this hard. A person can get cancer at any age. But a broken hip. That happens to old women.

Doc Adler comes out to the house to have a cup of coffee with Daddy the third day Mama is in the hospital. We've gone back and forth to Dothan the day before and are fixing to get ourselves organized to do it again when Doc pulls up in his Jeep and climbs up the steps, toting his black doctoring bag. Doc Adler replaced Doctor Shaw when he retired over fifteen years ago now. He's been treating Barrs ever since. This morning he talks Daddy into taking off his shirt and letting him press the stethoscope against his chest. It's been years since I've seen Daddy without a shirt, and it shocks me some to see how he's shrunk in on himself and how the mat of dark hair I remember has turned sparse and silvery. Makes me feel scared and small. Daddy fusses a bit, but he lets the doc take his blood pressure.

"I believe I'll take that cup of coffee y'all offered," Doctor Adler tells me once all the doctoring is out of the way. "And maybe a hunk of your mama's cornbread if you've got any in there."

When I return with the coffee, Daddy is staring at Mama's rose bushes like they hold the secret of life. Doc makes fast work of his cornbread, licks his fingers once he's finished, but he doesn't stay long after that, and when I walk him to his Jeep, he confirms my suspicions about Daddy's attitude change.

"I told your daddy he wasn't to be traipsing' back and forth to Dothan every day. He's gonna be eighty in few weeks. Be nice if he made it to the party I'm sure y'all are planning."

Until she fell off that stepladder, the only nights Mama and Daddy had spent apart in sixty-four years was that trip to Lookout Mountain on which Snickers and Candy and I dragged Mama all those years ago. Daddy is a mess without his wife. So when Colin shows up and enlists Daddy's help in making the changes the physical therapist in Dothan has recommended for Mama's recovery at home, it's a godsend. The two of them go all through the house, speculating on where they need to put handrails, what furniture needs to be rearranged to make a path wide enough for the walker. They plan and cipher and then disappear on a trip to the lumber yard that brings them back smelling of beer and raw lumber.

Colin has taken to walking across the creek, through the orchard, and on over to the house each day for a late dinner. He and Daddy are installing a winding ramp that leads slow and easy up to the front door. I was worried when they started in on it. I know there is no way Mama can handle the front steps right now, but I also know it is going to break her heart to see her roses and the rest of her garden destroyed to make room for an ugly ramp.

The smooth plank path they're building starts at the end of the driveway and winds in gentle curves, a wide tongue-and-groove path to the door. The incline Colin has designed is so gentle the fact that the front door is over three-and-a-half feet above the driveway is almost imperceptible. He and Daddy build wide planter boxes along the full length, and we carefully transplant Mama's roses and dahlias into good rich black dirt. The men discuss putting a roof over the whole thing, but decide the path is wide enough for three people to walk abreast. Somebody can hold an umbrella over Mama's head if need be.

Eight days after the surgery, when we make a doctor-approved trip to Dothan, Daddy brings along a picture of their work of art and shows it to the physical therapist. He's begun to worry that the length of the walk might be too much for Mama. The therapist is a little black woman named Angie, no bigger than a minute. She studies the pictures.

"That thar is one of the prettiest things I ever seen. It's a work of love is what that be. Won't be no problem for Miss Barr. Matter a fact, it be right good for her to have a somethin' like that. Walkin' slow along that path be good therapy a few times a day once she get home where she belongs."

For another two days, Colin and Daddy are busy installing handrails in the bathroom, figuring a way to move Great-grandma Powell's four poster to the first floor without destroying it and generally creating a ruckus while they rearrange more furniture than a new bride. Then, bright and early in the morning, they take off again in Colin's truck on a secret mission. At dusk they're back with a box near as big as an elephant squeezed into the bed of the 4x4. Right behind them comes a battered Ford truck with Jenkins Construction in block letters on the driver's door. They've stopped at the job site and picked up reinforcements for this project.

The Big Secret has to be uncrated and taken apart to fit in the house, but eventually they get'er done. They have replaced Mama's favorite chair—which is too low for her to get in and out of while she is recovering—with a recliner.

But not just any recliner. This one is higher than most, designed, according to my beaming daddy, precisely for people who've had hip-replacement surgery. The contraption has a button on the side that moves the entire seat of the chair slowly up and forward at an angle until you are standing just as easy as you please. The three of us and the two workmen, we all try the thing out until we fear we might do it damage if we keep it up. Best of all though, because I know Mama is going to hate anything that smacks of sickness in her home, no matter how much she needs it or how temporary it might be, they've had that recliner covered in the same homey chintz fabric as Mama's old chair.

I feed everyone pot roast, potatoes, green beans, and cornbread before the helpers go on home. Daddy scratches my cheek with his end-of-the-day beard and goes on to bed in the back bedroom where he's been sleeping since Mama's been in the hospital. Colin and I stand on the front porch and watch the stars flash through ragged clouds. I kiss him goodnight and send him on his way, then stand a while longer, watch the wind high above me move the thin clouds toward the distant sea, revealing more and more of the starry night. I wonder what I have ever done to deserve another good man in my life.

BLUE RIBBON (CAHOOTS) CORNBREAD

Most every woman in Noisy Creek has a signature dish, something she brings to potlucks, funerals, and church suppers. Mama always brings greens and cornbread. She generally carries Memaw Barr's thick platter the color of heavy cream rounded up nicely with fried chicken or pot roast as well, but the meat is in addition to her collards or turnip greens and cornbread.

As a brand new bride, Mama tweaked Grandma Powell's recipe for cornbread just a hair and carried it with her to the county fair where she won herself a shiny blue ribbon. A Texas upstart, not even from around here, winning the ribbon for something as doggone basic as cornbread didn't sit well with the local women folk until Mama happily shared her recipe. It's going on sixty-five years now, and she says I can give you the ingredients as well as the secret she's held back all these years.

Ingredients:

- 1/2 lb bacon
- 2 fresh eggs
- 1/2 t salt

- 1/4 c bacon grease
- 1 c buttermilk
- 1 c cornmeal

- 1/2 c sugar
- 1/2 t soda
- 1 c flour

Fry the bacon until it's crisp enough to easily crumple. Pour off 1/2 cup of the grease, and let set until cooled. Add the eggs and sugar, and blend it well. Add the soda to the buttermilk, and pour into bowl. Stir just enough to blend. Add everything but the bacon, and stir gently. Lastly add the crumpled bacon,and pour into a greased 8" square pan. Bake at 375 degrees for about 35 minutes.

That's the recipe.

Here's what Mama didn't share with the ladies: The bacon comes from Uncle Earl, and he makes it up special for Mama and her cornbread. It's honey cured, thin sliced, and Uncle says he always makes it from the year's gentlest hog. It's a good cornbread recipe even if you're not in cahoots with the family hog farmer.

Fifteen

We three Barr girls shared a bedroom growing up. It was a mighty large room, to be sure. When we got bigger and needed more space, Daddy and Grandpa Barr created the room simply by raising the attic roof a few feet to open one big, third floor. A Georgia Loft is what Mama called it.

There is another bedroom next to Mama and Daddy's, and Candy most definitely did covet that room. But Mama dedicated that room for her sewing projects and never relented to my oldest sister's campaign. Mama stuck to her guns. She'd wipe her hands on a dish towel, give Candy a no-nonsense stare, and deliver the verdict. "Not a one of you three girls can see your way clear to stay out of most any tree or creek or mud hole y'all might stumble upon. I need me a dedicated sewing room just to keep up with the mending and such for you three."

Years later, at some family gathering or another, when we were all middle-aged and married, Mama confessed. The bunch of us were snacking on Cousin Mary's watermelon pickles, the sweet tang still in my mouth, when Mama blushed and confided, "I liked the privacy of having your daddy and my bedroom on a separate floor from you girls."

Snickers shrieked like a mouse had run up her britches, but Candy grinned. "Good for y'all, Mama, good for y'all."

I can't remember if I added anything to this conversation or not, but I know it called up in me a vivid flash of memory from my childhood. I'd had a bad dream, and for some reason, instead of climbing into bed with Snickers or Candy the way I usually did, I came downstairs looking for the comfort of Mama and Daddy. I remember standing in the hallway outside the door to their bedroom, my small bare feet cold on maroon and gray linoleum. The locked door shocked me, like a fist to my chest. I was shut out, away from Mama and Daddy. Something so rare it seemed impossible for it to be happening. My crying progressed to wailing about then.

Daddy opened the door after a frighteningly long abandonment of no more than a minute. Tops. He scooped me up in his arms. My legs around his bare waist, I remember he wore navy blue and red plaid pajama bottoms. Mama had given them to him for Christmas. Except, silly Daddy, he had forgotten to put on his pajama shirt. Over his shoulder I could see Mama's bare arms against the white chenille bedspread, her shoulders pale and glowing in a slant of moonlight from the open window. She smiled at me, spoke my name before Daddy carried me back to bed.

It was an ordinary memory really. Nothing special. Except Mama's satisfied smile, the locked door, the unity and love in that bedroom, it all seemed a kind of grownup magic to me. A promise of things to come. A validation of the life into which Mama and Daddy were teaching me to step. A few years later when I heard Miss JoLynne, the fifth grade Sunday School teacher, talk about being sanctified, I immediately thought of bare feet on cold nighttime linoleum, that glimpse into Mama and Daddy's room.

Of course, I didn't sort any of this out back then when Daddy tucked me in bed, kissed my forehead, and returned to Mama. But the older I get, the more I ponder on how so many of the little things my parents did when I was a child seeped into me somehow, became a part of me.

Staying with Daddy while Mama is in the hospital, sleeping in my childhood bed with Grandma Powell's quilt tucked around me, listening to the familiar sounds of the old house feeling its age, I study on this legacy. Turn things this way and that, hold words like sacred and refuge up to the moonlight, fall asleep grateful.

Colin and I take to spending an hour or two together each night. I accuse him of wearing Daddy out with the building projects so he'll go to bed early. He is becoming accustomed to the Barr sense of humor, so he only pulls me tighter against him. He smells of new wood and paint overlaid with healthy man sweat. Ardell swears the scientific name for that particular combination of sweat and testosterone is Odor de Horniness. Whichever. I like it.

Saturday night under a half moon we follow the path to the creek. It's too dark under the trees to see the rope swing, but the flat rock where we always sunbathe shimmers in silver filigreed light. Colin and I stretch side by side on the smooth surface, our arms and legs wide open to receive the lunar blessing. The trees are a dark lace mantle, and the creek chants its own rhythmic hymn as it passes on its way to the sea. The air is thick and fecund with the smells of death, rebirth. Colin's fingertips brush mine. I turn my head away from him, watch a silent moccasin cleave the water with his triangular head, an undulating wave moving across the surface of the creek. I look across at Colin. His smile is wide and quick.

I don't mention the snake.

With soft words in the moist night air, he tells me again about how he came to love me before we ever met.

"I'd be sitting on my bunk over there in that giant sandbox. You think of a desert as hot. It's those cold desert nights I remember. Listening to the wind blow dry sand against the canvas tent wall and listening to Jimmy read your letters. I remember one letter where you told about taking a bunch of older kids from Royal Rangers to meet Jimmy Carter. You said the former president sat on a gray metal folding chair in the Plains High School auditorium and signed copies of his newest book. A book about how to live in peace with our neighbors."

He turns his head toward me, drops his voice to a near whisper. "My favorite part of that letter was when you told about walking the half block of wooden sidewalk that is downtown Plains, eating catfish at Mom's Café, and finishing the meal with peanut ice cream from a general store that sold postcards of Jimmy and Roselyn, boiled peanuts, and flat paper fans imprinted with scenes of nearby Americus, Georgia."

I don't move, allow his voice to mix with the warm, wet air and conjure a layer of contentment. Let that soft quilt float down over me.

"One whole letter, all you wrote about was how you sat on a shady bench in Confederate Square at dinner time. You told what trees and shrubs were blooming and who all walked past."

I had forgotten that letter, wrote it on the first anniversary of Johnny's death. Lying here now with Colin beside me, the two of us side-by-side in the moonlight on this familiar flat rock, I think about how, back then, most days I wanted just to curl up in a ball and sleep. Writing that letter to Jimmy had started as a chore. A family member in the military required regular letter writing. Simple as that. Like it or not. But the writing had turned out to be good for me as well, focused my thoughts outside myself, reminded me of how life keeps flowing along, shallow rapids eventually turning to wide deep pools in speckled shade.

"For me, away from home, those letters were a glimpse into another world. A world I needed to believe existed right at that moment. A couple of times you wrote, just a little, about how much you missed your husband, Johnny. You'd write about some memory or story of something the two of you had shared. I'd lie in the dark, listen to the sounds of the camp, wonder what the night and the next day and the day after that would bring. I just wanted more than anything to enter into that world you created with those letters. It made me ache for someone in my life who loved me the way you loved Johnny."

A breeze as light as a lover's breath tickles the wide leaves of the maples along the creek. Colin recites for me again the story of the first time he saw me.

"Jimmy and I, we were getting ready to pull out of the Piggly Wiggly parking lot. That redheaded stock boy, the one with the heavy black glasses he's half the time got held together with duct tape, he was loading brown bags into the trunk of your car. You were smiling at him, chatting, like you always do. I was watching the kid's face just light up under all that attention. I didn't have a clue you were the woman whose letters had worked their way into my dreams back in those long, cold desert nights.

"You were wearing this sort of simple, dark green dress, your hair all mussed in the wind. You seemed so much a part of this place. Something natural and

NOISY CREEK   121

beautiful. I was already watching a slight breeze glue that cotton dress to your body, already planning on finding out who you were and how to meet you. When Jimmy told me you were his Aunt Ruth, I grinned till my cheeks hurt."

He rolls on his side, traces the inside of my outstretched arm with his finger, props himself up on his elbow. The smooth, moonlight-softened granite becomes a dark pedestal for the pale glow of his beautiful form stretched on the rock's surface.

"This is going to sound weird, but, do you ever do jigsaw puzzles?"

I admit it does seem an odd question, but I go along and tell him I grew up in a place where nearly every single summer afternoon produces a rain storm, so, yeah, I have worked on a jigsaw puzzle or two.

He effortlessly lifts himself up, stretches himself along my length, his weight supported by his strong arms, the moon haloing his blond head.

"When I saw you there, when Jimmy told me who you were, it felt like a piece of the puzzle I'd been looking for a real long time—a complicated piece I had begun to think I was going to have to do without—just clicked into place."

He lowers himself slowly, kisses me. Lifts himself off me after a time so we lie side by side to receive the moon's blessing. I squeeze his hand and try to ignore the slither of worry about our twenty-year age difference that lifts its wedged head and flicks its tongue, testing the air for prey.

COUSIN MARY'S
WATERMELON PICKLES

A picnic along Noisy Creek is guaranteed to have a watermelon or two anchored side by side with the six packs cooling in the creek. The sweet taste of icy cold watermelon on a hot day, the joy of spitting the black seeds at your sister, that's about as close to paradise as we're likely to get this side of the mansion the Good Lord has prepared for us up yonder.

Watermelon season doesn't last more than a month or so, but these pickles are our way of carrying those hot summer days with us all year long. Biting into one of these crisp pickles is a way of reminding ourselves in the dead of the winter that summer will roll around again, it won't be that long before we'll once again be trying not to see Uncle Hershel flying through the air on the rope swing, his baggy bathing suit showing off the crack of his ass as he rattles the thick air with his rebel yell.

Ingredients:
- 7 c watermelon rind cut in slices about 1/4 inch wide and an inch long
- 1/4 c pickling salt
- 4 c water
- 2 c sugar
- 1 c white vinegar
- The rind of one orange, cut in long curling slices
- 1 cinnamon stick
- 20 whole cloves
- 1 lemon cut thin enough so that you can see through each slice
- 1/2 c maraschino cherries

Cousin Mary likes to use the small rattlesnake watermelon for this recipe. She says there's not a reason on earth for that preference, except that it's the type of melon her mama always used.

Trim the dark green and pink parts from the rind before you slice it. Soak the rind overnight in the water and pickling salt. You want every last piece covered. If it's not, add a little more water and salt, doing your best to keep the proportions the same.

Next morning, drain and rinse the rind. Cover with cold water, and cook until tender. While the rind is simmering in a big pot with a lid, combine the sugar, vinegar, orange rind, cinnamon, and cloves, and one cup of water. Simmer this for 15 minutes, then strain.

To your seasoned pickling water, add the rind, lemon, and cherries. Cook until the rind is translucent. Pour mixture into your hot, sterilized canning jars, being sure to leave about a half inch of breathing space at the top. Put the lids on loosely, and process in boiling water for five minutes. When the jars have cooled, tighten the lids.

Do your best not to think of Uncle Hershel on that rope swing while you enjoy these delicate reminders of summer.

Sixteen

Colin and I play at being children together for those ten days I stay with Daddy while Mama's in the hospital. We don't make love, do little more than kiss. I stomp hard on my worry about the difference in our ages and do my best to relax and enjoy his company. Soon enough reality will intrude, but I need to play for a few hours a day, and Colin is a good playmate. There will be time enough for the real world.

I do pop into the salon from time to time, but most of what needs my attention can be done by phone or delegated. Snickers has been telling me for years that the mark of a good manager is being able to walk away and know your employees will keep things running smoothly in your absence. Of course those workers are going to be collecting a king's ransom in overtime, but Snickers is right. The business keeps humming along without me or her. Still, I like to show up unexpectedly on occasion, human nature being what it is and the salon being my baby.

On one of these trips into town, while Daddy and Colin are putting the finishing touches on what we have christened the Love Ramp, I connect with Ardell. Living out in Leeville and cooking three meals a day for Daddy, I have gone off my lettuce diet. Ardell and I decide to skip lunch altogether and go for a walk. Up on Hummel's Ridge the trees are just beginning to turn. It seemed a good choice for a hike, except we forgot the part of the trail where the Cherokee loop comes near to disappearing into the embankment just above the old saw mill.

The two of us force our way through a game trail, swatting deer flies and cussing in a particularly un-Baptist manner. I may be the better cusser of the two of us. Ardell pretends to be shocked by my inventive vocabulary as I smash a nasty black fly that had been feasting on my bare arm. She attends the Evangelical Church of the Risen Savior out on MLK. Everybody in town calls it the Holy Roller Church. They have a woman preacher out there, and Ardell teases me that they only actually handle the rattlers and moccasins at the special Easter sunrise service.

A lot of the holy rollers are good clients at the spa and salon. They sparkle, these women. I have to say, if you study on the Book of Acts, the direct way this congregation makes decisions seems more biblical than the convoluted process we Baptists have adopted of late. Still, it takes a certain kind of person to do that shake, rattle, and roll they do with the tongues and all. At any rate, my vocabulary does nothing to advance the cause of the Baptist League as we slog our way up to the ridge.

Eventually, we gain the saddle and relocate the actual path, the one cleared once a year by Bobby Bradford's Boy Scout troop instead of the one maintained by the local family of white tail. Once we've captured our breath, Ardell asks about the Stud Muffin.

"I've decided to stop over-thinking the relationship."

I don't say that breathing the air of my childhood—that peculiar mix of red dirt, and ivory soap, and the mold endemic in every old house south of Macon— I have discovered once again the girl I was before three husbands abandoned me to the love of my family. I don't breathe a word, even to my best friend, that I am struggling daily to sluff off the responsibility of earning my salvation through hard work and pure mule-headedness and to simply enjoy Colin.

Not quite recovered from the climb, my breath burns my throat. "I've come to the realization that I have earned me enough money to provide my-self with vitals and doodads for the rest of my natural life. I am waking to the idea that maybe I don't need a husband to provide and protect me so much as I need a playmate."

Words are an inadequate, crippled way of communication at best. But then, this is the same woman who has held my hand and brought me Bible verses and margaritas through the deaths of three husbands.

Ardell leaps into the air. I mean the old broad's feet leave the stony ground. She grins beatifically at me. Her shout would not be out of place in a revival tent. "Hallelujah girl! You done stopped kickin' over the traces of love!"

Thank the Good Lord there isn't a snake handy nearby. I swear she'd scoop the serpent up and play with him. She is that filled with joy over her old stick-in-the-mud best friend loosening up a little. The woman is completely incorrigible in her belief in her own interpretation of the way the world works. She's delighted I've taken this small step to cross over to the wild side.

"You're not making yourself crazy nuts over whether he's after your money or your body or you high IQ?"

I shake my head and stretch the truth like a rubber band. "Not even contemplating on it."

"Not worrying yourself into a tizzy fit over the young Daisy Duke?"

"Only occasionally and only a small tizzy."

Once we make the ridge, we sit side by side and dangle our legs off the cantilevered limestone. The poison sumac is a blaze of crimsons and garnets against the deeper piney green of the hillside. We talk some about my worry over Mama.

"It's odd how, with Mama sick for the first time, Daddy seems suddenly old. Mostly I think it's my perception of him that's altered."

Ardell reminds me of the time when the two of us called Daddy from a pay phone in the gym where we were attending our very first high school dance.

"We hadn't talked of nothing else for a week," she remembers. "Made our own dresses. Yours was pale blue with a rounded collar edged in lace."

I loved the way the rayon swished over my butt every time I took a step. "Lord, I thought I was the prettiest thing in the county that night. You were a mighty close second in that peach chiffon with the daring V-neck. That dress showed not a smidgen of cleavage but, Lord have mercy, that fabric did cling in all the right places and hint at the glory that was yours under that soft fabric."

Ardell goes on with the reminiscing. "Mr. Crawley, the English teacher and junior class advisor, he put the two of us in charge of the punch bowl. That man was gorgeous, and didn't we all secretly love him? Fresh from student teaching up near Oglethorpe and filled with ideas. That special afterschool reading group he put together where we sat around in giggling bunches reading *Catcher in the Rye* and *Madame Bovary*."

The air up this high is crisp with the sharp astringent mix of pine and juniper. I reach across the limestone and take the hand of my best friend

Her voice is low, almost rote, but she doesn't flinch, keeps telling the story.

"Midway through the dance, right as Gary Mullens, the band's lead singer, was yelling 'I can't get no-o sat-is-fac-tion!,' Mr. Crawley asked me to go into the coach's office with him. Said he needed my help to carry out more bottles of punch."

Even after all these years, I can't help making excuses for not being with her. "He told me to stay there. 'Somebody needs to stay at the cle punch bowl,' is what he said.

God, that man was good-looking. If you had asked me just then, I'd have told you that Ardell and I would have done anything for him. I was young and once again wrong. Ardell came back from the coach's office ten minutes later, her eyes shiny, and her lipstick smeared.

"Soon as I saw you, I called Daddy. Didn't tell him anything. Just said we needed him to come and carry us home. Now."

A lot of years have come and gone. Ardell and I have had ourselves a fair number of adventures and what gets called life experiences since that night. But we both agree that nobody has ever looked as big or as strong or as wonderful as Daddy when he strode into the gym that night. There was no big scene, and we never did find out what happened to Mr. Crawley. When we came back to school, Mrs. Finkle had taken over his afterschool reading group as well as his regular English classes. Rumors flew for a while there about why he'd packed up and fled the county, but the man was never heard from in these parts again.

Perched on the ridge looking out over mountains that I know for a fact are filled with deer as well as the occasional black bear and solitary cougar, I hold Ardell's hand and listen to her wisdom.

"A man like your daddy, it's hard to see him as anything but the strong, virile man we remember from when we were kids. Hard to see your protector as someone who now maybe needs your help from time to time."

The two of us sit until the tawny yellows and ruby magentas no longer blur with the timeless green of the pines, then I get myself up off my cold butt in a most ungraceful fashion and lend a hand to Ardell. Starving after all that glorious fresh air and woodsy beauty, we head back down the mountain. As a reward for our strenuous exercise, we stop at Rebs and share an order of catfish.

REBS'
FRIED CATFISH

It's hard to imagine anything that looks as ugly or tastes as good as a catfish. If we have a totem animal here in Noisy Creek, this is it, the lowly catfish. You can catch him with a cane pole or a trotline. Use anything from cheese doodles to a hunk of tobacco as bait. How a catfish can eat the trash it eats and still taste as good as it does, well, that's a mystery you're gonna have to take up with the Lord.

Ingredients:

- 3 lbs of boneless catfish fillets, cleaned and dried
- Evaporated milk to cover the fillets when put in a pie pan
- Salt and pepper to taste
- 1/2 t cayenne pepper
- 1/3 t garlic salt
- 1 c flour
- 1 c yellow cornmeal
- 2 t paprika
- 1/2 pound bacon

Pour the milk into the pie pan. Add the salt and pepper and cayenne. In a bowl stir together the garlic salt, flour, cornmeal, salt, and pepper. Fry the bacon, and remove. It's the bacon grease you want. You can crumble the bacon and use it in your cornbread or save it for another use. Lay the fillets, one at a time, into the milk mixture, then gently drop one at a time into the bowl with the flour and cornmeal. Make sure each fillet is thoroughly coated. Fry the fillets in the bacon grease over high heat for about five minutes on each side. Don't crowd the pan. As always you want the grease as hot as you can get it without burning. Remember if you're using a cast iron pan, you'll probably need to adjust the heat as you cook. The catfish will flake easily and be a deep brown when it's done. Coleslaw and hush puppies are usually served with this meal.

Seventeen

Colin and I carry on like repressed teenagers for ten days. A stolen kiss here, a touch of the hand there, a longing glance, an answering wink, we are naughty in our minds for those few days while I sleep in my childhood bed and Colin helps Daddy make the house ready for Mama's return. We spend a good bit of time wearing down a desire line between the back of his new housing development and the Love Ramp. Maybe because the trail itself feels like middle ground, this is where we talk about what we have taken to calling the Other World.

I rant some about Kristen Yates. "That gal is like some trashy, wrecked Trans-Am convertible as compared to the classic Cadillac you are currently escorting." I don't mention all the pain and time it takes to keep this particular classic polished.

He squeezes my hand. "Kristen is a perfectly nice young woman in whom I have not one iota of romantic interest. Now I admit, out in California, before I ever met you, I did succumb to her brand of aggressive sexuality a time or two."

I jerk my hand out of his grasp, double my fist. He leaps sideways, just slightly more than an arm's length away. Maybe he saw a snake.

"Come on now, Ruth, as I mentioned, it was before I'd even met you, and

I swear I have been clear with her that I'm now in a relationship with you." He peeks over at me, inches closer. "I'm sorry I ever hooked up with her. I promise you, there'll never be anything between her and me but her daddy's business."

I decide to believe him.

On one of these walks through the wood between the worlds, Colin's battered thermos of iced tea sloshing against his leg with each long stride, I bring up the subject of money. Namely me having more of the stuff than him.

"Is it going to be a problem?" I come right out and ask him.

"You having more money than me?" He looks incredulous, "No. I think I can guarantee you that isn't going to be a problem."

He never once in all the time we spend together asks me for money. Plus, I know for a fact that the materials to build Mama's ramp were put on his account at the lumber yard. I probably had more money than both my second and third husbands, and I never once worried about it. Never even thought about it. So I know the real question isn't whether this beautiful young man is after my money. The question that wakes me in the night, heart pounding and hands cold with sweat is something else entirely. Can he really want me instead of a woman closer to his age?

On a Texas camping trip with Grandpa and Grandma Powell when I was maybe ten or eleven, we spent the night in a cobwebbed cabin where musty mattresses rested on wooden boxes built into the floor. As soon as the lights went out, something as big as a cougar began scratching its way up out of my bed frame where it had evidently gotten itself trapped. I was unconvinced by Grandma and Grandpa's assurances that it couldn't get out of the frame, did not share their confidence that the beast was not really trying to claw its way into my brain, using my ear as a conduit.

Eventually, they lit the kerosene lantern again, and in the globe of dim yellow light dangling from Grandma's steady hand, Grandpa removed the mattress and dismantled the entire top of the wooden frame. It took a long time, and I learned a few Texas words I'd not heard before, but eventually my trapped monster was exposed. A tiny, trembling mouse, no bigger than my thumb, crouched in the corner of the box, whiskers twitching, tiny body tensed in panic at his discovery.

I refused to let Grandpa kill it, though at that point he may have been thinking it was either the mouse or me—something was gonna die. Grandma threw a dish towel over the critter and carried it to the porch where she flung the poor thing out into a night of waiting predators.

This worry of mine about Colin being after my money feels like that tiny mouse scratching and nibbling his way into my ear in the night. I know it's my imagination moving down there in the dark box where I push the knowledge of my own aging. I understand that I am feeding the thing on insecurity and the twins of self-importance and fear of looking foolish. I know it is nothing but a tiny quivering rodent of worry, but still, there are moments when I lie in the dark and am certain a beast of epic proportions is scratching and chewing its way up into my life.

The green-housing project is creeping slowly forward through the forest of county permits, environmental protection laws, and financial requirements that surround all such construction endeavors. Colin is pleased with the progress, though to me, it just looks like a winding road through old trees and a bunch of stakes in the ground marking off imaginary happy home sites. The trenches for in-ground utilities will begin going in next week, and Colin is anxious to oversee this work as he doesn't want any more trees than necessary disturbed.

His original hope had been to generate all the power for the development with solar panels on the roof of each individual home and with a scattering of windmills that will line a small rise just out of view at the far side of the development. But Preston Yates and the rest of the investors have required hookups to Georgia Power and Southern Bell as part of the package. Colin still believes the houses will never have to flip this switch to the utility companies, but the option will be there, along with a number of straight paths of destruction through his pristine woods.

He has reserved a ten-acre, pie-shaped section at the back of the property with its tip dipping into the creek and pointing almost directly at Mama and Daddy's front door for a home of his own. A first for him. To this ten acres there will be no underground cable line. He plans a two bedroom cabin with a great room opened to the forest around it by two walls of windows. The exact alignment of these windows to maximize winter sun and minimize summer light while creating the feel of living in a tree house all requires more ciphering than I can follow. But the physical tracking of the light through the seasons, the careful recording of tree shadows and moonlight, this I love sharing with him.

His enthusiasm is a fascinating and powerfully sexy thing to watch. It reminds me of my excitement for my first salon. Thirty years ago. It stirs me to see the world again as a stage of infinite possibilities. Opens my eyes to the way settling-in can pass from placid to stagnation in the blink of a careless eye. He stands in the mottled light, paces leaf mold and the pollen of puff balls into tiny whirlwinds at his feet, and paints me into his vision. He throws his arms wide to demonstrate the dimensions of future rooms, strides through dead leaves to doors and windows that live only on paper and in his brilliant imagination.

I find him dazzling. His youth, his enthusiasm, his ability to take an idea and make it happen. All of it. All of him. In the middle of a discourse on the angle of the sun or a pronouncement about how easy it is to build a solar oven, how much more difficult to construct a solar home, I walk into his arms, and he makes me a part of his creation, weaves me seamlessly into the tapestry of dreams he is creating here in the dappled light of a South Georgia fall.

COLIN'S
SWEET TEA

This is about as simple a recipe as you can get, but with a couple of squares of cornbread to go with it, this has tided over many a Noisy Creek working man until he can get home to his supper and his woman.

Ingredients:
- 4 bags of Lipton tea
- 1 quart of water just brought to a boil
- 1/2 c sugar

Put the tea bags in the hot water, and let it sit until it turns the rich tannic color of oak-lined lake water. Remove the tea bags without squeezing. Squeezing will make the tea bitter. Add the sugar while the water's still hot, and stir until it's dissolved. Right now you have very strong sweet tea. Put it in the refrigerator to cool. When you're ready to pour it in a thermos, first fill the thermos with cracked ice. Ice cubes can be put in a dish towel and pounded with a meat mallet a time or two to get the right consistency. You want shards, not crushed ice. Pour the tea over the cracked ice. The ice will melt slowly and dilute the tea to the proper strength while keeping it frosty cold.

Throw in a square or two of cornbread if you've got it. We all know the way to a man's heart is a little lower than his belly, but good eats can't hurt none.

Eighteen

Even the extra freezer on the canning porch, the one Daddy uses mostly for venison, is smack filled with zucchini bread, casseroles, and enough pies and cakes to put us all in diabetic comas. Neighbors and relatives all make an appearance at the house while Mama's laid up in the hospital at Dothan, each and every one bearing offerings of community support. Once Daddy and Colin start on the ramp, folks come to sit on the porch, drink sweet tea, supervise the work, and swap stories. Uncle Earl arrives most afternoons with a faded red cooler filled with Pabst Blue Ribbon. He stays until the last top is popped. Uncle Neil spends four afternoons sizzling catfish in the twenty pounds of lard held in his turkey fryer.

"It ain't just for Thanksgiving anymore!" he proclaims each time he serves up another batch of golden nuggets.

We'd eaten all the gator at the Labor Day party, but Uncle promises Colin he'll "wrassle up anoder'un right soon."

If it sounds like Mama's hospital stay is an occasion for a ten-day party while she isn't there to scatter the hooligans away like a farm woman shooing chickens out of her flower bed, well, in a way, it is. Is it more work than if the well-wishers, the curious, and the just plain bored stayed at their own homes.

Of course it is. Does it accomplish its purpose of surrounding Daddy with the love of a community who cares about him while entertaining folks for miles around? You betcha.

But all this ends the day Snickers and Candy carry Mama home. They had planned on getting to Noisy Creek just before noon, but at the last minute there were extra insurance forms that needed filling out, one more social worker who was required to sign off on Mama's release, and some confusion with the physical therapist who had scheduled an additional session. My sisters keep calling from the hospital, their voices more worried and stressed as the day wears on. They report that Mama waits in a wheelchair all during the extra three and a half hours of bureaucratic hoopla fully dressed and itching to go.

The pale yellow light of the autumn sun is already filtering through the kudzu at the edge of the piney woods when they pull up the gravel drive to the house. Daddy and I have given up and eaten Mama's favorite pork roast and apple dumplings hours earlier. Before the dust of the driveway kicked up by the tires of Candy's Volvo settles, Snickers rushes to pull the walker from the trunk. She snaps the locks in place and wheels it to Mama so she can support her weight on it as she scoots herself out of the vehicle.

If you didn't know Snickers, you might only see the professional manner she's using for all this fussing–the positioning, the helpful arm, the brisk but encouraging whispered words. You might miss the firm set of her jaw, locked to prevent any distracting crying. Those dark patches at the corners of her eyes and mouth, like the bruises left by fingers pressed too hard into tender skin. The tension in the way she carries her shoulders, high and stiff with the weight of seeing Mama changed by the aging process that stalks us all, biding its time, smiling at our efforts to outrun it.

"Welcome home, old woman," Daddy says, his eyes glistening in the slanted afternoon light. "We done ate your apple dumplings, but I believe we saved you a bite a pork roast."

Things get confusing then for a while. Mama exclaims over the ramp and her transplanted roses. She balances on the ugly metal walker, her wrinkled face shining with tears and the joy of being home. Daddy is a schoolboy on his first date with the homecoming queen. He fusses around her, gets in her way more than he helps, backs off and then is propelled forward again by his need to touch her arm or brush an imaginary hair from her face. Snickers gives orders in her sergeant major's voice. Candy and I roll our eyes a bit, but we hop to it like good soldiers.

We bring in the plastic bags of hospital paraphernalia we all hope never to see again. The puke yellow kidney-shaped vomit catcher. The plastic torture device designed to prevent pneumonia by forcing the patient to play a morbid game of "can you make the little blue ball float to the top of the clear plastic tube before you pass out from hyperventilation." The square gray boxes of rough tissues. The rectangular pads to protect against unthinkable leakages. All this and more Candy and I cart into the house.

"Does she need all this stuff?" This right here, this is proof that Mama is vulnerable, and I hate every single tissue and plastic doodad.

"No." Candy touches my arm in what I take as reassurance. "But she paid for it, and you know there's no way she was gonna leave it there."

There is an edge of hysteria in our laughter. We catch the evil eye from Snickers when we rejoin the convoy on the ramp, but laughter seems our best option at the moment. Mama shuffles along for a few yards, stops to catch her breath, regain her strength. I say maybe we should have brought the wheel-chair, but Snickers quickly instructs me that the doctor said that was the worst thing possible for Mama. She has to build up her muscles, or she'll never re-cover. The look Snickers gives me makes me think of mean schoolmarms and naughty children in pointy dunce caps.

I shut up.

One of Mama's Wyandottes, the one she calls Lucy, has worked her way around the side of the house and is clucking and scratching and carrying on like a house afire to see her mistress. Her squawking alerts the rest of the little flock, and they come at a chicken trot, straight for Mama. Of course they're looking for a handout. Though admittedly more than once I've come up on Mama sitting on the back porch, one of her hens squatting beside her, the two of them staring out across the fields seemingly enjoying each other's company.

There are four cell phones among the welcoming committee. Everyone we know calls to check on Mama during the half-hour it takes her to make the walk to her new space-age recliner. We finally switch the phones to vibrate. Our pockets and purses twitch and quiver like we're transporting mice, but we make it inside without any further interruptions. Mama sobs into her hands once Daddy gets her ensconced on her new throne.

"I am just so happy to be home. The ramp. The chair." She flutters her hands through the air. "Everything y'all have done. I am plain overwhelmed by all this effort and support."

Dwarfed by the recliner, she looks plumb tuckered out.

We phone the well-wishers and the curious.

"Mama's home and resting," we tell everyone. "We so very much appreciate your concern but we are not receiving phone calls or visitors until further notice." This reduces the calls to five or six an hour, and only four people show up with casseroles and house plants. By then, Mama is sleeping in her new mechanized chintz chair with Daddy stretched out next to her on the sofa. Candy and I hunker down on the back porch steps and pass a cold beer back and forth. Because there is no way we can stop her, Snickers is on guard duty at the front gate. She has her a lawn chair set up under the magnolia out yonder at the end of the drive where our gravel meets the county dirt road.

Candy aims the neck of the brown bottle at our stubborn sister. "That there is the Barr version of a yeller junkyard dawg."

When I go inside to get us another cold one, Mama and Daddy snore a soft duet in the living room. I pull aside the ruffled kitchen curtain over the old porcelain double sink, just make out the gray image of Snickers out there, potted plants and casserole dishes around her feet, doing everything she knows to keep our family safe from the inevitable.

Uncle Wally and Aunt Emma May make a red dust storm as they turn their Old International Pickup around in a lazy circle, having left their offering with the watch dog and been denied access to the palace. I fetch Candy, and we carry two more chairs and a six pack of lights up the driveway to keep Snickers company as night closes the first long day of a new era.

APPLE
DUMPLINGS

In the fall, we go out past The Big Johnson Super Store and turn onto Route 4 until we see the peeling red sign in the shape of an apple. Under this sign on a chalkboard is where Cousins Hugh and Nancy list what apples are ready for picking. Daddy likes the Gravensteins, which are usually ripe by late August, but for dumplings we always pick apricot apples which ripen in late October and have a pale orange flesh and a crisp taste just right for this treat.

Ingredients:
- 2 c flour   • 2 t powder   • 1 t salt
- 1/2 c leaf lard or Crisco
- 6 small apples peeled and cored
- 3/4 c buttermilk • 1/2 c brown sugar
- 1/3 c butter
- Dash of cinnamon and nutmeg

We girls always liked a few of those red hot cinnamons from the candy counter of the Dixie Circle Market tossed in, but Mama only added those if we'd been extra good.

Sift flour, powder, and salt. Cut in lard. Add buttermilk. Stir and then, on a lightly floured surface, knead the dough until it's no longer sticky. Roll out to 1/8 inch and cut into 6 squares. Place an apple in each square, and fill the hole where the core has been with butter, brown sugar, cinnamon, and nutmeg. If you have a child who's been good, this is where you'll add those red hot candies. Pull the dough up, and seal around the apples. Place on greased pan.

Combine the brown sugar, butter, nutmeg, and cinnamon with 1 1/3 c hot water. Stir until the sugar is dissolved and then pour this over the apples in their greased pan. Bake at 450 degrees for 20 minutes or until done. Save at least one for your mama.

nineteen

Colin and I sway in our own peculiar courtship dance, making up the moves as we go along, revising, revisiting, backing off, moving closer. As autumn days shorten we grow accustomed to the joy of joining our bodies and the comfort of falling asleep in each others arms. But the worry mouse continues to scratch its way into my ear in the dark of the night. Kristen Yates is still in town and hot to trot with my man. The girl has been in the spa twice. She complains about the horrible, rough towels we use. Moans about the way Mona, who is our very best stylist, has butchered her hair. Threatens to sue because the avocado facial has completely ruined her flawless complexion. The last time she made an appearance, LuAnne threw her out on her cute little Yankee butt. We're all expecting a phone call from her attorney any day now. In fact, I believe Snickers's exact words when I mentioned the possibility of a lawsuit were, "Bring it on!" My phone rings in the dead of night, scaring me into an early grave. I knock over the beside lamp, the alarm clock, and nearly bloody Colin's nose getting to it, only to hear Dear Little Kristen's voice.

"You old bitch. You'd better stay away from Colin if you know what's good for you. Do you hear me?"

Colin changed his cell phone number and threatened to get a restraining order if she didn't learn how to behave like a normal human being. Evidently she's decided now to try her charms on me.

All this we endure. Then her daddy tries an end run.

Preston Yates strolls into the salon on an overcast Tuesday morning in early October, one of those early fall days that remind folks to carry that old winter coat to Millie's dry cleaner over in Aiken. We don't get many men wandering into the mauve and ivory reception area, so when a six foot four, silver haired, gold and diamond bedecked man in city clothes shows up, it gets the attention of nigh on every single women in the place. Heck, Marleene Fostnick from the hardware store even runs across the street faster than a scalded hog and sticks her head in the door.

Basically, we behave like estrogen-challenged hillbillies. In our defense, we don't see many men who have paid more for their clothes—in particular if you count the flashy Rolex—than we paid for our homes. Not including, of course, what it cost to remove the wheels and screen that aluminum siding in with a nice sitting porch. So when Preston Yates arrives, with his sparkling white teeth and his arms filled with an overdone arrangement of orchids and yellow roses, the ladies at the spa are delighted with the day's free entertainment.

I am less thrilled.

LuAnne fetches me from my office, her eyes all big in her head and a grin that promises something to liven up the morning. Snickers and I have been fighting about her desire to give up her job as manager to stay full-time out at Mama and Daddy's, an ongoing argument from which I am happy to walk away. The two of us follow LuAnne's bouncing rump out to reception. Preston Yates looks like a pedigreed coon dog at a possum fest. He is right pretty, but he surely is out of place. Plus, it is looking like the possums might be fixing to turn on him.

The flowers are for me, and he must have dragged them all the way from Atlanta. There is no way Bessie's Florist and Baubles over on Lee put that arrangement together.

"I am here to request the pleasure of your company over lunch today." For a second I think he's going to bow at the waist, but no, he lets a low bob of his perfectly groomed head suffice. "I would appreciate the opportunity to properly apologize for that unfortunate misunderstanding about the payment of that hotel suite in Savannah."

What nonsense. First of all that little incident was months ago. More importantly, men like Preston Yates have no interest in the hurt feelings of a woman unless that woman has something they want.

I accept the flowers and listen to the words floating out of his mouth like so much minty nonsense. He takes good care of himself, I'll give him that. His skin is small-pored and smooth, his hands soft, the moons of the nails fully exposed. Lots of facials and manicures have gone into the making of this here man. His right hand sparkles with two gold rings, one appears to be some sort of ruby-eyed lion encircled by two rows of diamonds. Surreptitiously examining that sparkling king of the beasts, I notice something else a whole lot more interesting—my sister Snickers.

Sexual attraction is a funny thing. No matter what our brains and our common sense may tell us, desire can by-pass the whole kit and caboodle. In men, we call this thinking with the little head. In women, well, we mostly deny it happens. But looking at Snickers right now, I expect her to fan herself at any moment and inquire, "Is it hot in he-ah or is it just little ole me?" She appears positively smitten by a man who is so far from her usual type as to be from another universe.

I am struck with a brilliant and evil idea.

Which is how Snickers ends up in a silver Bentley on her way to dinner with a Yankee. I accept the gracious invitation of Mr. Yates, but stipulate the inclusion of my sister. At the very last moment, just as we are all three ready to leave for the fancy La Vive la Reina over in Greenville, Ardell calls me from out of the blue with a personal emergency that requires my immediate assistance. Can't be helped. I wave Snickers on without me.

I know what I have that the big money man wants, and I know for whom he wants him. I can even see it as a nice fatherly gesture to try and distract the competition so little Kristen can move in on Colin. We rednecks ain't near as dumb as city folk think we are. What I want is a distraction for Snickers who is driving us all nuts with her over-protectiveness of Mama.

"Putting Preston together with Snickers will provide a nice diversion for my obsessive sister," I tell Ardell. She looks at me over the top of her rhinestone glasses, gives me the evil eye. "It seemed like a harmless thing to do."

"Them there," Ardell says, "are probably the words most often heard at disaster sites."

At any rate, with Snickers out of the way, I drive out to Mama and Daddy's for dinner. Snickers has defrosted Maribelle Spaulding's ham and lima bean casserole and Daddy has seen to it the dish got put in the oven at the precise time instructed. Against orders, Mama has stirred up a batch of cornbread and a bait of collards to go with it. Colin and Daddy clean their plates and then break up the corn bread and use it to sop up the pot liquor, but Mama and I make do with mostly the greens and sweet tea.

She is recovering faster than any of us dared hope. That ramp has turned out to be wonderful physical therapy. She is up to walking it three times a day now. Daddy has set up raised benches at the end and the middle so she can rest when the need takes her. Her roses are in full, fall splendor and are a glorious motivator for getting her out and moving along their fragrant length. She and I head to the ramp and leave the men to their second and third helpings of dinner.

The Cecile Brunner is in full bloom, and Daddy has positioned the middle bench under its pink arch. I walk beside Mama as she scrapes her walker along on her way to the shade of that climbing rose. When I was a kid, those delicate pink blossoms grew all mixed in with the old red cabbage blooms known here abouts as outhouse roses. Mama has worked for years to separate the two, but each year a few of the incorrigible blousy red blooms appear amidst the more ladylike delicate pink.

Mama is working toward trading her walker for one of those claw-footed canes by Daddy's birthday. The physical therapist is coming out tomorrow, and her plan is to convince the woman to take "this danged nuisance contraption" with her. Mama is upset by the scrapes in the paint on the walls of the house already made by miscalculating the width of the walker, sick of pushing it along in front of her like the unruly mascot of an invalid.

She walks right past the bench under the Cecile Brunner. We don't stop to rest until she has settled herself on the seat at the end of the ramp, the one where the Climbing Iceberg meets the Mary Washington, providing us a narrow tunnel of speckled shade.

"I don't know what to do about your sister," she tells me as she deadheads the old blooms within her reach. "I wouldn't hurt her feelings for the world, but I don't need or want her moving in here to take care of your daddy and me."

This is old family material, worn thin here lately as Snickers's fear of losing Mama rubs daily against Mama's desire for independence. Candy and I are both of the opinion that Daddy and Mama are fine living alone. We are united in our belief that the problem isn't that our parents have reached an age when they need full-time assistance. The fly in the ointment is our middle sister, who has somehow married her need for a life's purpose with her irrational belief that she can keep Mama alive forever if she just loves her enough—as though the grim reaper can be turned away by sacrifice, deterred by vigilance.

I tattle to Mama about her dinner with a Yankee, happening right now, as we rest in that narrow band of leafy shade. I tell her everything. The expensive clothes, the whitened smile, the Bentley, her blush, the ruby-eyed lion.

Mama smiles like a girl. She pats my hand. "You have always been my most wicked child."

Colin has already cleaned up the dinner dishes when Mama and I make it back to the house. Mama fusses over him doing it before she hugs his neck and sends us both on our way. I walk him back to the Jenkins Development, where the infrastructure is officially in place and work has started on four houses. He is excited that two more lots have sold in the past week. His gamble seems to be paying off. People do want to retire to small, well-built, energy-efficient homes in the country setting of a small town. Even though we've known for years that there is no better place to live than Noisy Creek, it still shocks me a bit that city folks are intrigued by and drawn to the life. As my Uncle Earl would say, "Who'd a thunk it?"

I drone on a bit about my suspicions about Preston Yates's motivation for the flowers and invitation to dinner.

Colin kisses me thoroughly. When he releases me, his face is dappled in sun, his smile brilliant. He pulls me back against him, murmurs into my ear.

"There exists a very good possibility that Mr. Yates came looking for you simply because he wanted a date with the most beautiful woman in South Georgia."

It ought not to feel that good when a man blatantly lies to you. But Colin and I, we are going through a good patch, so I just pretend to believe him, let him lean me up against an old rough barked pine tree and take advantage of my good nature.

BARR FAMILY
COLLARDS

Folks here abouts eat collards four or five times a week. It would not surprise me one bit if scientists one day discovered that eating these greens sops up all that grease we insist on taking with every meal and is the reason our clogged arteries don't sent us all to our heavenly reward by our fortieth birthdays. France has medicinal red wine and dark chocolate. Southerners have collards.

Ingredients:

• A bait of collards, about 2 lbs—Mama says a bait is as many greens as you can hold in your two hands coming in from the garden. Daddy says it's as much as one grown man can eat at a sitting without plumb busting.

• 3 T onion chopped

• 3 cloves garlic minced

• 2 t bacon fat—Some folks use salt pork, but that there is really for making turnip greens. Collards don't need nothing but onion and a little bacon grease for flavor.

Clean the collards, discarding any leaves that are yellowed. Roll the leaves so they look like long cigars and slice on the diagonal. Place all the ingredients in a pan, cover with water, cover the pan, and boil until the collards are tender. The time to cook them will depend on the age of your greens. You can add a pinch of sugar just before taking them out of the pot with an unslotted spoon. You want some of the pot liquor to end up in plate for sopping up with cornbread.

Always serve these with pepper vinegar—small bottles of white vinegar with whole hot peppers inside. Remember to add enough vinegar to cover the peppers so they have time to spice things up between servings.

Twenty

Snickers has always been the best looking of us Barr girls. Candy and I are pretty. Snickers is downright beautiful with luscious curves, a heavy mane of thick red hair, and an ivory complexion that jumped a generation and came as a gift from Great-grandma Branson. That sublime beauty though has been more of a curse than a blessing to her over the years. Folks, men and women, are blinded by an involuntary attraction to her. They step all over themselves doing for her. They occasionally resent it, but can't seem to help themselves. Beauty demands worship. Which was all well and good when she was younger.

Now that she's edging up on sixty, her looks are softening around the edges, doors no longer open miraculously, baggage and groceries remain where they are, wait for her own arms to lift and move. Two years ago I found her in tears over an incident that wouldn't have fazed a less attractive woman, or to my way of thinking, one less vain, either.

While looking for our accountant's office in Atlanta, Snickers accidentally walked into the wrong room, stumbled into a meeting of business men seated around a long, gleaming wood table. At her entrance, their talk ceased, a covey of well-groomed male faces looked up at her and registered annoyance at the interruption. Not a single man jumped up to see if he could be of assistance to her. None of them even asked for whom she was looking. Not one pair of eyes flashed in recognition of her beauty, no involuntary sexual attraction hiked up the room's tension. I'm here to tell you, it was a shock to poor Snickers.

She was sobbing when she told me all this. This big dramatic tragedy. A bunch of self-important men didn't stop what they were doing and fall all over themselves to help her out.

"It was a nightmare," she wailed. "Those blank faces. They were angry, you can't tell me any different, at being interrupted by an... an... old... woman."

Well, I had no intention of telling her any different. To me, her reaction was bizarre at best, though I was leaning toward insane. I called Candy for help.

"She's never learned to rear-up on her haunches, stand up for herself, and demand respect," I bitched. "She's as smart as we are, but she's had very little experience using that intellect to get what she wants. She's skated through life on her beauty."

We divided the personality assets up evenly, Candy and Snickers and I. Candy is the practical sister, the good girl who can be counted on to employ good sense and judgment. She's the perfect Baptist minister's wife. I am the feisty one. The one with the temper and the sense of humor. Snickers is the beauty. As the three of us age, it becomes more and more obvious that Candy and I have the more age-resistant attributes. Snickers feels tricked by nature, as though the world has reneged on a personal promise. She's handicapped by her inability to adjust to her new status, the slow move from what folks describe as a fresh young beauty to someone referred to as a handsome older woman.

This difficulty in adjusting to aging, coupled with her special relationship with Mama, makes her a royal pain in the ass. When I set her up with the rich Yankee, is there some tiny bit of my getting even with her going on? Some payback for the wringer she's been putting the rest of us through with her obsession over Mama? As Kristen Yates would say, "Well, hello? Like, duh?" It's Ardell who sympathizes best with Snickers. By which I mean that Candy doesn't live in Noisy Creek, and I don't sympathize much at all. Ardell was my second call on the day of Snickers's meltdown over being ignored by busy men.

"Well, darlin," she had cooed to my sister when I handed her the phone. "It was pouring down buckets all day. You were soaked to the skin, I bet. None of us look that fetching after being caught in a downpour. And anyway, honey, Atlanta! Why that's near about Yankee territory. Fools wouldn't know how to treat a lady, less'un you lumped em up with a big stick first."

All of which sounded like the kind of cooing nonsense you tell a dog whose tail you've accidentally shut in the screen door, but Snickers perked up some.

I think about that day of infamy while I wait for Snicks to return from her dinner with Preston Yates. Talk about the ultimate Carpetbagging Philistine. The man is from Los Angeles, but it wouldn't surprise me none if he knows Ted Turner. What in the world was I thinking turning the Beast loose on my defenseless sister?

So, okay, I am feeling a little guilty.

Snickers does not return to work that day. She does call, just at dark-thirty, to say she and this darlin' man are in Savannah, at that cute little ole hotel Preston paid for when you and Colin spent the weekend. I don't believe my blood pressure jumps any more than fifty points at this news. I sputter.

Snickers elaborates, in a giddy voice I had so hoped she'd outgrown. "We have separate rooms. Of course. But there's a naughty adjoining door."

"Like knotty pine?" I can't resist. Can a door really be described as naughty?

Snickers isn't amused. "We're staying a few days, might even go up the coast a ways, explore some. Why not? Like you and Candy keep telling me, it isn't like anyone in Noisy Creek needs me."

Which isn't quite what I recall either Candy or myself saying, but I let it go. Mainly because she hangs up on me when the Bejeweled Carpetbagger himself comes to the door. They are going to supper at a friend's house in Hilton Head. Probably Ted freakin' Turner.

What I really want to do when I hang up the phone is run out to Leeville and tattle on her to Mama and Daddy, but I am pretty sure this would elicit some mention of the fact that it was me that hooked my sweet, naive sister up with the Yankee. Probably better not to worry Mama about all this. I go on home and call Candy and Ardell while I wait for Colin.

Ardell is no help whatsoever. In fact, she is downright rude.

"Well now," she drawls, "like the preachers tell us, no evil deed goes unrewarded. At least Snickers knows going in who paid for the room."

Candy, on the other hand, is of the opinion that the entire fiasco is somehow my fault. "You're the one tricked Snickers into going alone with the man. You know how that gal is around handsome men! I cannot conceive of how you couldn't have foreseen that he would suggest that dinner wasn't enough time to spend getting to know one another. You might have used your head and predicted that she'd let herself be swept away in his fancy silver car for a few days of fun and games at the shore."

Ardell calls back. "Hey," she shouts into the phone, "if Snickers and Preston get married, you'll be related to the Faux Daisy Duke."

All I can think to mutter before I hang up the phone is, "Not blood kin! Just one more half-assed relative!"

I unplug the house phone. Set my cell on vibrate. Both phones have caller ID. If Mama or Daddy call, I'll pick up. Otherwise, I'm done talking for the night. I reheat collards. A pork roast is already making the house smell good, though it's not going to be ready to eat until after dark.

Colin arrives fresh from work and still in his ratty gray sweatshirt with the broken zipper. I'm on the lounge chair in the backyard. No moon, and under the grandeur of the stars, I feel small and insignificant, doing a fine job of convincing myself that I am not responsible for the decisions Snickers or anyone else makes in this brief life. Am I my sister's keeper?

My first words of the evening to Colin, however, are, "Is that the only sweatshirt you own?"

A clue perhaps that there might be a smidgen of jealousy swirling around in all that guilt. I take him to bed to apologize. We have time before the roast is ready, and I am, after all, the feisty sister.

DRUNK
PORK ROAST

This recipe is Great-aunt Edna's signature dish. There is a reasonable assumption in the family that dear Auntie samples a good bit of the Jack Daniels as she's cooking. At any rate, she's generally a bit wobbly by the time she arrives at the family gathering to which she's toting this offering.

Ingredients:
- 3 lb pork roast
- 3 T honey
- 3 T orange juice
- 4 cloves of garlic, sliced thin, lengthwise
- The peel of one orange
- 1 T flour
- 1 t paprika
- 1/2 t salt
- Ground pepper
- 1/2 c Jack Daniels whiskey

Cut slits all over the roast, and insert your garlic slices. Rub the roast with the orange juice. Mix together the honey, orange peel, flour, paprika, and salt. Rub this mixture into the roast. Place the roast, fat side down, in a roaster, and generously sprinkle with fresh ground pepper. Pour the whiskey over the roast. Cover, leaving a vent, and roast for 3 hours at 325 degrees.

Auntie says you're supposed to baste this roast every half hour, but the night I made it, I never once opened the oven door until Colin and I stumbled back into the kitchen on shaky legs about three hours after I'd put it in the oven. I suspect the reason for Auntie's frequent basting instructions is that she sips a bit from the bottle at each basting.

Twenty-One

Nine days before Daddy's eightieth birthday, Megan Molly Jenkins blows into town. Colin wants me to ride with him to pick his mother up at the airport in Atlanta, but I think they need a little time alone. Also I am busy metaphorically covering my windows with plywood and hiding in the basement. I admit it. I am nervous about meeting the mother of this much younger man I am dating.

"What d'ya think she's gonna do?" LuAnne asks. "Slap you silly for taking advantage of her baby boy?"

Actually, my fear is related to Snickers's experience with the uninterested Atlanta businessmen. I am afraid his mother's judgment of me as an older woman luring a beautiful young man into bed with my money and experience will force me to see myself not as Colin's lover but as a predator, or worse, as a pitiful old woman. Nervous that, if she sees me as a cradle robber, my relationship with Colin will slip off center.

The night before her arrival, I dream I am walking down a red dirt road with one of those poles Johnny and I saw people in Asia using to carry burdens, equal weighted bundle at each end, the whole deal balanced on their shoulders. Colin is with me under the little balance beam. It is summer. A drought summer, evidently. In the dream my bare feet and legs are coated with a film of red dust. I am inordinately pleased with myself for balancing this weight in tandem with Colin. As though we've invented this means of conveyance all by ourselves.

There follows one of those moments in a dream when I know I've moved away from happy rambling and am headed inexorably into nightmare country. This particular moment is heralded by a gusty breeze. I smell honeysuckle and dirt and the musty odor of rotting leaves. The balance of the load shifts, one side instantaneously heavier than its opposite. Colin and I stumble. Recover. The bucket on my side is old and dented. I begin to worry that it might be leaking. Colin's bucket is shiny new. The metal glinting in the sun. Even in the dream I understand the meaning of this little discrepancy, the blaring symbolism involved.

Then, in front of us, blocking the dirt road is an old tree. There is no way Colin and I are going to fit around this ancient tree with that pole balanced on our shoulders. In the way of dreams, the tree becomes an old woman. Colin drops his end of the pole and runs joyously to his mother.

I wake to the smell of sawdust and sex, Colin's heavy snores anchoring me to my bed. When my eyes adjust to the dark, I watch him sleep, wonder how he'll hold up his end of the relationship once his mother hits town. Fear my reaction to her disapproval.

I offered to have her stay at my place, but she declined. "I'd prefer you reserve a room for me. Someplace I can relax into my own brand of weirdness without worrying about freaking out anyone."

I am relieved she won't be staying with me and intrigued by just what she is planning on doing that might disturb the locals.

When I ask Colin, he says, "She meditates and does tai chi at dawn, and yoga every evening. That's all she means by weirdness."

That's all? Lord love a duck, are we going to be required to rustle up tofu and organic granola to feed this woman?

"So, um, is she some sort of hippie?" I ask him in a completely respectful voice. I don't judge folks. If Colin's mama wants to hang by her heels and whoop like a Gibbon, it is of no nevermind to me. I'm just wondering is all. So I can warn other folks who might not be as tolerant as myself.

We reserve a room for her at the Thelma and Louise Bed and Breakfast. It really is owned by two woman named Thelma and Louise. Well, it is now that Susan Louise Parcell goes by her middle name. Both women go by Parcell. They moved here to Noisy Creek from Atlanta seven years ago and bought the old Clarke mansion out near the new Big Johnson Supermarket. They're very affectionate with one another. They've even been seen kissing on the big wrap-around porch with the rounded corners. Noisy Creek folks pretend to think they're sisters. Very close sisters. Thelma and Susan Louise don't pretend anything at all. They just go on being who they are and, I assume, enjoy laughing at the rest of us.

Colin knows Thelma and Susan Louise. He says it's because he did some remodeling work for them. Ardell assures me he knows them because the man is attracted to peculiar individuals. She tells me this over the phone so there is no way I can throw anything at her. She's not near brave enough to say it to my face, or more accurately, to my throwing arm.

At any rate, when I mention it to Colin, he says, "The Thelma and Louise B&B will be perfect for my mother. It's just her kind of place."

I suppose my eyes may have widened some. He immediately laughs and puts me out of my misery. "No. My mother is not a lesbian." He can't resist a small dig at my redneck roots, though, and adds, "Though she's not going to feel it's necessary to pretend to believe Thelma and Susan Louise are unusually close siblings."

The room he reserves for his mother has its own private garden. Evidently she does her Chinese contortions outdoors. To better absorb the earth's energy. The more details I report to Ardell, the harder she laughs. I should probably stop revealing the particulars to her, but Colin is so matter-of-fact about all this, I am beginning to think my wackometer is on the fritz.

Maybe I'm the one who can't differentiate between odd and normal.

Ardell chortles. "Darlin', it ain't a question of normal. Your lover boy is from California. None a them folks out there is what we'd call right in the head."

Colin calls me from Columbus. "Mom and I will be at your place by three. Do you want to go out to dinner?"

"Honey," I tell him. "Ah have been cookin' all day. Worked ma little fingers to the bone. Have me a ham in the oven and my heart set on whippin' up some cornbread and a bait of turnips." For some reason my accent had become so thick even I can barely understand what in God's name I am saying.

Colin, bless his heart, just whispers into his little cell phone, "Calm down, baby. You two are going to love each other."

Before he folds his flat phone shut with a click, I catch Colin's CD of the Lovin Spoonful rasping out "Jug Band Music." A lusty female tenor is harmonizing with Colin's baritone as the two of them belt out the lyrics.

They get to my place a bit after 3:30. Just before they arrive, I run around the house and freshen the bowls of honeysuckle and vanilla potpourri. As I'm counting out the last ten drops of fragrant oil for the koa wood bowl in my living room, it occurs to me that there is some similarity between what I am doing and a female wolf pissing on everything in her territory before the arrival of an invading female.

I absolutely have to stop watching Animal Planet.

Colin's truck pulls into the driveway, giving me just enough time for a quick check that my hair doesn't look any different than it did when I checked it thirty seconds earlier. I take four slow, deep breaths, and the door opens. I don't know why I never asked to see a picture of his mother. The woman on my front porch is strikingly beautiful. All that earth's energy she's been collecting over the years, coupled with the Georgia humidity, has made her ash-blonde hair into a wreath of curls around her face. For the briefest of moments, I see Colin standing beside a Madonna, a halo of gold framing a face that can not possibly have seen sixty-eight years of this old world.

Then this earth mother steps forward, wraps me in some musky scent that has me thinking of primal forests and new beginnings. Megan's voice is low. Not soft exactly, but quiet. As though she's used to folks paying attention to whatever gems of wisdom might drop from her mouth. I think of Jackie Kennedy and all the photos of world leaders leaning toward her, their good ear cocked toward her soft words.

Into my ear she whispers. "You and I need to talk."

I jerk away like I've been snake bit. Her eyes are the same blue as Colin's. They flash in what I take as a warning before she releases me, takes her son's arm and murmurs, "I've been looking forward to meeting you, Ruth. Colin has told me so much about you."

Colin grins and kisses my cheek, leads his mother to the French doors of the sunroom where they stand side-by-side and stare at the shiny leaves of my magnolia. I stand dumbfounded, my shoes rooted to the floor. I've had months to build up worry about this woman's visit, and now, less than a minute after her arrival, I'm no longer concerned about her approval at all. I'm pissed off is what I am.

You and I need to talk? Oh, this old California hippie and I will talk all right. She can take that to the bank.

I had planned supper with just the three of us, but Colin calls Daddy and Mama and plans get changed. Daddy speaks on the phone with Megan Molly, and without so much as speaking to me, he officially welcomes her as a member of the family by christening her M&M.

Mama asks to talk to me. "I haven't been further than the end of my ramp since I got home from the hospital. I'm itchy for company."

Just that quick, Daddy loads her in the car and carries her to town. Which means I just about have to call Snickers and give an invite.

In the sweetest little passive aggressive voice y'all could ever hear, my sister says, "I just wouldn't miss it for the world. How much older than you is his mama again?" When I ignore her, she tells me, "Preston and I are spending the weekend together. He is just the sweetest man. Would it be all right with y'all if he tags along to dinner?"

"Sure. Bring The Great Yankee Satan. I'll set a place for him at the table."

Which leads to Daisy Duke being in my home on the day I meet Colin's mother for the first time.

I am sorely tempted to freshen up all that potpourri again, but instead I pull out the big guns. I call Ardell and LuAnne. Candy is fit to be tied that she is missing out up there in Stone Mountain. Sunday being her husband's busy day as a minister and all. I promise to call her before I go to bed and fill her in on all the details. I fully intended to do so. The road to hell no doubt being paved with just such good intentions.

TURNIP
GREENS

These greens have a little bite to them, just a tinge of bitter. Closer in taste to dandelion greens than to collards, they're best when picked young and fresh from the garden. Mama trims the edges from the greens several times before harvesting the root.

Ingredients:
- Bait of turnip greens, washed and trimmed
- 1 lb salt pork, diced
- 1 diced Vidalia onion
- 1/2 t red pepper flakes

Fry the salt pork until it's crisp. Add the rest of the ingredients, and just cover with water. Bring everything to a boil, then turn down the flame, cover, and simmer for about 45 minutes or until the greens are tender. A teaspoon of sugar can be added now if desired. Just like with collards, make sure you get a good portion of pot liquor with each serving. You'll want to have corn bread and vinegar with pepper sauce to go with these greens.

Twenty-Two

Preston Yates turns out to be more like a minion of the Devil than the actual Great Satan. He might even be revealing himself as an ordinary human man, but I am blinded by all that flashing gold and jewelry and miss the revelation. I swear his teeth nearly glow. Perhaps that makes it easier for Snickers to find him in the dark. Personally, I find Braille to be a better method, but to each her own, I suppose.

The Money Man does do his level best to be personable the evening we welcome Colin's meddling hippie of a mother to Noisy Creek. I return the favor. In my own way. I seat him between Snickers and Ardell and directly across from LuAnne. I swear to him in my best Dixie drawl that he is sitting in the seat of honor. Snickers glares mightily, but what can she do? She's not the only Barr to excel at passive aggression.

Megan Molly, or M&M as everybody has taken to calling her, is the hit of my dang party. I seat her between Mama and Daddy and across from Colin. Within moments she and Mama are chatting like old friends, and Daddy acts like he's never had the good fortune to chat with a woman of such wisdom and insight in all his natural life. The entire display makes me mad enough to chew nails. This woman thinks she can just trot into my house and tell me what I can or cannot do with my love life? She and I need to talk all right and then she'd best just fly on back to the land of fruit and nuts where she belongs.

M&M has a doctorate in comparative religions. There's a hippie-dippie college major if I ever heard one. Mama, however, smiles into this information as though gazing on the Holy Grail. She tells M&M how she herself attended college in Texas for a short spell and then transferred on up to Athens for two and a half years with a major in men, and a minor in flirting. Colin's mother has studied with Tibetan monks in Nepal, a Hindu Maharishi in India, a La-kota medicine man, a witch doctor in Rwanda, and lived with Maryknoll nuns in El Salvador for two years.

Mama tells Megan Molly that she's attended the Baptist Church almost every Sunday of her life. Hospitalization for childbirth or hip replacement be-ing her only valid excuses so far for staying away. The two women take to each other like long-lost sisters. Terrific. Two old bossy women thinking they can run my life. Honestly, dinner parties are one of my favorite things in the world to host, but with M&M and Daisy Duke and the Great Satan, I am a hot mess. Even I hear the sharp edge in my voice, see the way I keep fidgeting with my pearls, escaping to the kitchen every four seconds for another dish of butter or more sweet tea or extra pepper vinegar.

I try to seat Kristen Yates at a special child's table I am willing to arrange just for her. I am thinking maybe in the neighbor's backyard, next to Scarface, the pitbull they keep on a rusty chain. Snickers vetoes that idea. I settle for seat-ing the child as far away from Colin as I can get her. I sit between the two of them grinning like Dinah Shore interviewing a man from backwoods Missis-sippi explaining how he's been abducted by aliens. Southern woman know how to be polite, no matter how much it makes our teeth hurt to do so.

Actually, little Miss Fake Daisy Duke doesn't turn out to be any more both-er than a toothache at a pie-eating contest. She is young and spoiled, but a good many of us sitting at the table have been in her high-heeled sandals, or some-thing very like them, at some time in our lives. Admittedly, it has been a long time ago, but even so we make allowances. I take her under my wing, and long before the last bite of cornbread has sopped up the final drops of pot liquor, she has been smothered in enough attention to numb a billy goat. She is an easy mark. Snickers glares at me when I prompt Miss Daisy Duke with, "Well, I'll be! Whatever did you do, then?" Or, once, "Why, aren't you just the bravest little bitty thang! I've heard tell our southern squirrels can be right vicious."

LuAnne is the gourmet cook among our little group. She says baking is better than any ornery ole boyfriend as a way to relax herself in the evenings. She always has some delicacy in her freezer she'll bring along to a last minute invitation that'll blow your culinary socks off. Her contribution to my simple dinner is chicken pasties. These melt-in-your-mouth delicacies are filled with chicken, brown-sugar-cured ham, golden raisins, and just enough spice to make you remember to breathe through your nose.

Toward the end of the meal, when we are all picking at our plates, filling in the edges of our gluttony, Kristen's shrill voice squeals into the silence like chalk on a blackboard with a question directed at LuAnne.

"So how come you stay here? Down south and all? I have lots of black friends in California, and they tell me there is no amount of money big enough to get them to live down here, in, you know, a backward place like this?"

Forks stop midway to mouths, the only sound a heavy fatherly sigh and Snickers's soft hand tapping Preston's gray linen slacks. Pat, pat, patty pat.

"Some a us darkies ain't really all that bright," LuAnne says straight-faced. "How ya like them itty bitty pies I done brung?"

"They were the best thing here? I ate two?" the naïve child enthuses. "I don't care what anybody says, you people are just the best cooks? Are these pies some sort of soul food?"

Ardell snorts peach daiquiri up her nose and has to be beat on the back by Snickers, who pounds a little harder than is strictly necessary.

"I'se right proud you like em," LuAnne goes on in an accent I have never heard come out of her mouth before tonight. "That'air is possum pie. I been sweetenin' the meat some. Keepin' the critter under a big ol' warsh tub out back by the outhouse."

Kristen's eyes are wide, like one of those Beverly Hills women who've had one too many facelifts. Her little rosebud mouth is a near perfect O.

LuAnne shows no mercy. "They'se nasty critters if'n ya don't sweeten em some afore ya kill em. I gots me a big ole round a oak setting on the tub. Ya unerstand, to sort a anchor it down and keep them wily critters from gettin' away. I'se been feedin' em corn for nigh on at four days now. T'was just luck that I had em nailed up on a side a the outhouse a gettin' ready to skir em when my white friends called and give me this here special invite."

Preston Yates has turned a dangerous magenta color. Snickers is wearing a hole in his nice gray trousers with her patty-pat routine. Kristen herself is a peculiar pea soup color. The rest of us have rounded the bend into knee slapping, tears streaming down our faces, belly muscles going to be sore tomorrow laughter.

Snickers looks ashamed of the whole bunch of us. "Honey. It's not possum. LuAnne's just kidding you. The recipe is probably from Martha Stewart, for pity sake. Heavenly Chicken Pasties or some such."

"Had you going there for a minute though, didn't I?" LuAnne smiles wickedly at the child just before the Little Dear flees the table.

Snickers follows behind her, calling over her shoulder, "Y'all ought to be ashamed of yourselves."

LuAnne speaks for all of us when she mutters, "I ain't no such a thing,"

We've cleared the table by the time Snickers and a subdued Kristen return to the living room. The child really isn't all that much trouble. I've kept her daiquiri glass topped off from the pitcher that as luck and design would have it, ended up on the table between the two of us. Now she curls up in my wingback chair and is snoring with her mouth hanging open by the time the grownups have finished dessert. I cover her with an old blanket I keep for when I dog-sit Paris, Aunt Ginny's snowy white miniature poodle. It isn't as bad as it sounds. I've washed the blanket since Paris used it. I'm almost sure I have.

By the time the table is cleared, my anger and anxiety at just what Colin's mama might have to say to me is mixed with enough booze and good food to allow me to take the bull by the horns. I slam the refrigerator on the last of the leftovers and stomp over to where she sits.

"Okay, Ms. Molly Megan, let's you and me go on outside and have us that come to Jesus meeting."

She looks across the kitchen at me. Haloed by the overhead light shining through all that curly hair, her face is a study in puzzlement. Brow furrowed, head tilted. Beside her Mama shoots me a look that could curl nails. I'm beyond caring. Done with worrying about how this old broad from California feels about my sleeping with her gorgeous young son. It ain't about winning or losing anymore. Not about consequences or logic or nothing else but getting this over with so as I can move on with my life in whatever direction it's going to take after tonight. A gentle settling into old age or one more wild ride with a man who plum steals my breath away every time he touches me.

Molly Megan glides across the kitchen, slips her arm through mine, and we leave my dinner guests staring after us. The French door opens to a night lit by a moon hung in the branches of my magnolia. Warm air wraps around me, rich with jasmine and honeysuckle. I breathe deep, do my best to convince myself I don't care what his mother thinks. Colin and I love each other, and that's all that matters. Really, what on earth is wrong with me? Have I learned nothing in my fifty-five years of life? Do I honestly believe the opinion of his mother can alter how I feel about Colin or how he feels about me?

She lays a warm hand on my arm. "Have I done something to offend you?"

"What? No. I—you said you wanted to talk. I thought we should get things out in the open between us." In the moonlight her blue eyes look as soft as a dove's wing, her wide mouth accented by dimples. Have I misunderstood her intention in wanting to talk to me?

She slips her arm through mine. "Things seem quite simple to me." Her voice is soft and grates on my nerves less than the accent of most Yankees. "My son and you are in love, are you not?"

"Well, yes. Of course. But. . . ."

So *this* is her game. To make me be the first to mention the age difference. Well, fine. So be it. I exhale, straighten my shoulders, feel myself stiff and unyielding and hate that knowledge.

"I'm twenty years older than your son."

She squeezes my arm, lays her head on my shoulder, her soft warm body pressing against my rigid side. "Is this a problem for you?"

Damn this woman and her hippie-love-beads-can't-we-all-just-get-along ways!

"Of course it's not a problem for me. I'm the one gets to sleep with him." My voice comes out louder than I intend. I don't have to turn around to know every soul in my house is staring out into the dark and praying Baby

Ruth Barr doesn't make an ass of herself in front of this charming, educated goddess from California.

Laughter thunders out of Megan Molly like the braying of goats, and for the first time since she walked into my house, I like Colin's mom.

"Has Colin mentioned that I live with a man twenty-eight years my junior?"

"What?" I twist my neck to stare into her grinning face.

"Oh, Ruth. Love has nothing to do with age or race or gender. Love wants what it wants and is only happy in the arms of the beloved." She pinches my waist. "For the love of God and Colin, lighten up, and enjoy your good fortune."

The door opens behind us, and Snickers is the first to venture outside.

"Everything all right out here?"

"Everything is just glorious." M&M's skirt swirls around her as she turns to Snickers. "I was just about to suggest we do a little after-dinner tai chi."

I step deeper into the darkness, take just a moment to say a prayer of thanks that God did not allow me to muck up the best thing to happen to me since Johnny's death. When I turn around Molly Megan is demonstrating Tai Chi to a bunch of rednecks who for years thought the spa's spinning class involved looms and wool.

Between Ardell's peach daiquiris and LuAnne's mojitos, the general feeling appears to be mellow joy. The whole bunch of us kick off our shoes and do our best to mimic the movements M&M demonstrates. The moon is nearly full. It hangs low in the sky, its pink light peeking through the bottom branches of my magnolia, spilling a little pool of magic on the grass.

Colin and Preston carry my loveseat out back so Mama can join the fun. The rest of us scatter in the moonlight, stretch on lawnchairs or perch on upturned boxes, or stand loose-limbed and do our best to follow along to Parting the Horse's Mane and Crane Spreads Wings. M&M makes the poses look fluid, like water over smooth stones. The rest of us come closer to the jerky movements of a stroke victim. Ardell and Colin aren't bad at it. LuAnne gives up and keeps Mama company after Mixing the Cauldron when she falls in my dahlia bed.

"This is not the dance of my people," she proclaims as she mixes herself a final mojito.

She redeems herself in a bit though when Colin puts on some Lynard Sky-nard and Creedence and Elvis. With that inspiration, the whole mess of us make fools of ourselves while the moon follows its ordained path in the night sky. Later, with Mama long tucked into my bed, Daddy switches the mood and finds some old CDs of Johnny's, and we all sway in slow circles to Tony Bennett and the Chairman himself. It is still a few hours from dawn, the moon long hidden behind my neighbor's scabby pines, when the party breaks up.

Daddy joins Mama in my bed. Kristen, still passed out in my wingback chair, is awakened and loaded in the car with Preston and Snickers. Ardell and LuAnne call Tommy Holmes over at Yellow Cab, and he hurries on over. I'd have been happy to have them stay the night, but LuAnne is keeping company with Tommy, and I believe she has an ulterior motive for having him carry her home. Colin and his mother leave last. I am sorry to see them go and am asleep on my couch less than a minute after I close the door behind them.

LUANN'S
POSSUM PASTIES

LuAnne uses puff pastry for this recipe that she buys up in Dothan when she visits her sister. She says you can use Mama's pastry dough if you can't lay your hands on the puff pastry.

Ingredients:
- 2 T butter
- 1 finely chopped onion
- 1 t red curry powder
- 1 peeled and grated carrot
- 1/2 c golden raisins
- 1/2 c country ham, diced
- 1 T flour

1 1/2 c chicken stock
- 1 1/2 c cooked chicken breast, cubed

Melt butter in pan. Sauté onion until transparent. Add chicken and ham, and brown. Add everything but the chicken stock, and stir well. Add the liquid, and simmer the whole mess until it thickens good.

Use about 2 T of this filling for each of your pasties. You should end up with about 20. Place on greased baking sheet, and cook at 325 degrees for about 25 minutes.

In case you're interested, you really do sweeten the meat of a possum by keeping the animal caged for a few days and feeding him corn. After that you just skin him like a rat and cook the meat like anything else that tastes some like chicken. Roll it in flour and spices, and deep fry.

Twenty-Three

The day after Megan Molly's welcome party, well into the afternoon, I finally call Candy to give her the Barr Report. Daddy and Mama have gone on home where Daddy predicts they are going to sleep for a week. Sunday had been crisp and cool, but today is overcast. The weather fits my mood. As the hostess I only indulged in two of the frothy peach concoctions Ardell blithely calls peach daiquiris, but which I today believe need to be renamed Potent Peach Poison. The woman must have tripled the usual rum content.

Or perhaps I no longer handle a hangover as gracefully as I once did.

I am well-fortified with coffee when I finally get in touch with Candy, beginning to convince myself that I want to live to see another day.

"What china did you use?" The first question my preacher's-wife sister asks me when she answers the phone.

This has nothing to do with dish patterns. When Memaw and Papa Barr passed away, God rest their souls, Memaw's china went to Candy as the oldest Barr girl. Just over three years later Gramma and Grandpa Powell joined them in paradise, though I'm pretty certain neither couple know the other has taken up residence since both would be worried sick about the decline of the heavenly neighborhood. At any rate, Snickers inherited Grandma Powell's good china.

With only two sets of grandparents, as the youngest of three girls, I should have had the good fortune to choose my own china. I had the pattern all picked out from a boutique shop in Buckhead. Snowy white with the thinnest ring of silver along the edge. Very plain, wonderfully elegant. But I forgot about my daddy's brother's wife, Brenda Rita Barr. Uncle Herchal–that's right, we all call him Hershey Barr—is still alive and as fine a man as you'd ever want to meet. His wife, on the other hand, was a piece of work. Daddy used to say she was the Barr with nuts. Lots of em. Technically, Aunt Brenda wasn't crazy. She came from money, so she was eccentric.

Boy, was she ever.

Her furniture was custom made up in Atlanta. Which might have been only a waste of money, except that she had the taste of a wild boar. The woman was as kind as the day is long, but she wouldn't have recognized quality if it jumped up and bit her on the snout. Candy and Snickers couldn't stand her pretensions, but I always found her entertaining. Big mistake on my part. She left me her plates, her silver, and her horrendous living room set.

I'm ashamed to say I unloaded the furniture on a perfectly lovely couple from our church who'd lost everything to a fire. They pretended to be grateful when the truck showed up with the oversized purple and orange flowered mess of a couch, love seat, and, Lord have mercy on my soul, four high-backed chairs. They do still speak to me, but their smiles always seem a bit tight.

Family tradition and common courtesy require that I use Aunt Brenda's china at all genuine family gatherings. Planned gatherings. So often at my home things are just thrown together at the last moment, giving me no time whatsoever to drag out the exquisite china and the fabulous silver that good old Auntie has left me. What Candy is really asking when she inquires about the place settings is if I have honored Colin's mom by using these atrocious family heirlooms, thus welcoming her into the real Barr family—warts, crazy aunts, and all.

"I'd already laid the table with my own lovely everyday dishes before people started arriving." I tell Candy. "Snickers, bless her evil little heart, had other ideas. While I was giving Molly Megan a tour, our fast thinking and diabolical sister reset the table with Aunt Brenda's china and silver. I could have cheerfully killed her. Was eyeing the electric carving knife when Ardell handed me my first daiquiri."

Aunt Brenda purchased her dishes while on her honeymoon in England. The manufacturer, Royal Doulton, also makes toilets. We all believe they tried a blend of the two—fine china and bathroom fixtures—when they filled the order for this particular pattern. The plates are heavy. Not quite as weighty as a toilet tank, but close.

The center of each bowl, cup, saucer, and plate is adorned with heavy gold calligraphy proclaiming BRB. Brenda Rita Barr. Baby Ruth Barr. Lucky me. To prevent the possibility of the lettering being covered by food and enabling the guests to forget for a moment at whose table they are dining, around the scalloped edges of each and every piece marches the same, and only slightly smaller, gold lettering in an endless circle of bad taste.

As if all this weren't enough, in a design Aunt Brenda came up with herself, interwoven in all these gold swirlycues are tiny and decidedly odd animals. Unicorns peek through the gold leaf side by side with yetis and sea monsters. Platypuses frolic with narwhals, golden frogs ride on the broad shoulders of a creature which is either a large ape that walks on two legs or possibly Bigfoot. Aunt Brenda always said the image came to her in a dream and the rest of the family felt it was prudent to let it go at that.

I actually use my BRB china when I'm alone. I know it's tacky, but beauty really is in the eye of the beholder, and I find it so outrageously ugly as to be cheerful. More whimsical than awful. While it's not a side of our family I usually expose to folks I'm just meeting, I forgave Snickers fairly quickly for setting the table with what she calls the "more money than good sense" china. Besides, in Noisy Creek we're right proud of our crazy relatives. They add spice to the stew of life.

Relating family events to those members not in attendance always feels like flipping through snapshots. No matter how good the photographer, some moments get lost, and others seem more important in the photos than they did at the time. When I tell Candy the BRB china story, her laughter roars over the phone, cementing in my memory an event that I otherwise might have forgotten over the years.

"After dinner, Mama and M&M sat on my good sofa out under the stars." I do my best to make her see the two women.

"Honey, it was something precious to see, their heads leaned back looking up at the sky, the tawny light through the window blinds casting their faces in a linear pattern of gold and shadow."

I try to make her hear the whisper of their conspiratorial voices, the way their laughter floated out into the night like soft-winged moths. A rare thing of beauty you catch in your peripheral vision and wonder ever afterward if it was real or part of a seductive dream.

I rat out Snickers.

"I caught our sister in the kitchen with her Yankee. The two of them with their tongues in each other's mouths. In my kitchen! Where I prepare *food*! He had her leaned up against my tiled counter, the two of them going at it like randy teenagers."

"I'm telling you the old coot must have been seeing everything through a blue Viagra haze. He was that happy to be with her."

Candy, with her own knowledge of Viagra side effects, whoops like one of those Asian Cranes we'd all been drunkenly imitating the night before. I know she'll be equally amused when Snickers relates her own version of the party.

Three is such a good number for sisters.

"Kristen Yates threw up in the gutter before her daddy got her loaded in the backseat of his Bentley."

I do so enjoy relating this detail of the party.

"As her hostess, you probably should have paid a little more attention to how much that girl was drinking." She does her best to shame me. "You know that child is no bigger than a minute, and, bless her heart, doesn't have the brains God gave a goose. You need to speak with Jesus about settin' that full pitcher of peach dynamite right in front of that child." She lectures me just as though I give a rat's ass.

Her little sermon tells me she's already spoken with the Minion of Satan's main squeeze.

"What did Snicks say about Megan Molly?" I ask, just to let her know she isn't fooling anybody with the time line of Barr Reports she has tuned into today.

"Tell me what she was wearin," she orders, skipping right over the fact that she's given away having already spoken with our sister, "'cause Snickers had nothing bad to say about the woman, although she did have some interesting comments about your behavior toward her. But tell me about her outfit, 'cause to me it sure did sound like mutton dressed as lamb."

There's no way I'm telling Candy or Snickers about my little meltdown with Colin's mama.

"She looked gorgeous."

And no way I'm letting my sisters bad mouth M&M for acting or dressing younger than she really is. Hell no. Not with me sleeping with her son who's young enough to be my gorgeous and very sexy young nephew.

"She arrived at my front door wearing a long flowing dress. Leopard print with lots of lions and zebras and a monkey or two woven subtly into the silk. Her sandals were flat and had tiny bells on the strap that went between her big toe and the piggy that stayed home. There was a lot of silver and gold jewelry too. Earrings that hung to her shoulders, little metal links that reflected the light when she moved. She wasn't wearing any rings, but her wrists and ankles jingled with flashes of charms and pendants and Mexican milagros, you know? Those little tin images of dogs and cats and angels and what not."

"Yeah, yeah." I picture Candy fluttering her hands to hurry me along in the story. "What else was she wearing?

"I'm not sure how many necklaces she had on. More than a half dozen. Mostly intricate chains set off with dull earthy stones or what looked like seed pods strung with some reddish dried flowers. For certain, nobody thought she bought her outfit in Noisy Creek, but it looked custom made for her. Not flashy, not too young, just earthy and comfortable."

"Earthy is the same word Snickers used to describe her. Which," she says, "is really kind of funny, since it's also a word very often used to describe you. I wonder if Colin sees that similarity?"

I am not interested in exploring the line of thought that leads to me reminding Colin of his mommy.

"I'm exhausted. Need a nap before Colin and M&M get here this afternoon. We're going out to supper. Colin called and left a message on my cell

earlier that his mom wants to try Goggins Barbeque. I guess the woman is looking for the full southern experience."

"Ruthie?" Candy's voice has that warm molasses quality that means she is
not going to be able to resist sticking her nose into my business. "Whatever was
bothering you about meeting his mama? Did you get that resolved?"

"Uh-huh. It wasn't anything. Just me being silly and worrying for nothing."

"Well that's good, honey. That's real good, 'cause you know Colin is that
woman's only child. It'd be right natural for her to be some protective of him
and maybe downright mean and sneaky with somebody she thought wasn't
right for him. You know what I'm sayin', Ruthie?"

"No worries," I say and hang up the phone quick. But not before that
little worry mouse pops up and nibbles some at my self-confidence. This
here—this pickin' in the name of love and support—this here is why sisters
are such a dang blessing.

GOGGINS
PULLED PORK BARBECUE

If you picture a rack of ribs slathered in sauce when you think of barbeque, then you are in for a treat. Rule of thumb: Texans do ribs. Southerners do pulled pork.

Which raises the question as to whether Texans are Southerners. Since half of my relatives hail from the Lone Star State, I believe I can answer that question with some authority.

In 1836 Sam Houston was the president of the country of Texas. That sovereignty only survived for nine years, technically. But, in truth, Texas is still a nation unto itself. Oh its residents are Americans, to be sure, and they hail from below the Mason-Dixon for a fact, but they are always Texans first. As for the rest of us Southerners, we treat Texas like any other half-assed relative—when they do something of which we approve, we claim em. When they do some God awful fool thing, well we remind ourselves that they ain't really blood kin. Texas, after all, is a whole nother country.

Dry Rub:
- 1 T each: paprika, cayenne pepper, salt, garlic powder, onion powder, black pepper
- 1 t each: thyme, oregano, and basil

Trim some of the fat from a 4 lb pork roast, and rub this mixture into the meat. Refrigerate overnight. Cover, and cook at 300 degrees for about 4 hours. The meat should be falling from the bone, but not dry. Remove from oven, and let cool enough to handle.

Sauce:
- 1 T butter
- 1 chopped onion

- 6 cloves chopped garlic
- 1 c ketchup
- 1/2 c molasses
- 1/2 c honey
- 3 T Worcestershire sauce
- 3 T cider vinegar
- 1 T dry mustard
- 1 t each: liquid smoke, salt, and cayenne pepper

Cook the onion and garlic in the butter until tender. Add the remaining ingredients, and simmer about ten minutes.

Pull the meat apart with your fingers. Stack this pulled pork on the bottom half of a hamburger bun, spoon a generous portion of sauce over the top, place the top of the bun on the sandwich. Serve with cole slaw and extra sauce for dipping.

Twenty-Four

It isn't until Tuesday that Molly Megan and I get a chance to talk without Colin hovering in the background. Candy's comment about Colin being the only child of a woman not that dang much older than me has me twitchy, tensed for trouble. Like waking in the night and waiting for the sound that disturbed your sleep to come again, this time closer. I treat M&M to a morning at the spa, and afterward I drive us up to the Chattahoochee Hut for a late dinner. I have confused her some by inviting her to dinner. Molly enlightens me with the information that, in California, dinner and supper are both names for the evening meal. Which I suppose I should have known. You never hear anyone on one of those TV sitcoms saying, "Let's do dinner."

The Chattahoochee is running high and red and muddy. This time of year, after a good rain, it looks more like a mud slide than a river. LuAnne is always threatening to collect its red clay and use it for facial masks. Swears we could make a fortune if we just packaged it in tiny jars with fake gold lids and stuck an exorbitant price tag on the bottom. Maybe stick a little brochure with testimonials on the side. Get us up one of them websites. She's only half joking.

The Hut serves only a daily special. Tuesday is pork chops with sweet potatoes day. Which is why we're here. The meal comes with biscuits and honey and sweet tea. I'll be eating greens for a week to even out the calories in this meal, but it will be worth every bit of the sacrifice.

M&M tells me a good many interesting tidbits as we plow our way happily through the food.

"I've been married only once and then only briefly. Colin's biological father left me when the evidence of the pregnancy moved from the bigger boobs stage to the swallowed a small watermelon period. Good riddance to a youthful bad decision."

She takes a bite of biscuit and moans in pleasure before telling me, "My dad, Colin's grandfather, invested in a few properties on the outskirts of Los Angeles in the 1930s. When he died and I inherited them, they were worth enough that I didn't have to worry about how I was going to support myself and a baby."

She polishes off the last of the pork chops, watches the pink-apron clad waitress refill our teas. "I was working on my Ph.D. Took Colin with me to New Mexico where we lived in a mud hut while I interviewed Little Cloud, the Navaho medicine man who taught me about herbs and dreams and Turtle Mother and rain and sky. It took a while, but eventually, I converted that knowledge into a dissertation.

"More importantly, the knowledge that old man shared enriched the rest of my life. Once, I remember, I strapped a bundled-up Colin to my back in a willow-root canopied basket and followed Little Cloud as he walked along a high desert mountain ridge with the rain beating down like pellets and the sky black and swirling around us.

"When I caught up with him outside a neighbor's hut, I asked, 'Is the rain god speaking to you?'"

"Nope,'" he told me flatly, "ran out of coffee and forgot my umbrella."

We lay our hands against our hard bellies and contemplate dessert.

"My entire year in that adobe hut was like that. Me doing my best to make every experience mystical and other-worldly, and Little Cloud explaining to me in a thousand different ways that the miracles were in the commonplace. That old man was so patient demonstrating that the scorpions and red ants and stones beneath our feet knew more than me about the Great Turtle Mother.

"Still, that worldview did rub off on me some. Not much, but enough that

I remembered it over my life since then, built on it in Nepal and India. Life is such a process. That's what I've learned in twelve years of college and forty years of traveling the world, availing myself of the teachings of the wise. Wisdom isn't about answers. It's about the process of living."

Seems like that would be a hard philosophy with which to fill the church pews, and I don't find it as compelling as Jesus's love for us sinners, but it seems to work for Molly Megan. The only woman I know that comes close to possessing her calm and inner peacefulness is my own mama.

We talk about Mama and visit some about Colin. I swallow hard and ask her outright, "Are you bothered by the age difference between your son and me."

She takes her time giving me an answer.

"I admit when he first told me I had a moment or two when the great bear of motherhood rose up and wanted to take a swipe or two at you." Her dimples lessen the weight of her words. "But Colin's happy. The two of you seem to be enjoying each other, learning from one another. Why would I care about your age?"

I exhale, think of several dozen reasons why she might care very much about her only son getting together with an old broad like me, but decide not to mention them. No point in looking a gift horse in the mouth is the way I figure it.

The outward evidence of our artery-clogging dinner has been removed. We sip sweet tea. My hope is that the bloated feeling in my belly will dissipate if I ignore it long enough. Molly Megan, God love her, gives me a little gift.

"I want to share something with you in confidence." She leans across the table and runs her finger along the top of my hand. "Colin recently received a rather large inheritance. It's something he never talks about. Sees the money as tainted. My belief is that he's trying to clean the money somehow in a spiritual sense by refusing to use it for anything except his environmental development project."

"Money from his grandpa? What's so dirty about Los Angeles real estate?"

"Ah, that inheritance from his grandfather is mine. The money he's trying to clean is from his own father.

"After the man disappeared from our lives, he got himself involved in a very lucrative business. Pornography. Not child porn or bestiality or anything like today's brand of triple X Internet extravagances, but for its day, pretty raunchy stuff. The most famous was The Sunshine Girls series. He made a lot of money for ten years or so, then when the Internet took over and every nasty fool with a video camera jumped on the band wagon, Mr. Sunshine took his earnings and ran. Strip malls were his next moneymaker. The man had a sort of genius for pandering to the lowest human common denominator.

"Except karma caught up with him as he was leaving a joint in the desert just off the grapevine, a place called Butt Naked Girls where he was entertaining three Japanese business men, hoping to convince them to invest in his latest project—increasing the cement jungle outside Los Angeles. An eighteen wheeler hauling beakless chickens out of Arkansas lost its brakes, and the driver made the fateful decision to slow the rig down by running it off the freeway and up the incline into the gravel lot around the club.

"The attempt might have worked without mishap, except the investors had brought gifts of brand new iPods with them. Bluetooth cordless earphones, very high tech stuff back then. They were all four—Colin's dad and the investors—plugged into the music. One of the Japanese was swiveling his narrow hips in the parking lot, doing a drunken karaoke rendition of 'Jail House Rock.'

"At the part he was translating as 'the whole peep hole section was the par boil gang! Let's rock! Everbody let's rock,' right about there in the song, Mr. Sunshine himself joined in the merriment so that they all four had their backs to the eighteen wheeler when it came rolling through the gravel.

"Even then he might have cheated destiny if at the line, 'little Joe was blowin' on a slide trombone,' he hadn't turned to the right and extended his arm in pantomime of little Joe's musical gifts.

"The chrome bumper took his arm off just above the elbow. My ex-husband bled to death in the gray gravel while the florid green Butt Naked Girls neon sign flashed above him, three foreign business men chattered in a language he didn't understand, and a truck driver with a Santa beard cried into his hands."

Hard not to believe in poetic justice after a story like that.

So Colin inherited a lot of tainted dollars from a man on whom he never laid eyes. Parental love can be expressed in so many ways.

I knew Colin had graduated from Cal Poly two years earlier and struggled to design the kind of homes he envisioned while earning his living turning out fake Tudors and Victorians in gated communities known as Buena Vista Estates and Mansions on the Hill. What I didn't know was that when his dad died, he took his inheritance and started his own business. That was eighteen months ago, and his company's first project was that development out by Mama and Daddy's place.

"If he inherited so much money, why is Preston Yates in on this deal with him?" I ask.

"The construction project in Columbus, the one with the McMansions that Colin and your Cousin Jimmy just finished? That was the first part of a twin agreement Colin negotiated with Preston Yates before he inherited the money from his dad. At the time, it seemed like his only hope of being able to design and build the kinds of houses and developments in which he wants to be involved."

"So he doesn't really need investors for this project?"

"No. In fact, he'd get rid of Mr. Yates if he could, but by now the man can see that those energy efficient homes are going to make a pot full of money. Colin's stuck with him. He'll have to share the profits on this first project."

So my stud muffin has more money than I do. Has no need of my little stash of dough at all. My brain is working its way toward the conclusion that the man is actually interested in me for the same reason every other man I have ever loved has been interested in me. He likes feisty, independent women who give him grief on a fairly regular basis. There is simply no accounting for taste. I feel a little like Gidget at the Oscars. He likes me. He really likes me.

PORK CHOPS
WITH SWEET POTATOES

By now you may be wondering why everyone in Noisy Creek doesn't weigh four hundred pounds and suffer from diabetes. Well, to be fair, a few of us do, but most of us avoid that fate by feasting occasionally, eating a lot of salad and greens, and by working our tails off. Some of us, like Daddy and Colin and most all my uncles and male cousins, burn off the calories by working outdoors from dawn to dusk. The rest of us hike, drip sweat on a Stairmaster, and car pool in a plump little convoy over to Aiken once a week where a Jenny Craig representative transforms our money and good intentions into semi-svelte bodies.

What I'm telling you here is that while every one of these recipes is delicious, don't try them all in the same week. Also, I have given you the traditional use of lard and bacon grease, but many of us substitute other oils most of the time. Why, last time I opened a cupboard in LuAnne's kitchen, the woman had walnut and grape seed oil in itty bitty jars right next to her extra virgin olive oil. Feel free to twist these recipes around some and make 'em your own. Heck, you can't get any more southern than that!

Ingredients:
- 4 thick cut smoked pork chops
- 1/2 t cardamom
- 1/2 t cinnamon
- 4 whole cloves
- 1 Vidalia onion, sliced thin
- 6 cloves garlic, sliced lengthwise
- 2 apples, cored peeled and sliced
- 4 sweet potatoes peeled and sliced lengthwise thinly

Rub the chops with the herbs and some salt and pepper, and brown in skillet. Remove the chops, and in the same pan caramelize the onion and garlic by cooking over a low heat in a little oil, stirring often to prevent burning. When the onion and garlic are ready, add the slices of sweet potato and apple, a little more of the herbs, and stir. Place chops in a baking dish, spoon the mixture over the top. Pour 1/4 cup of water into the skillet and then gently pour this over the top of the chops. Cover, and bake at 400 degrees for 40 minutes. Remove the cover, and cook an additional 15 minutes or until the potatoes are tender.

Twenty-Five

Be careful what you ask for. With Snickers distracted by Colin's current business partner, I am taking up the slack with Mama and Daddy. I'm doing my best to think of Mr. Yates in a positive way. Thus I vow to stop labeling him with any name that includes a reference to Beelzebub. One big difference between Snickers and myself is that while Snickers gets positively glowing over lemon wood cleaner and new-fangled toilet bowl brushes, I hate housework. Snickers and Candy maintain this demonstrates a lack of character on my part, a pride that needs to be tempered. I'm sure they're right.

Nevertheless, I hire the oldest Williams girl, Bessie, to help Mama each morning for four hours. Bessie's job is to keep the house spotlessly clean and to assist Mama with the cooking when she'll allow it, which most days she does not. I drive out at dinner time and do nothing but visit with Mama and Daddy while I munch on the rabbit food I keep in the produce section of their old Frigidaire. I tell my sisters it's a Mary and Martha thing, and they need to get over themselves. When your parents are pushing up on eighty, it's time to sit at their feet and soak up as much love and wisdom as you can stomach. Screw the housework. Or hire it out. Most days, Colin joins us for whatever dinner Mama and Bessie have put together. Midweek they're enjoying chicken pot pie, a sure sign Mama is feeling spry. No way she'd let anyone else make the pie crust, though there's a little sadness in her eyes when she tells me she let Daddy kill the hen. One of her old Wyandottes. The first time she hasn't dispatched one of her brood with her own hand.

Mama's philosophy of chicken raising is to let them run wild all day, scratching and pecking and being fowl. She locks them in the hen house at night to protect them from weasels and opossum and raccoons and the occasional fox that still patrol this bottom section of Georgia. She steals their eggs, except for one or two clutches a year reared by the brooders.

This year's chicken mother of the year is Matilda, an Orrington who dodged the stew pot by spending her spring being followed around the yard by twenty-eight tiny yellow chicks, most of whom came from eggs not her own. Mama set up a special brooding box for Matilda. She had Daddy replace the slats with screen so the hen could get the afternoon air while still being protected against marauding varmints in the night. More than once, I saw Mama perched on a wooden crate, the door to the chicken house thrown open to the sun and breeze, taking the shade with Matilda, the two of them watching the rest of the hens scurry around the yard being pursued by the two handsome roosters, Brad and George.

Mama gives her chickens a good life and then, when the time comes, kills them quick and clean. I hope it is the way God will look down on us as well. A life well lived. A purpose served. A quick trip to glory. The difference between us and Mama's hens is that our bodies don't make anyone a fat chicken pot pie. Later when I relay all this to M&M she tells me that in Tibet, the final funeral act is to throw the bodies of loved ones over a high cliff as food for the circling condors. Tibetans believe when the soul has already moved on, the only purpose the body can serve is to be food for another being.

I don't believe I'll mention this to Pastor Coleman next Sunday, but it is an interesting, if macabre, notion.

The physical therapist has approved Mama's use of the claw cane for short walks each day. She maneuvers her way down the ramp with it while I push the walker along for her stroll back. We're sitting in the thin green shade of Mama's Iceberg Rose when The Devil's Spawn herself roars into the yard, throwing red dust and evil intentions into the breeze. Colin and Daddy are inside enjoying the last of the hen's contribution to our day. Kristen checks herself in the rear view mirror before slinking out of the low-slung, purple Lexus.

Mama takes my hand in hers, issues a command. "You be nice now."

She may have seen me reaching for her cane. I was thinking I might use it the way a lion tamer employs a chair. Back now! You get back!

"Hi? I need to talk to Colin?"

Does the child not understand the ordinary use of courtesy, not to mention inflection in speech?

"We're just fine. How are you?" I cry out.

Mama's hand is strong in mine. She is hurting my fingers. She never uses a hatchet on her hens, just quick as love gone bad, wrings their necks before they know they've scratched their last bug.

"Colin's inside," Mama calls, "Would you care for a glass of sweet tea? Ruth'll fetch it for you."

When there's ice skating in hell.

The back porch screen slams, and footfalls head our way. Kristen's face lights up like, well, like a young girl turning toward her lover.

"What's up?" Colin sounds nervous.

Miss Kristen has dressed to match her car. She is wearing a purple hand-kerchief disguised as skirt. It does cover her working parts, but not by much. The skirt, paired with a top that barely covers her pert little nipples, rides low enough to reveal that flash of belly ring I'd noticed the very first time I had the pleasure of meeting her out at Rebs Café.

She stamps her little foot in the red dirt drive.

"I thought we were going to lunch," she whines at my man.

"I don't know why you thought that." Colin's nervousness seems to have crossed over into the territory of fear. He comes up behind me and rests his hands on my shoulders. I suppose Mama and him think they can secure me to the bench, save the clueless purple Seed of Evil from the wrath of Ruth.

"I told you this morning that I always come here for dinner."

"For dinner? But this is lunch. I hate this awful place! They're so stupid! Supper, dinner. Whatever! I wanted to drive up to Atlanta? Or at least Columbus?"

"So," I say. "I guess that's a no on the sweet tea."

Mama is cutting off the circulation to my hand. The woman is freakishly strong for her age. Comes of wringing hen's necks and living in the sticks her whole married life.

Miss Yates has a little tantrum in the red dust there in the Leeville end of Noisy Creek. She really isn't cut out for this life. The girl needs to go back to California before something really bad happens to her. A day on the Pacific Ocean would do her good. Maybe she'd enjoy a little surfing. Colin mutters, the hens cluck, the dust settles over purple, high-heeled sneakers.

It is time I take some action.

I extradite my hand from Mama's, rub it to get the blood flowing again, turn to Colin, and give him a warm wet kiss.

"I have got just nothing at all to do today that can't wait," I announce.

Before the shock wears off and somebody stops me, I come down the ramp, throw open the driver's door to the grape colored Lexus, and, as I slide behind the wheel, yell at the brat, "Well get in! Are we going to Atlanta or what?"

Nestled into the creamy, unnaturally colored leather, I can see Colin's wide grin, the shrug of his shoulders. I also have a fine view of the fire-breathing dragon tattoo winding its way up the small of Kirsten's back. It takes no imagination whatsoever to figure out where the lizard's tail is resting.

Fire-eating dragon my ass. The girl has no idea with whom she is dealing.

I lean out the window and offer encouragment in my best honey-drenched voice, "Honey'chil', if you're fixin' to make Atlanta by suppa time, you better shake yo tail."

Mama and Colin wave bye-bye. Both know better than to waste their energy standing on the tracks, waving their objections in an attempt to stop a southern woman already moving fast on the rails between Jealousy and That's-Just-About-Enough-Ville. Also Colin may be a teeny bit afraid to step in front of the vehicle as I've already found the keys in the ignition and have the Purple Wonder cranked up and dancing impatiently.

MAMA'S
CHICKEN POT PIE

If the only pot pie you have ever tasted is one of those frozen messes where they've just waved the chicken over a slimy filling of mostly peas and carrots, then bless your heart, you are in for a fine treat.

Ingredients:

- 1 chicken recently dispatched
- 1 carrot, chopped
- 1 celery stalk, chopped
- 1 onion diced
- 2 t salt
- 1/2 t cayenne pepper

Put the hen in a pot, cover with cold water, add these ingredients. Cook about an hour. Remove the chicken, and let cool. Keep the stock bubbling. You want to end up with about 2 1/2 cups. No more. When the chicken has cooled, remove the bones. There's no way to do this except with your fingers.

You're going to use Mama's pie dough recipe for this, so if you don't have a batch frozen, better make it now.

Filling Ingredients:

- 3 T butter
- 3 T bacon grease
- 1 c onion diced
- 6 carrots thin sliced
- 1 1/2 c milk
- 1 t thyme
- 1 c fresh peas
- 2 t salt

- 1 t Tabasco
- Dash of Flour

In fry pan, melt butter and bacon grease, cook onion and carrots about 10 minutes. Add the boned chicken meat. Add flour, and blend well. Pour in 2 1/2 c chicken stock and the milk. Decrease heat slightly, and keep stirring, or you'll end up with lumps. Simmer for about 10 minutes. Add the remaining ingredients, and stir well.

Mama uses a regular 9" pie pan. Place your bottom crust in the pan. Pour filling in, and cover with top crust, trim dough, and seal edges. Don't forget to cut some slits in the top so the steam can vent. Cook at 375 degrees until the crust is golden. About 30 minutes. Let cool, and serve. If you have filling left over, add some chicken stock, and serve it the next day as soup.

Twenty-Six

Kristen seems stunned. Of course, the girl is just naturally flighty. The poor thing is not in her element. My plan is to return the child to her true home. It's like rescuing one of those purple clawed crabs you sometimes find on a day at the beach stranded in a shrinking tide pool. It is a mission of mercy I am on, if you think about it right. I have Merle cranked up on the satellite radio before The Spawn of a Philistine can click her seatbelt around her skinny, bare belly.

It is a ten-minute drive to the mini-mansion on Jeff Davis Drive in which Kristen and her daddy are making do until their super-sized monstrosity of a house is completed. Colin has managed to isolate the seven thousand square foot castle from the rest of the homes in his dream project. Last I heard, he was frantically planting fast-growing Oleander around its ten acre perimeter to protect the Yates family from a view of the unwashed masses. Or vice versa. The boys of Montgomery Gentry and I are screamin, "Hell, yeah!" as we pull to the curb on Jeff Davis Drive. In full-commando mode, I order Kristen to go inside and pack all her clothes.

"Your little sojourn here is done. Pack everything, and have it loaded in this car in ten minutes, or I'm coming inside to get you."

Sweet Jesus, let Preston and Snickers be away from home. Because there is no way I am backing down, and this little mission has the potential to get real ugly right fast.

I call Molly Megan and tell her I'll be gone for the night, but that we are still on for our girl's night out tomorrow. Candy and Bill are driving down for Daddy's birthday party this coming weekend. Candy, Snickers, LuAnne, M&M, and I are congregating at Ardell's tomorrow evening for a combination women's philosophical rap group and bitch session. Also Ardell's daiquiri machine has just been overhauled, and it seems wasteful not to give it a spin. My plan is to put the Devil's Spawn on a plane, turn in the rented Lexus, spend the night in the city, and catch a ride back to Noisy Creek with Candy and the Preacher as they pass through the next day.

I hit Candy's number on my speed dial next. I'm brave on the phone. Something about the option of disconnecting if talk gets too heated often endows me with nearly superhuman stupidity. I watch the front door, pray not to see a Snickers-shaped tornado headed my way. Candy picks up, and I tell her my plan. Her response is so quick I wonder if Mama hasn't already called her.

"Lord, Ruthie, it's about freakin' time you pulled yourself together and started to fight for what you deserve!"

Can minister's wives say freakin' now? I missed the memo.

The front door of the mini-mansion swings open, revealing a stack of suitcases that probably are not going to fit in this amethyst low-rider. Jesus protect me, instead of bare legs topped by a purple tea towel, taking direct aim at me comes the unmistakable pale yellow linen wrapped stride of the middle Barr sister. Snickers is down the winding cobblestone path and to the Lexus before I recover enough to hit the switch to lock the doors and roll up the windows. I do turn down the radio, even though Miranda Lambert is wailing fine.

"Kristen says you threatened to give her a free ride to fist city." Those are her first words to me. I'm kidnapping her lover's daughter. The modern equivalent of riding her out of town on a rail. And Snicks is quoting Loretta Lynn. With a lovely smile on her beautiful face. "Thank God! That girl is seriously getting' on my last nerve."

Preston is next. He has a suitcase in each hand. Ever helpful, I pop the trunk for him. The Lexus sinks down some with the weight of the first load of luggage. Preston comes to my window, squats down in a position from which I am certain he is going to need help getting up. He opens his mouth to say something, thinks better of it, pulls his wallet from his hip pocket, and hands me a credit card.

"Put the plane ticket on my card. Whatever else she needs," he says in a voice that makes me think this isn't his first fling with the misbehavior of his only child.

He pulls himself up, using the side of the car and Snickers's discretely offered arm for leverage, and returns to the house for the second installment of luggage.

Ten minutes later we pull away from the curb with Snickers's promise to ship the luggage that can't be squeezed into the sports car.

"Y'all drive real careful now!" she trills out as I wave good-bye. She has her arm looped around Preston's waist, her head on his shoulder. Preston looks like he's been hit by a truck and hasn't quite realized yet that he is bruised up mightily. I am sure Snickers will take fine care of him.

Me, I am trying to figure out why I suddenly feel so guilty when everything is going so well on this tar and feathers expedition. It might have something to do with the tears tracking through all that expensive makeup of the child sitting in the passenger seat beside me who looks out the window and hiccups between sobs. Nothing cuts through anger quite like seeing your enemy as an actual human being.

From my current position as the lead bitch, I can afford to cut the girl some slack. Her view isn't all that great. Which is how I learn that the scantily clad, pierced, and tattooed young woman sitting beside me, the one who ends every sentence with the intonation of a question, who can't complete a thought without putting the words "like" and "duh" in the verbiage at least three times, she ain't as dumb as she pretends to be.

"I'm not some hick." She glares across the car at me. "I, like, graduated in the top twenty percent of my class at UCLA." Her lower lip protrudes in a pout.

Ah hell, who am I kidding, this young thing is sexy as all get out, even when she's behaving like a mangy possum trying to steal the back porch cat food.

"What's your degree in?"

A college graduate? I am slap-my-grandma surprised.

"Daddy wanted me to major in, like, economics or business. But I'm an artist. A sculpter. So I was all like, well duh, like I'm not going to major in art?"

So she's smart enough to understand what I'm going to tell her next.

"You've behaved like a spoiled brat," I explain to her in the same tone of voice I usually reserve for the neighbor's pit bull, Scarface, when he breaks his chain and pisses on my morning paper. "I'm taking you to the airport and putting you on a plane for California. You'll be happier there. All of Noisy Creek will be happier with you there. Except possibly your daddy, and the two of you are gonna have to work that out for yourselves."

She stares out the window without speaking. I turn the radio volume back up. Coming into Ridgewood, just as we pass the old tin peanut-shaped sign letting us know that a turn on the next dirt road will lead us to an old wood shack where we can buy a soggy paper sack of the best boiled peanuts in the state, Kristen starts to talk. For the next five hours, I listen to the hopes and dreams of a young woman who reminds me of someone I knew a very long time ago. She is a little more spoiled than I was, but then, not everyone can be lucky enough to have my parents. Plus, her daddy has a whole lot more money than mine ever did, and that's a burden about which I know nothing. She's also an only child, another hardship I've been blessed to avoid.

If Daddy had raised me by himself and if he'd had the money that Preston Yates had, well, he still wouldn't have spoiled me to ruination, but I can see that the temptation might be there.

She flips her hair to the side. "My mother was a Las Vegas show girl."

Which I gather is a California euphemism for hooker.

"She was afflicted with some, like, chronic disease. No way she wanted to leave me, but she, like, had to obtain the medication she needed. To, you know, like, keep her alive."

So the woman abandoned her baby girl to run off with her drug dealer. Well, you can dress a pig up and even teach it to dance, but it's still gonna be Easter dinner.

"Poor Mom, when I was four, she had, you know, a really bad reaction to her medicine and died in, like, some horrible run-down motel room on the outskirts of Reno."

So her mama died of an overdose when Kristen was in pre-school.

Even though I hear all this in sentences that sound like questions with, like, so many, like, Californications it's difficult not to, like, scream, I am nonetheless feeling more and more guilty. I mean, like duh, maybe it's not her fault she turned out so whiny. I fish around in my purse and hand her a hankie. White cotton. One of Colin's.

"Dad was, you know, super busy with work." She wipes her eyes, careful not to smudge the liner. "But he almost always made time for me at, like, holidays." She brightens a bit, fishes in her purse for a tube of purple lip gloss which she applies to her pouty lips with her middle finger. A move that provides insight into why Colin succumbed to her charms.

"One time he flew me to Switzerland. Another time I met him in Morocco. Once we were going to spend, like, two days at Disney World. Except he ended up having to leave to close this, you know, like, multi-million dollar business deal. But I got to stay in Florida at this great hotel. I had my own room, even. A suite. His girlfriend, Trixie, she kept his room. So she and I, we got to, like, you know, hang out."

It is a sad little rich girl story, and I am inclined to sympathy until she blows her upturned nose on my hankie and whines, "Daddy, like, promised me I could have Colin? I told him and told him about what a bitch you were being, and he promised he'd take care of you? Instead he's like all lovey with your stupid sister who's like even older and more decrepit than you! What does Colin see in an old woman like you, anyway? I'm, like, duh, young and firm and beautiful?"

It feels some like letting myself trust a tiger who has subsequently managed to get one of my body parts in its mouth. Time to take the shot and rejoice in getting away with only a scar. I turn the radio back on, but she talks over the top of Willie and Waylon and Kris and even Johnny. By the time I am following the blue and white signs for the Delta terminal, I have discovered that, against my better judgment, I like Kristen Yates. She is intelligent and beautiful and might even turn her life around and make something of herself over the next few years. But until she does, I don't want her anywhere near me or those I love. My belief is that she needs therapy and a new California lover.

Of course, I will never get her on the plane to Los Angeles if she doesn't want to go. But without Colin to play with her, she is good and sick of rural Georgia. I am only providing her with the excuse to get back to the civilization she's been increasingly more desperately seeking for well over two months.

As the spoiled brat herself explains it to me, "You're like not the boss of me? This stupid ecological housing development Daddy wants me to help with is, like, too hard! I'm going home where people, like, speak actual, like, English?"

Security no longer allows non-ticketed passengers to stand at those big plate glass windows and marvel at winged metal containers as big as buildings as they pull up off the runway and disappear into the smoggy air. But I know Kristen's flight number, and position myself at a Starbucks where I can sip my own jet fuel while keeping an eye on both the exit door and the departure board. Her plane leaves at 8:48. I stay right where I am for another half hour, making sure a sweet little thing barely dressed in purple doesn't walk back through the security doors.

The Lexus is a dream to drive now that my passenger has departed. The Ellis on Peachtree has valet service and a suite on the women's-only floor. Room service delivers a petit filet mignon with a green salad and a half bottle of Merlot. Once fed, the Italian votives arranged along the black granite counter of the bathroom, I kick my clothes to the white limestone floor and step under the rainforest shower. Refreshed from my frolic in the tropical downpour, the bed is a welcome oasis of plush pillows and soft sheets. A nap seems just the thing.

Just before midnight I wake long enough to leave a message for Candy, asking her and Bill to pick me up the following morning. One additional call to the concierge and a refined voice assures me that panties, a pair of jeans, and a lovely sweater in my size will all be delivered to my room precisely at 8:00 the next morning.

The entire night goes on the credit card the Great Satan gave me when I relieved him of the responsibility of caring for his only child. My sleep is that of a woman without one single thing on her conscience.

OLD JOE'S
BOILED PEANUTS

When I was a girl we stopped for this treat on near every trip to Atlanta. Back then the stand was run by Joe Washington himself. There used to be a small wooden hand-lettered sign at the entrance to the dirt trail that identified it as Nigger Joe Road. The sign has been gone now for a number of politically correct years, but the peanuts are as good as ever, and the stand is manned during the summer by a succession of old Joe's grandkids.

When Candy and Bill and I stop on our way home from Atlanta, it's Shamelle who lifts our hot peanuts out of the salty water with a slotted paddle and hands us our brown paper lunch sack.

"How's your grandpa doing?" I ask.

"He's doing well. Up in Athens right now getting my sister, Darleene, settled into her dorm room." Shamelle's wide grin demonstrates his justifiable pride in his older sister.

"You goin' up yonder to Athens before too much longer?" Bill squishes open a warm peanut. Pops the salty legume in his mouth like a dog catching a treat.

Shamelle ducks his head to the side, bestows on us another beatific smile. "Yes, sir. I'll be joining Darleen next year. Be working on earning me a degree in engineering."

By the time Candy and Bill are finished giving out free advice and swapping tales of their son's engineering degree from the University of Georgia at Athens, I'm already half way through my soggy bag of peanuts.

Ingredients:
- 2 lbs raw peanuts in the shell
- 1/2 c coarse ground salt

If you're not lucky enough to live where peanuts are grown, you may be able to buy them raw from your local health food store or order them over the Internet.

Rinse the peanuts until the water runs clear. Put in a large pot, cover with water and salt, and bring to boil. Reduce heat, cover, and simmer until soft but not mushy. Start checking the peanuts closely after 30 minutes, though it may take an hour or more before they're ready. It depends on the variety as well as the freshness of the legume.

When they're tender, taste one or two for saltiness. If they're not salty enough, leave them sit in the water a bit before draining. I like them best warm, but have eaten a fair amount pulled cold right from the refrigerator. Either way they don't keep well, so eat them all or share em within 24 hours.

Twenty-Seven

Ardell lives next door to the house in which she grew up. When we were kids, the candy store was on the site. Truth be told, one of the reasons she and I were such good friends is that candy store. That and the fact that we both could, and did, beat the bejesus out of any boy dumb enough to tease us about girl cooties. The Dixie Circle was actually a small general store. Ardell's mama would give us two quarters and send us next door to buy a carton of milk. That left us four cents for candy.

Miss Wynonna kept the penny candy along the front counter in those round oversized fish bowls with lids. "Y'all ain't foolin me," she'd tell us each and every day. "Little uns has got sticky fingers."

Which never made good sense to us as kids and confused me about half-to-death years later when the devil's own band put out an LP with the same name. Candy bought the Rolling Stones album on a trip to Atlanta with the family of a friend. We hid it in the underwear drawer under my day-of-the-week cotton panties. The album cover was a male pelvis, covered in skin tight denim pants, with a zipper that actually opened. In Noisy Creek, this was the equivalent of a house call from Satan himself. Half the female population in the school district trooped up our stairs to see this abomination.

I cannot tell you a single song that was on that album, but I can still feel the anticipation as we built up our courage to pull that zipper down. Like an electrical current running south by south-west, zaps of estrogen taught us that naughty is indeed titillating. The disappointment Ardell and I felt when we slowly, as though braving the gates of hell themselves, edged that zipper down to reveal nothing but undershorts, well, that is a disillusionment that neither of us has ever forgotten. If we'd only known, that gyp of a zipper turned out to be a fair and clear warning of what sex was going to be like for the next few years. But hope and hormones spring eternal, and that was a lesson we both had to learn the usual, more painful, way.

But all of this was far in the future when Ardell and I lusted after Miss Wynonna's penny candy, making our big decision of how to spend our two cents each. The big jawbreakers gave you a long time with something sweet in your mouth, and the bright colors were enticing, but they always made my jaw hurt, and I'd spend the rest of the day worrying that maybe I had indeed broken my jaw with Ardell singing out, "Hence the name! Jawbreaker! Get it?" She was a smartass even as a kid. The miniature Sugar Daddy suckers gave the same long, sugar-drip effect, but I pulled out a filling with one when I was eight, and I still woke nights worrying that Mama and Daddy were going to find out I had not done the damage while eating a crunchy peanut butter sandwich that Ardell's mama made for our after-school snack.

Ardell usually settled on two red licorice whips and two black ones. I generally ended up with two miniature peanut butter cups and a free stick of Black Jack gum that Miss Wynonna threw in, "just to get you two whippersnappers out a my dang store." We learned quickly to buy the milk after our hour-long decision-making process, not before, and that if we looked sweet and adorable enough, we could usually get one customer or another to throw in some change so we could broaden our choices. This worked until Daddy found out what we were up to. A month of coming in after school and sweeping up for Miss Wynonna convinced me that the manipulation of good hearted folks wasn't as great an idea as it had seemed at the time.

The Dixie Circle closed down when Miss Wynonna died in '74. Heart failure. Possibly exacerbated by four generations of Noisy Creek kids clogging up her store to make their endless penny candy choices. Though I did talk with her niece at the funeral, and she insisted us kids stopping by after school was the highlight of her aunt's life for years.

"I feel like I know ever last one a y'all," she said from the lectern, "even though Mama moved us on up to Alabam' when I was a itty bitty thang, ever single Sunday phone call Auntie Wynonna would tell Mama one tale or 'nother 'bout one of you chil'en and that penny candy."

The store sat boarded up for a while, like childhood come to a dusty vacant end. Ardell bought the building in 1987. She saved the small-paned, wrap-around front windows and the cash register only slightly smaller than a young elephant. The windows now look out on Main Street from her sitting room, and the cash register is a fixture in her living room. She keeps her mad money in the thing. An antique dealer once told her the ivory-keyed monstrosity was worth well over $5,000. Lots of folks have got more money than brains, so it could be true. Ardell has a little porcelain plaque over her front door that proclaims her house to be officially named after Miss Wynonna's old General Store.

Candy and Bill are staying out at Mama and Daddy's, so Candy picks up M&M on her way to our girl's night out at the Dixie Circle. Snickers, LuAnne and I walk over once we close up the salon and spa. We arrive a little later than we had hoped. Four large-boned women from the Dothan Church of The Agape Love of Jesus Christ Our Almighty Savior have traveled up for a full spa day. We gave them a deal on the Southern Pride package. They were delightfully enthusiastic about the experience, but sipped white wine from the moment they walked in the door at 8:00 this morning. I don't mean to be cruel, but getting them out of there so we could close up was, if I've learned anything at all from Animal Planet, like herding four drunken hippopotami across a long barren stretch of savanna.

By the time the three of us step through Ardell's front door, laughter floats over the whirring of the blender. A fire crackles in the living room. The flames dance clear blue edged in glowing orange around a chunk of the wind-downed oak Daddy brought over after last year's big October storm.

LuAnne calls into the house, "Y'all started without us!" just as the blender shuts off. Candy pours each of us a peach smoothie with a kick, and Ardell wraps her arm around my waist and proclaims, "Let the games and merriment begin!"

The six of us put only a small dent in the bottle of rum that night. We are mostly drunk on companionship. M&M is a wonderful addition to our estrogen-challenged group. The woman knows stuff. Interesting ideas about different cultures and religions. She is the oldest of us and mostly seems like the youngest. She claims that's what comes of teaching at a university. You either stay young, or you strangle one of the spoiled little pukes you are being paid to teach and end up a bitter old woman trying to live off your writing.

Ardell has a salad bar lined up along the kitchen counter, and we all help ourselves to four or five thousand calories of grilled chicken, blue or feta or cubed Gouda cheese, garbanzo and kidney beans, artichoke hearts in garlic and olive oil, roasted red peppers, tomatoes and avocado, all arranged on fluffy beds of guilt-free greens. We top the whole mess with olive oil and balsamic vinegar and arrange ourselves on couches and chairs and, in Snicker's case, on the living room carpet.

We gossip about Kristen. M&M expounds about transference and projection, enabling and inappropriate behavior, and setting limits. We all secretly watch Oprah and Doctor Phil, so we know, more or less, what she's saying.

At some point though, she stops lecturing, looks around the room at us rednecks, and politely dumbs it down for us, "When you let her get away with being rude and mistreating you, you encourage her to be a spoiled rotten brat. Putting her on that plane was the best thing that could have happened to the little twit."

"How on earth did you convince that child to pack her bags and get in that purple rental car of hers?" LuAnne asks.

"It never occurred to me that she wouldn't do what I told her," I say.

"My belief," Snickers says, "is that the child thought she was just going to Atlanta when she got in the car."

"That's pure nonsense," I tell her. "That young woman was ready to get on back to her own neck a'the woods. Plus she knew for a natural fact that she had pushed me about as far as she could push without being snatched bald."

"She may also have been responding to you, Ruth, as a mother figure. You put an end to her nonsense. I would guess she was quite relieved finally to have limits set for her," Molly Megan speculates.

"Could be," I admit. "It's true, she has called twice since she got to Los Angeles. At a normal hour. She was even mostly pleasant. Only a little whiney just before I told her I had to go and hung up the phone." I sip at my spiked peach smoothie. "She said she had a good trip back, met a man in first class who makes his living putting together start-up companies. Oh, and also that she was looking forward to a Hollywood Hills Rave with a bunch of people whose names sounded like dogs. Chippy and Momo and Lefty."

"A rave is just a new word for party," Ardell says. "Makes it sound wild, doesn't it? Like a collection of raving lunatics all gathered together to let loose."

"I kind of like Kristen," I confess, "now that she lives over two thousand miles away from Colin and me."

"What can you possibly find to like about that spoiled brat?" LuAnne asks.

"Well, yes, Kristen is selfish and rude, no denying that. But she's also straightforward and has a certain vulnerability I can't help but find refreshing. I actually feel a little guilty about running the girl out of town."

Over the hoots and moans, I amend my position. "A little guilty. Nothing I don't plan to get over lickety-split."

We focus on Snickers and give her a bad time about Preston Yates.

"The man only dresses like a Yuppie asshole because in Los Angeles if you don't wear a Rolex with the price tag of an economy car, folks don't take you seriously as a businessman," she swears, straight-faced.

"It is indeed a sad truth in the City of Angels," M&M confirms. "If you want to be successful, you are required to look successful."

We drink to our own simpler life in Noisy Creek.

"So," Ardell asks, "what's it like to ride in a silver Bentley? Does The Philistine have any other awesomely cool cars?"

Snickers giggles. "In Los Angeles he has a Silver Ghost Rolls Royce."

"Cool!" we all chorus over M&M's, "Sweet!"

"Really, Snicks," Candy asks, "you've never been that impressed with money. What do you see in the man?"

"He dotes on me." She blushes shyly. "It's nice to be with a man who reach-

es out and makes all my little wishes come true. When we got back from Savannah, I mentioned, just in passing is all, how I missed the chocolate-dipped
strawberries we'd enjoyed so much from this little shop we stumbled into to
get out of the humidity. Now every morning, a half dozen of those wonderful
candy-coated wonders arrive by FedEx, right to my front door before I've even
had my first cup of coffee."

The rest of us are rendered speechless by this tale. In part because it is such
a blatant example that the rich really are different from the rest of us, but, more
importantly, because Snicks hasn't offered to share a single one of the glorious
confections with anyone in the room. Preston Yates certainly does have all the
outward signs of success that society can bestow. Maybe the attention of a man
like that is exactly what Snicks needs right now. Maybe her vulnerability over
her slowly fading beauty needs this over-the-top attention.

"I know you don't like him," Snicks says to me, though I swear there most
definitely is not an expression of disgust on my face. I'm having a little heart-
burn, that's all. "You," she accuses, "hold Daddy up as measurement against
every other man in the world."

Well that's true. I do.

"The thing is, Ruth, while you were always Daddy's little princess, I was the
one who never quite got enough attention from the man."

My mouth hangs open like I'm trying to catch flies.

"We grew up in the same house," she says softly to Candy and me, "but we
had different childhoods."

Snickers is already sitting on Ardell's beige carpet. Candy and I join her in a
jumbled heap of hugs and tears and back rubbing. Ardell hands us a box of tissues.

"Honey, I'm sorry," I tell my sister. "You have been nothing but supportive
of me and my relationship with Colin, and here I am being my usual judgmental self about you and Preston. I truly am sorry. I just want you to be happy."

The three of us stay on the carpet, wrapped together in what Mama calls a
puppy pile. LuAnne informs M&M in a deadpan voice that we three sisters do
this every time we get together.

"They ain't happy unless they end up a crying mess," she explains.

I lean my head against LuAnne's bony knee, snake my hand up to find hers.

As the evening winds on, I forget M&M is Colin's mother. The woman is not like any mother-in-law I've ever had. Not that Colin and I are getting married. That's certainly not what I meant to imply. It is Ardell who brings up the subject of younger men with older woman. I'd kick her, but I am still sitting on the floor next to Snickers, and my legs have fallen asleep. My butt too actually, but the point is, I can't move to give her the swift kick she deserves.

"There are a good many tribes where young men are sexually trained by older women," M&M tells us.

I feel the color moving up my chest, consuming my neck and face.

The incorrigible Ardell shouts out, "Sweet!" before the rest of us release little fits of nervous giggling like random machine gun fire into a dark night. We are a group of older, southern Christian women. It's not that we deny having thoughts of sex. God, no. But we rarely talk frankly about it in groups of more than two. And rarely without a good deal more alcohol than what has been consumed here tonight.

"In some African tribes the names of whom, by the by, sound like a series of clicks and whistles, age holds no importance culturally to sexual unions. Marriages are arranged based on the compatibility of the bride with the groom's mother."

I am known for opening my mouth before thinking.

"Maybe I'll marry Colin to get you as my mother-in-law."

While the Georgia contention is mulling over my last remark, M&M, unfazed, comes back with, "Don't you think that part of your appeal to Colin is your big wonderful family? Love and lust are always multi-dimensional."

Later, we rinse the blender, clean the kitchen, and arrange ourselves in plastic lounge chairs in Ardell's tiny back yard. The moon is absent from the night sky, the stars muted by the lights of town. We are all cupping mugs of Ardell's Feel Good Magic Tea, the steam rising up to warm our faces.

"We look like a coven of good witches," Snickers says.

Candy opens her mouth, and I know she's thinking of challenging the theology of a good witch. But she forces her jaw shut, sips her tea, and keeps quiet. She's good at choosing her religious battles, is Candy.

The radio is tuned to some classic rock station out of Athens. When the DJ announces the next song is "Brown Sugar" from the Rolling Stones Sticky

Fingers album, every last one of us old Georgia broads break up in laughter. Following ten minutes of convoluted reminisces, M&M gives up and pretends to understand the story.

An hour later, as we are making ready to go home, Ardell laments, "It was a rip off! That Sticky Fingers! Wasn't any preparation at all for Bobby Joe Nelson and the real thang!"

ARDELL'S
FEEL GOOD MAGIC TEA

Ardell buys this stuff at a back street shop in New Orleans where they also sell voodoo dolls and black candles, and where, if you ask me, a nice holy roller girl has no business setting her foot, but you ought to be able to make it up yourself if you can't get to the Crescent City. The hand-written lapel on the baggie says it's a blend of kava, ginger, peppermint, and chamomile. We've been drinking it at these gatherings for years,and it does put a nice gentle end to the evenings. It should, however, be said that M&M thought the brew smelled remarkably similar to something she called Humboldt Gold.

Twenty-Eight

My young lover is a coffee snob. The first night he stayed over, he rolled out of bed in the morning in all his glory and headed for the kitchen. He was back before I could steal his pillow.

"Where's your coffee?"

I opened my eyes to see him standing at half-mast. I don't remember thinking too much about caffeine at that moment, but I did rummage in my sleep-clogged brain for an answer.

"Cupboard. Left. Next to sink."

I may even have reached up a hand still warm from the covers in an attempt to get a full salute out of him. He was not to be distracted, though walking away, he did look better than Granddad's young rooster. I closed my eyes and hit my mental snooze button. I have a cloudy memory of him returning to my room, pulling on his jeans and T-shirt, and whispering, "I'll be back in a few with actual coffee, not that Juan Valdez crap in the can."

Three notions did manage to filter through my sleeping brain with this declaration. One, he was a little grumpy in the mornings without his coffee. Making him the more functional of the two of us, since without caffeine, the mammalian part of my brain is still under the control of my fat, lazy iguana cortex. Two, the man took his coffee California serious. Three, he left his black briefs lying on the floor next to the bed so when he got back with the fancy coffee he evidently required, he'd be even easier to undress than he had been the night before. Plus, we'd both be hopped up on gourmet java.

Over the next two months I learn about Peaberries, shade-grown versus sun-blasted, organic as opposed to chemical ridden, dark and light roasts, Panamanian boutique coffee farms and Kona blends. He buys me a French press when it becomes apparent that indeed I do intend to perform the sacrilege of putting his fresh-ground dark roast peaberries through my old Mr. Coffee. In July, I couldn't have told the difference between Folgers and Costa Rican Dark if my life depended on it.

By October, I am doing the West Coast nose wrinkle of disapproval over anything that doesn't cost as much per cup as a full breakfast at Rebs, cup a Joe included. Of course, both Colin and I still sit around the kitchen table in Leeville and drink Daddy's chicory-laced cowboy coffee with faces as wrinkle free as the butts of newborns. I teach Colin how to use his front teeth as a sieve to filter out the inevitable grounds, tease him that Daddy doesn't need a fancy device from a foreign country to make him a cup of real coffee.

Colin is the only man I've ever been with who isn't from Noisy Creek. Ordinary things like cowboy coffee, package stores, boiled peanuts, and enough kinfolk to populate a Central American country are all new to him. Showing him my world makes it new to me all over again. Explaining the way we do things here in my neck of the woods leads me to re-examine traditions I stopped seeing years ago.

Like the fact that Noisy Creek is in dry Humley county. Dry having to do not with rainfall but with alcohol. You can't buy alcohol here. Not legally. Fortunately Monroe County, just past Leeville on Route 4, is a wet county. So we all just drive over to the conveniently-located package store not ten feet across the county line.

"Don't people just buy the booze by the case so as not to have to make the trip across every time they want a drink? Doesn't that increase the consumption of alcohol rather than discourage its use? And why is it called a package store?"

The man does occasionally seem deliberately obtuse. At such times I raise my voice a hair, shake a school teacher finger at him, and end the discussion with, "I don't give a rat's ass how you do it up north, damn it. You're in Noisy Creek now, boy!"

Sometimes he pulls my leg with outrageous stories about where he grew up in Northern California, painting scenes of a ravioli restaurant with checkered table cloths, fat-bottomed, straw-covered wine bottles, and a machine gun range outback. He swears the State of California built its first nuclear power plant directly on top of the active fault line that runs through his hometown. He insists that each Earth Day they hold an All Species Parade where folks dress as their favorite animal and take a solemn vow to communicate in a species-accurate manner for the entire day or until the beer kicks in. He expects me to believe that on the Fourth of July the local micro-breweries sponsor a beer tasting that ends with attaching wheels to bar stools and racing them down the middle of Main Street.

He bemoans the fact that there are homeless living in the dead trunks of ancient redwoods in the city parks, under bridges, and behind the one and only mall. He insists that the city fathers addressed this issue by installing arm rests in the middle of all the city benches so the homeless can't use them as beds, while the state politicians handled the crisis by passing out camouflage blankets treated with a scientific coating which renders anyone hunkered down under them invisible to surveillance satellites or night vision goggles—a high-tech, out-of-sight out-of-mind solution to the homeless problem.

He talks about a place of extraordinary beauty where the fog rarely lifts and the trees are older than Christianity. While I rest my head on his chest and listen to his heart beat against my ear, he talks into the dark of lagoons and wild rivers and rugged coastlines. He runs his fingers along my arm and tells of hoary bull elk protecting their sleek cows from marauding and dangerously frustrated bachelor bulls. I fall asleep listening to his lullaby of desperate leaping salmon, waddling black bear, white-tailed deer, and the very occasional cry of a cougar like a woman's scream in the night.

"I'm a little homesick," he admits.

"Do you think of moving back there," I ask. "It does sound beautiful."

"No." He shakes his head. "The Humboldt County of my childhood only exists now in small pockets of resistance. The twin gods of consumerism and Los Angeles-based greed occupy the area now. It's become a place of shiny political correctness and hidden marijuana gardens. I'd love to bring you back to see the place, though."

"We'll go back for a visit. It's the only way I'll believe your description."

"Noisy Creek," he whispers in my ear, "is more like the town I grew up in—more like the Arcata of my childhood—than the town itself is now."

We both hope Noisy Creek is far enough away from Los Angeles and its Confederate cousin, Atlanta, to remain a dirt-dusted small town of rednecks for at least a while longer. We talk a lot about our fear that his green project could change the flavor of the town by introducing seventy-five retired yuppies into the mix. We pray not. So far and knock wood, the home buyers are all country people who have endured one city or another throughout their working lives and are now content to come back to their country roots to retire. Of course, they've been contaminated some by all those years in a big city, but I am certain that we Noisy Creek folk are abrasive enough to wear that veneer of sophistication off their hides right quick.

I was never married to any of my husbands long enough to completely wear off all the newness. With Johnny there were stretches of time when we coasted some, but we always managed to find in each other some fresh corner of shininess we'd not noticed before. The adventure of discovery is part of the fun of marriage and the reason old married couples often end up looking and thinking alike. All that unique individual coating ends up shared, rubbed into both the man and the woman, me and you becoming a blend of us.

I expect that Colin and I will have a very long and exciting time of exploring each other, finding new grooves and hidden knobs against which to grind. It is true that I occasionally make reference to something like The Brady Bunch or Get Smart, and he replies that he's seen it on Nick at Night.

Once, with him half asleep and depleted of most of his bodily fluids, I mention Jimi Hendrix and Purple Haze as a way of trying to explain the eerie cloud of happy exhaustion in which I find myself, and he comes back with, "Jimi Hendrix? Is he the Muppet guy?" This precipitates a crucial moment in our relationship. Throw him out of bed and come to my senses once and for all, or laugh like an old fool, spoon against him and go to sleep. Since I didn't have the strength right then to toss an alley cat out of my bed, let alone 182 pounds of adorable muscle, I chose to laugh and snuggle. I still believe it was the correct decision.

Two days after the party at the Dixie Circle, I demonstrate my recently acquired expertise at coffee making by pressing us a second cup of Sumatran Dark Roast. "Your mother suggested that you might be as attracted to my family as you are to me."

He ponders that while the clear water in the French press grows as dark as a tannic-stained swamp, kisses my forehead.

"I'd take you without your family," he says. "But Mom's right, I like the whole package."

We decide that no matter what happens between the two of us, his mother will always be my friend, and he'll be stuck like slobber from the jowls of my uncle Neil's bulldog to every last one of my kinfolk. Bless his heart, he claims to have gotten the better of that deal.

DADDY'S
COWBOY COFFEE

Daddy makes this coffee in a dented aluminum camping pot. The kind with a detachable handle and a lid that fits down into a groove. He uses cold spring water and a fistful of whatever coffee is on sale that week at the Piggly Wiggly. He says he adds the pinch of chicory for a little Cajun mischief.

Ingredients:
- 5 c water
- 5 T coffee, coarse ground (real cowboys never actually measure this, just know by the heft when they've collected the right amount in their fist)
- 1 t chicory
- 1 egg shell crushed (this cuts the bitter taste).
- 1 c water

Put the 5 cups of cold water in a pot, and bring it to rolling boil. Toss in the rest of the ingredients except for that last cup of water. Bring the whole mess to a boil again. Remove it from the heat, and let it set a spell. Slowly add that last cup of cold water. This will settle the grounds some, make less work for your front teeth as a sieve. Lighten with evaporated milk to taste. Daddy says he generally likes his about the color of Riley Creek after a right hard rain.

Twenty-Nine

The day before Daddy's eightieth birthday party, Snickers shifts into over-drive on the preparations. It's possible I may strangle her with my bare hands. I love my sister dearly, of course I do, but she's a perfectionist, and when every little thing isn't done the exact way she wants it, that ole girl can scald the hairs off a hog with that tongue of hers.

"I know y'all are doin' your natural best," she growls at me when she inspects the hundred Chinese lanterns I've been ordered to produce out of nothing more than ordinary paper bags, "but Ruthie, those look more like smashed hats than lanterns."

She has thirteen of our nieces and nephews arranged at a long table strewn with paper bags and multi-colored construction paper, scissors and glue, felt tip pens and crayons. Each and every one of the little show-offs is turning out lanterns superior to mine. I sit next to Cousin Enid's eight year old, Jake. The thick crew cut his mother has inflicted on him feels like stroking a boot brush. "You have the Traveller epistle memorized for Granddad's party tomorrow night?"

Cousin Pauline's girl, Susie, who's going on twelve years old, tells me, "We've decided to do General Stonewall Jackson's last words instead." Her grin is pure Barr mischief.

She and her little brother Lester jump up from their chairs, stand side by side, adopt an expression of sorrow, and intone, "Let us cross over the river and rest in the shade."

For young Barrs this quote is the equivalent of the "Jesus wept" Bible verse. Namely, it's short. Plus this recitation has the added bonus of a little bit of irony since moments after speaking these words, the great general was mistakenly shot and killed by his own men. Susie and Lester bow to hoots of irreverent laughter.

Cousin Dale's boy stands at attention, places his right hand stiffly along his eyebrows, and proclaims, "They couldn't hit an elephant at this dist...." at which point, he clutches his heart, widens his eyes, and falls to the floor.

His little sister, Mary Ellen, rises solemnly. "Last words of Union General John Sedgwick before a Confederate sharpshooter shot him through the heart and killed him daid at Spotsylvania."

Snickers glares in from the kitchen, her look firm enough to bend every little Barr head back to work.

M&M says our family, with its traditions and emotional intimacies, reminds her of some of the African tribes. An observation which I find fascinating, but after glancing around nervously, advise her not to share with any gathering of my relatives where sharp implements are handy.

The evening before, with two dozen or so kinfolk from out of town—though none live any further away than Candy up in Stone Mountain—already gathered at Mama and Daddy's, camped out under the Chinaberry tree in RVs and tucked into rooms at Snickers's and my houses, Colin and I talked about children. He has given up his funky airstream rental and is living at his construction office. I walk him over there from Mama and Daddy's after supper.

It's still warm enough for fireflies. The grass and trees are miniature galaxies of cold blinking light, the males desperate with the desire to mate before the first frost. Earlier, I watched from the kitchen window as Colin investigated a spider's activity with my nephew, Justin. The spider had woven her small miracle between Mama and Daddy's rocking chairs. Whether as a matter of routine or triggered by the unusual rumpus of the evening I don't know, but as Colin and Justin watched, she unwove her web, pulling the threads back inside herself to use again the next day. Man and boy wore identical expressions of wonder as they stared at this reverse spinning process. My hands immersed in the hot soapy dish water, a chill entered my body, a low dull ache.

On the walk to Jenkins Development, amidst flashing reminders of the universal need to reproduce, I ask Colin if he wants children. Over the last couple of months he has ceased to be my young lover and has become simply my love. The change in status makes me frightened of his response, knowing it will determine our future together.

He stops walking and turns off the flashlight. We've been holding hands, and now he draws my hand up to his mouth, kisses the inside of my wrist, exactly like I've taught him. He pulls me to him and puts his mouth butterfly gentle on the inside bend of my elbow, the back of my neck just at the hairline, behind my left ear, then my right. He runs his hands down my back, leaves them at my rib cage, a promise resting just under my breasts.

My heart is fluttery, knocking against my chest. A hot flash gone south.

"Do you want children?" Too scared suddenly to wait for his answer, I rush on with a possibility I haven't considered in twenty years. "We could adopt. Maybe."

"I'm quite content to play with your forty or so nieces and nephews and then send them home at the end of the day. The better to give my undivided attention to ravishing their aunt."

—

This afternoon Candy and Snicks ban Mama from her own kitchen. Snickers has relieved me from craft duty, muttering rudely, "If you're going to just deliberately mess up every little thing I ask you to do, you may as well go on into the kitchen and help with supper."

Candy has one Valium left over from when she had her cataract surgery, and she's threatening to slip it in Snick's sweet tea. I may take the pill myself.

The kitchen is filled to bumping with cousins and aunts, all of us doing our own choreographed dance as we stir pots, move pans in and out of the ovens, mix batter, and make gallons of sweet tea. The back door is open with just the screen to protect against light-seeking bugs. A cool breeze lifts the hair off our necks. I'm in charge of the black-eyed peas. The onions are browning nicely in the bacon grease, when I catch a glimpse of Daddy and Colin standing out by the calves.

Whatever they're discussing looks serious. Daddy is offering his hand. Colin takes it. Then the two of them do that man hug where they pat each other on the back twice, careful not to allow any body contact. Aunt Beatrice distracts me by asking if we're offering any new spa packages at the salon. I tease her that after seeing what great shape Molly Megan is in, I'm thinking of offering yoga classes and maybe the masseuses will soon be aligning hillbilly chakras.

By the time I look back toward the pasture, Daddy and Colin are silhouetted by the last of the sun's reflection. Colin has one leg propped up on the lower fence rail, and Daddy stands with the slightly bowlegged posture that makes me smile with recognition. The sunset is all lavenders and deep blues with a line of murky black already claiming most of the horizon.

After dinner and the cleanup, I carry a couple of plates out to Traveller's Park for Uncles Neil and Earl who are keeping the coals hot over the roasting pig. The leftover ham bone wrapped in a greasy paper towel is my special treat for the bulldog, Beauregard. The uncles are glad to see me, happier to get supper. Beau however is insulted by my offering. Uncle Neil slips the jowly beast chunks of ham and bites of chicken as I drive away and leave them to another night of tending the fire. Uncle Earl is just back from a run to Texas to visit some relative or other and has returned with a pickup bed of Pabst Blue Ribbon, so they have plenty of beer. Between the two of them there is no way they're going to run out of stories to tell.

Daddy's waiting for me in his front porch rocker when I get back to the house. A three-quarter moon is just showing itself over the jagged edge of Sawtooth Mountain. When Daddy suggests we escape the house full of relatives and take a little walk, I am tickled to have him all to myself. What with all the activity of preparing for the party, it's been days since the two of us have had five minutes to talk.

One of the ancient pecan trees fell in the night a few weeks ago. Daddy has trimmed the limbs with his chainsaw and left the trunk to cure for a while before he cuts it. It makes a nice place to sit and listen to the breeze rattling the remaining leaves, watch the fireflies flicker half-heartedly, and breathe deep of the last smells of autumn, the earth readying itself for the long cold sleep of another winter.

His voice is rough in the cooling night, low and growling, "I want you to know how much I like Colin."

I take his hand. "I know how you feel about him. Understand that in the beginning, you were only worried for me."

The waxing moon makes its slow, certain path across the sky, and I listen to Daddy tell me what he needs to say.

"Candy was always an independent little thing, even as a baby. When Snickers came along, she fastened herself to your Mama and never let go. By the time you showed up, your mama was just plumb wore out. Three babies coming so close together was just too much for her to handle. You was colicky, fussy in the hours of deep night. You'd wake like clockwork at just after two a.m., and no way we could get you to settle back to sleep until just as dawn was staining the morning with red and gold."

Daddy holds my hand out there in the orchard with the constellations jagged through thin trailing clouds.

"I took to holding you through those night cries. Grew to love those private, middle of the night times with just the two of us so much that, when you outgrew the colic, I'd still get up in the night and walk with you through the house.

"Was your mama who found me at the kitchen table holding the warmth of a sleeping baby girl against my chest, staring down into your peaceful face. It was your mama who put you gently in your crib and took me back to our bed where I belonged."

He shakes himself some, as though bringing himself back to the moment.

"Baby Ruth," he says. "I think I did the same thing with you and Colin. I had come to enjoy having you all to myself so much after Johnny died that when I warned you off that man, I believe I was thinking more of myself than I was of you."

We sit a while longer with my head on Daddy's shoulder, the glow from the house lights just visible from this distance, before I kiss his scratchy cheek, and we walk back across the field and into the chaos that is family.

BLACK-EYED
PEAS

We eat this side dish all year long, but on New Year's Day, it is traditional to have a big bowl of black-eyed peas with hog jowls for health and wealth in the New Year. This is the everyday recipe, but y'all can substitute smoked pig cheeks for the holiday if you want.

Ingredients:
- 4 c cooked black-eyed peas

If you're making them for New Year's Day, boil the jowls until tender before you add the dried peas.
- 1 onion chopped
- 6 strips of bacon crumbled

I'm sure you know by now to save the grease.

Cook the onion until soft in a little of the bacon grease. Add the cooked peas, a cup of water, and salt and pepper to taste. Simmer for 30 minutes. Add the crumbled bacon and a little more of the grease if needed for flavor. Cook another 5 minutes to melt and distribute the extra grease.

Thirty

Snickers has hired a professional photographer from Dothan to spend the entire day of Daddy's eightieth birthday with our family. This young woman's job is to capture candid shots of us Barrs pretending not to be aware of the two foot camera lens whirring in our faces like the most annoying mosquito on the face of God's green earth.

"It's for posterity," Snickers claims. What she really means is this might be Daddy's last birthday party.

The older Mama and Daddy get, the more our fear of their death causes us to blanket them with an increasingly palpable aura born of our need to shape and preserve each remaining moment of their lives. Since Mama's fall, none of us girls walk away from either of our parents without hugging them good-bye. Each phone conversation ends with "I love you." The unspoken knowledge hazing every interaction is that sooner rather than later, we will need to be able to say, "The last thing I said to him was that I loved him."

Which is why Snickers is out of control with the birthday party plans and why neither Candy nor I have the heart to rein her in. Each time we attempt to point out that Daddy is really a simple man who just wants his family and friends around him to raise a glass of muscadine wine in celebration of the passage of another year of his life, we are met with the same hard stare, followed by Snickers's teary proclamation, "This might be Daddy's last birthday. His very last one."

I am reminded of Ardell's mama. At the end, doing poorly with the cancer, the wonderful old woman took to responding to anyone foolish enough to ask how she was doing, with "I'm not buying any green bananas, and I'm brushin' up on my hymns of praise."

Mama and Daddy have been practicing their praises for a spell now. It's the three of us—Candy, Snickers, and myself—who are clinging in the hope of keeping them on this side of the Jordan.

Mama is recovering well from the hip replacement, just as the surgeon promised, and Daddy is in fine health. For his age. Nobody is talking about dying. But we are all striving to squeeze every last drop of joy out of life for these two people who have shown us how to live so richly. Snickers, though, has crossed a line and lost touch with what is important. I yearn to blame Preston Yates's ostentatious influence for this leap of hers into the dark side, but the truth is Snicks has always had a tendency to overdo things. It is one of the things we all love about her. Her perfectionism only rarely makes us want to strangle her with our bare hands.

"What are you gonna do if he makes it to his eighty-first birthday?" Candy asks as she inspects Snickers's latest bright idea. "How are you going to top this? Book a world cruise for the whole family?"

The look on Snickers's face when she hears this suggestion is not encouraging.

Candy and I back away from the crazy person and allow her to continue to supervise the nieces and nephews over whose heads she is cracking the whip, a yard boss from hell. The kids have now been given the task of making eighty gold stars. These are to be cardboard, eighteen inches from point to point and covered in gold foil. Each star is to have dozens of holes punched in its shiny surface. A yellow Christmas light will be fitted behind each one. Her plan is to string these heavenly bodies from the trees closest to the table where Daddy and Mama will be trying to eat, blinded no doubt by the over-attentiveness of their loving family.

By Saturday morning, the PowerPoint collage of family photos is ready. The three-tier cake has been loaded in Aunt Enid's six-year-old Cadillac after a two-day argument between her and Aunt Myrtle over which of their vehicles could provide the smoothest ride. Aunt Myrtle has an eighteen-year-old Land Rover.

The discussion is ended when Uncle Bobby promises to put the frosted monstrosity in the open bed of his '68 International if the two of them don't shut the hell up and let him watch World Wrestling Federation in peace. I have threatened bodily harm to the next person who renews Snickers's subscription to Martha Stewart Living. Candy mutters about obsessive-compulsive disorder.

M&M, in that whispery voice of hers, explains to Snickers, "It is the tradition of Japanese brides that they and their family create for their wedding day a veritable flock of one thousand origami cranes."

I pray to the great Buddha himself that Snickers might never remarry, cause you just know that thousand crane idea will come back to bite us in the ass.

LuAnne has checked in earlier. "I'll be carrying two hundred possum pasties to the party," she teases, "but otherwise, my intention is to stay away from you crazy white folks until the booze is flowing strong."

We get reports that Beauregard has taken a fancy to an aggressive chipmunk. Last we heard, the rodent and bulldog were eating out of the same bowl of dog food, and Uncle had given up on Beau's training as a huntin' dawg. We've been told the uncles have two pigs and a gator tail roasting in the pit. Uncle Earl hints at other exotic cuisine that does not bear contemplating, but which makes me a little sad that Kristen won't be here to enjoy the fine southern delicacies.

Pickup trucks—their open beds laden with covered food, tables and chairs, and other assorted paraphernalia—have been pulling into Traveller's Park since dawn. Preston Yates has acquired for himself a gleaming new black Dodge Ram Diesel long bed.

Snickers confides, "Those leather seats adjust to twenty-two different positions, and the truck is an automatic, so there is no annoying gear shift to get in the way of any spontaneous hanky panky."

This report creates a visual on which I do not want to dwell. Though I do appreciate the thirteen trips the man makes from the house to the park, delivering whatever Snickers orders him to fetch and carry.

Mama, who overhears Snickers's comment about the gear shift, asks, "My question to you girls is this. Do y'all think God's commandment against fornication only applies to those young enough to risk gettin' pregnant?"

I ponder on that a moment. "Well, yeah," I admit, "come to think of it, I guess that pretty much sums it up for me."

"'Sides," Snickers insists, "that there commandment is against adultery. The fornication thing is not so much a law as just sort of a little suggestion."

This interpretation renders both Mama and Candy speechless, while leading Snicks and me into a fit of unseemly laughter.

By noon the entire Barr family, half-assed or otherwise, has relocated to Traveller's Park. The radio has warned for two days that a storm front is headed our way from the Great State of Alabama. Snickers is of the opinion that it wouldn't dare rain after all her preparations.

I'm not so sure. Watching a thick gray line of clouds rob the sky of its gold, I send the uncles and their trucks out to scour the countryside like good Confederate soldiers.

"No one gets one bite to eat or pops a single top," I tell them, "until we have tarps over every table."

By 2:02 blue plastic and florescent yellow ropes, stained moldy canvas, and hemp has obliterated Snickers's dream of turning the park into a cover shoot for Southern Living. The first raindrop doesn't fall until 2:12. By 2:15 we are in a deluge, rain pounding the canvas so hard it drowns out the music from all four strategically placed speakers. Before Snickers can come completely undone, Ardell shows up with one of those blue cooler barrels of peach daiquiris, takes the loudly wailing Snickers under her rum-pushing wing, and we are ready to party.

Snickers is right about the professional photographer. The photos from that day are priceless family treasures.

There's one of Cousin Melinda's two-year-old, Brendan, spraddle-legged on the picnic table, naked but for a towel wrapped around his middle. His mom is attempting to put dry clothes on him after he has stretched himself full length in a mud puddle as big as a catfish pond. Looking at the photo of that beautiful scrawny child, I will always hear Daddy saying, "Ya ain't a very big bird without yer feathers are ya?"

Here's Uncle Earl, a shit-eating grin on his wide face, extending his hairy right arm with an offering of a glistening chunk of marinated and sautéed rattlesnake.

The photographer captures all the couples. Some we didn't know were couples until we saw the pictures.

My favorite of Preston and Snickers has them framed with those ridiculous gold-foil stars. They're holding hands, but Snickers is turned slightly away, and by the look on her beautiful face, I know she's watching Mama. Preston Yates is focused on my sister, caught in an unguarded moment of pure adoration.

Candy and Bill's portrait catches them looking at each other across a table heaped with food. I can pick out Aunt Minnie's homegrown string beans, Aunt Enid's spicy cornbread, and Memaw Barr's heavy cobalt-blue platter, the one with a small chip on the side. That heirloom is holding an offering of five of Mama's Rhode Island Reds butchered after last night's sunset, soaked in buttermilk, drenched in the Barr blend of flour and spices and fried golden. In the picture, Candy and Bill are smiling directly into each other's eyes, oblivious to the food and the hundreds of relatives around them, the rain making a silver veil as it falls from the canvas behind them.

The best shot of Mama and Daddy shows Mama with her head on Daddy's shoulder. It's late in the party. Already dark. The rain has finally let up for a spell. Children are sprawled on dry blankets under tarps or snuggled in some relative or another's lap, tired adults absently stroking their soft hair. Daddy's traditional toast with homemade wine is over. The children have reverently and very proudly recited General Lee's ode to Traveller. In the picture, the photographer's filter has turned the foil-wrapped cardboard around Mama and Daddy into a universe of falling stars. Daddy's hand covers Mama's. Her crepe-paper wrinkles are a soft contrast to his more deeply lined face. They seem the calm center of a world they helped create.

There are a heap of pictures of Colin and me from that day, but the one I framed and hung in my living room is of Colin and Molly Megan. They are encircled by wet and bedraggled children. M&M has become the story lady with Colin as her faithful sidekick. They're reciting tales passed on from Lakota, Navajo, African, and Asian keepers of wisdom. The best image of Colin and me from that day doesn't come until the very end of the party, and it is never printed on slick Kodak photo paper.

Candy and Bill carry Daddy and Mama home just before midnight. By 2:30, most all the revelers had gone. It's a misty false dawn before we've transported the left-over food, tables, chairs, lights, and tarps back out of Traveller's Park. Uncle Neil and Beauregard are spending another night with the chipmunks. They've volunteered to do the final clean up in the light of morning before they go on home.

Colin and I make a final run with a load of coolers and miscellaneous plates and serving dishes we'll sort out and return to their rightful owners in the light of day. The last to leave Mama and Daddy's, Colin and I sit in the front porch rockers, taking a rest before heading home, when the rain gets serious again.

We run, hand in hand, for the cab of his truck. Colin cranks up the engine. Hot air blasts the already fogged windows as he fiddles with the vents and switches on the radio. The rain hits the metal cab in a roaring downpour. True to tradition, the local disc jockey already has Trisha Yearwood crooning about Georgia rain. We exchange a look of delight at this perfect end to the day. I scooch over, straddle the gear shift. Colin holds me away from him slightly.

I have come to love this man. The way he makes me laugh at myself when I get up on my moral high horse. The way his mouth tastes after his first cup of coffee in the morning. The way he talks so fast with that California accent of his that I have to lay my hand on his arm, signal him to drop it down to Georgia speed. It surprises me that I no longer feel whole without him. The ordinary experiences of life—a joke Ardell tells badly over lunch at Reb's, south-flying geese in a lopsided V against a pure blue sky, Uncle Earl's latest coon hunting story—none of these seems complete anymore until I've shared the moment with this man.

The house is quiet. I know Mama and Daddy are lying side-by-side with no fear of what the dark might hold. Trisha sings, the rain keeps up its rhythm on the roof of the truck cab, and Colin reaches into the pocket of his Carhartt jacket and presents me with a choice. I hold up my left hand, feel the thin band of gold and Colin's warm touch mark me again as a woman loved by a good man.

With my head tucked into his shoulder, the rain still serenading, we watch a new day turn the sky from inky black to indigo blue. When Mama and Daddy's bedroom window spills a path of tawny yellow light into the dawn, we walk out back and open the door to the chicken house, watch the groggy hens and strutting roosters pour out to claim a new day. Then we go on in to make our announcement over a hot cup of Daddy's cowboy coffee.

RED-VELVET CAKE & CREAM CHEESE FROSTING

This is milestone celebration cake. Birthdays that end in zero. The birth of long-awaited babies. Engagements and weddings. The return of a son or daughter from a place of danger—war or some big northern city.

The taste of this mild chocolate cake on my tongue triggers a hundred lovely memories. It's the cake I serve to those I love when Colin and I officially announce our impending marriage.

Ingredients:
- 2 1/3 c flour
- 1 1/3c sugar
- 1 t baking soda, salt
- 1 t powdered cocoa
- 1 1/2 c butter
- 1 c buttermilk
- 3 eggs
- 2 T red food coloring
- 1 t white vinegar
- 2 t vanilla

LuAnne, who has promised to make this cake for my engagement party, uses three nine-inch pans. She's says to be sure and remind y'all to generously butter and flour the pans before distributing the batter, or better yet, get you some parchment paper, and line them pans.

Sift together the dry ingredients. Add the softened butter and liquid ingredients. Using a wooden spoon, stir just until well blended. Bake at 350 degrees for 30 minutes or until a toothpick inserted in the middle comes up clean.

Let the cake rest in the pans for five minutes, then remove the layers, and let them cool.

<u>Frosting:</u>
- 1 lb cream cheese
- 5 c powdered sugar
- 1 1/4 c softened butter
- 2 t vanilla

Put the ingredients in a bowl, and using a mixer, blend until fluffy. Refrigerate for a few hours while the cake cools thoroughly. Once the cake is frosted, press chopped pecans into the sides of your tiered cake.

Think of Colin and me while you enjoy this sweet Noisy Creek favorite. We'll be enjoying our slice, encircled by family and friends, out at Traveller's Park.

Pamela Foster fell in love with South Georgia twenty-five years ago when she visited her husband's home town of Americus. Over many years, her experience there gave rise to the stories that eventually became *Noisy Creek* and its sequel, *Redneck Goddess*.

After over two decades of travel, mostly in Latin America and Asia, Pamela has since returned to her hometown of Eureka, California, where she wakes each morning to fog draped redwoods, the ebb and flow of Humboldt Bay, and the comfort of finally being home.

www.pamela-foster.com

www.ingramcontent.com/pod-product-compliance
Lightning Source LLC
Chambersburg PA
CBHW020408210626
46816CB00006BB/2182